KIRSTEN RYAN

SNOWFALL

The Last of Her Kind

For my Mother, Susan.
Thank you for being my biggest fan
and loving this story as much as I do.

Contents

Acknowledgement

When I first began writing Snowfall I barely told a soul, I was too afraid this would become another project I would never finish. When I finally built up the courage to share my draft with family and friends, I was overwhelmed by their response. I may have started this story on my own, but I couldn't have finished it without the love and encouragement I've received over the past year.

Andrew, thank you for encouraging me to follow my dream of becoming an author—rather than being a responsible adult and going back to work. I appreciate everything you do for me and our boys. Thank you for always listening to my nonsense and helping me research the many weird questions I have had while writing this.

Mum, thank you for annoying the hell out of me until I finished this book (just kidding!) But really, your love for Snowfall has kept me motivated to share this story with the world. Thank you for always letting me borrow your brain when I needed it and always helping out wherever you could. I honestly couldn't have done this without you.

To my family and friends who read the draft—Ryal, Jen, Barbara, Kell, Natalie, Lauren, Cheryl, Terina and Caryl. Your excitement and love for this book has been appreciated beyond words. Thank you for taking the time to read it and share your thoughts (as well as laughing with me about my Google searches). I am so lucky to have each of you in my life.

To my Dad (who should have a bigger mention, but I asked him not to read it out of embarrassment over the love scenes), thank you for not reading it and being so supportive nonetheless.

Lastly, I want to thank all of the family and friends who have reached out with kind words and support, your enthusiasm has meant the world to me. I hope you all love this story just as much as my mum does.

Prologue

The Fall of Panthera

The cries of a baby could hardly be heard over the battle outside.

"Hush my sweet Tilly." Queen Alwyn paced back and forth, rocking Matilda in her arms.

A flurry of snow drifted through the open window, she trembled and stopped before it. Smoke and snow veiled the cityscape, but she could see the fight growing closer to the palace. Her heart sank in her chest—she was running out of time.

Queen Alwyn sat at the edge of her bed, carefully laying Matilda in her lap. Matilda stopped crying and stared at her mother curiously. Queen Alwyn rested her hand over Matilda's tiny chest and wrapped her other hand around her own moonstone amulet. Her hands glowed as she drew the magic out of Matilda, directing it into the amulet. She removed the necklace and placed it in a velvet box beside her.

Staring down at Matilda's doll-like face, Queen Alwyn tried to imagine what she would be like as a toddler, as a child, as a woman. She bowed her head and began to sob. "I'm so sorry," she whispered. "This is the only way to keep you safe." She wiped her eyes on the sleeve of her gown and cleared her throat. "Celia, come quickly please."

Celia hurried into the room, wringing her hands. Her petite body was hidden under a thick, white, fur-lined cloak and her short black hair was tied back carelessly. Celia's golden eyes widened as she took in her Queen's appearance. "Why haven't you changed?" she asked. "They are getting closer Alwyn, we need to leave."

Queen Alwyn lowered her head, unable to meet her friend's eyes. "I can't leave, but you must take Matilda away from here."

Celia rushed to her side. "What are you saying? I'm not leaving without you."

Queen Alwyn met her eyes, watching her carefully. "You've been awfully quiet since Matilda arrived. What have your dreams shown you?"

"Please," Celia whispered. "You know I don't see everything."

"But you have seen something."

A pained look crossed Celia's face. "I saw Princess Matilda, in the arms of a loving human couple."

Queen Alwyn paled, it was the answer she had feared, but in her heart, she knew it was true. "Then we know this is right," she said. "You will take Matilda, and I will remain here." She stood abruptly and hurried to her wardrobe, retrieving a brown leather backpack she had already prepared. She placed the velvet box inside and handed it to Celia. "I've packed everything you'll need, and I've taken Matilda's magic as a precaution. Please give my amulet to her when she is ready to know the truth. I trust you'll know when."

Celia took the bag and shook her head in anger. "I don't

care about the dream—I won't leave you."

Queen Alwyn smiled sadly. "We have no choice. If I leave, this fight will follow me across Valuna. This is the only way to keep Matilda safe. No one knows she was born and it must stay that way."

Celia closed her eyes, nodding slowly. "Yes, my Queen."

Queen Alwyn wrapped an arm around Celia and pulled her close. "Thank you, my friend, for everything."

Celia sobbed quietly on her shoulder. "I promise I'll take care of her, but what will you do?"

Queen Alwyn didn't want to lie, but she couldn't tell her the truth. "I'll make sure you can escape."

She wrapped Matilda in a thick blanket and kissed her one last time—breathing her in. "I love you Tilly, I wish I could have known you."

While holding back tears, Queen Alwyn placed her whole world into Celia's arms. She focused her magic and ran a finger down Celia's forehead, making them both disappear before her eyes. Once she'd heard Celia's soft footsteps leave the room, Queen Alwyn dropped to her knees, sobbing into her hands. Her heart was completely broken.

Chapter One

Silverleaf City

Nineteen years later

The afternoon sun cast an orange glow across the city, it had been a sweltering day. Tilly Norris hurried down the street, checking over her shoulder nervously. On a normal day, the Cultural Precinct was her favourite place to visit. Tall trees lined the sidewalk, with leaves like melting drops of silver. Boutique stores and galleries were nestled between the many cafés and restaurants, with street art decorating the alleyways in between. People dined outside in the sunshine, while buskers performed on every corner. But mostly Tilly loved it because it smelt of roasting coffee and all classes and species were welcome there. She passed the bakery and quickened her pace—glancing over her shoulder again.

"Heya Tilly."

Tilly jolted back, almost falling to the ground. The baker stood before her, watching her with amusement. She'd been so distracted she hadn't even noticed him. Tilly rested her hand over her heart and laughed nervously. "Hey Veer, you do know it's rude to sneak up on someone don't you?"

Veer wiped his hand on his apron, smiling at her with his small, sharp teeth. His mischievous, green eyes never missed a thing. He poked the cake box in her hand. "And here I thought you were the one sneaking—are you cheating on me?" he asked dramatically.

Tilly laughed and held up the box. "Don't be silly, it's one of Mum's. I'm taking it to Eleanor and I'm running late," she added, hoping he would take the hint. Like most Fenx, Veer could talk for hours.

His velvety, pointed ears shot up with interest, he moved aside and ushered Tilly along. "Why are you still talking, get out of here, and tell Eleanor to call me anytime."

She said goodbye and hurried off. When she glanced back, she noticed Veer hadn't moved. He stood there with hopeful eyes and a goofy smile. "Anytime!" he yelled after her.

Tilly grinned and shook her head, poor guy she thought, he'd been trying for years with no luck.

She turned a corner and that's when she felt it again, the same feeling that had kept her on edge for the past three days. Tingling in the back of her neck, warmth enveloping her body and a knowing sense she was being watched. Her heart began to race, she looked around anxiously. Everyone was going about their day, not paying any attention to her. "Where are you?" she muttered—this was really starting to piss her off. She reached the end of the street and crossed the road toward a brick apartment block. She raced up the front steps and knocked on the first door. "Eleanor? It's Tilly."

A moment later, Eleanor opened the door, beaming. "I

thought I might see you today child."

Tilly could understand Veer's fascination, Eleanor held other-worldly beauty and grace. She was forty-six years old, with smooth, golden skin and straight black hair to her shoulders. Flowing around her petite body was a sheer-sleeved, black and gold embroidered dress. She wore a matching blindfold wrapped around her head. Although they joked about it, Eleanor had never told her what happened to her eyes and Tilly had never asked.

Tilly stepped into her cramped living room, quickly closing the door behind her. She leaned down and gave Eleanor a hug, breathing in the familiar scent of herbs. "You know I'm not a child anymore—I'm almost nineteen."

Eleanor chuckled. "You'll always be my child, child."

Tilly held up the cake box. "Well, this child brought you some honey cake."

Eleanor clapped her hands excitedly. "Your mother is an angel—I'll get the tea." She headed towards the kitchen, using her cane to guide her.

Tilly placed the box down and sank into the sofa, resting her black boots on the coffee table. She glanced around Eleanor's apartment fondly. Her furniture was mismatched as if each piece had been collected from different parts of the realm. Timber shelves were scattered around the walls, holding books, trinkets and jars of herbs. Tilly had spent many days with Eleanor as a child, reading her books and listening to stories from when she had travelled Valuna. Tilly picked up a snow globe from the windowsill behind her. Inside was a shimmering city covered in moss. Eleanor swore it was a real place, but it was hard for her to imagine. Tilly had never left Silverleaf City.

"I saw Veer on my way over," Tilly called out. "He said to call him...anytime."

Eleanor laughed as she walked back in with a glass pot of blue tea, swirling it around and sniffing it twice. "That Fenx never gives up. Tea?"

"What kind of tea?" Tilly asked suspiciously.

"One of my medicinal blends, good for the nerves."

Tilly returned the snow globe and tied her long black hair out of her face. "That actually sounds perfect right now."

Eleanor poured them each a cup and placed the teapot on the coffee table. "Get your feet down child, this isn't a farmhouse."

Tilly burst out laughing. She pulled her boots off the table, shaking her head. She only did it because Eleanor always caught her, but she could never work out how. She took a sip of her tea and was pleasantly surprised, it was floral and sweet. "That's nice Eleanor, one of your better blends."

Eleanor sat in the armchair beside her and smiled. "How have you been? You sound anxious."

"That's why I came to see you," Tilly said quietly. "I think I'm being followed."

Eleanor sipped her tea slowly. "Have you seen them?"

"No, but I can sense them." Tilly knew how crazy she sounded, but she knew Eleanor would believe her. "I thought you might know something," she added.

"Hmm," Eleanor said, tapping her cup thoughtfully. "I don't know much, but I can tell you it is a young man. He means you no harm."

Tilly frowned. "If he's harmless, why has he been freaking me out? What does he want?"

Eleanor laughed softly. "He definitely isn't harmless, but he won't harm you. My dreams aren't always clear, but I can see he will come to you when the time is right."

Tilly shuddered at the thought, Eleanor was never wrong. "How do you see so much without eyeballs?"

Eleanor scoffed. "How many times do I have to tell you I still have eyeballs."

"I'm still not convinced," Tilly said doubtfully.

Eleanor laughed loudly. "I'm guessing you haven't told Orvyn about this?"

"There's a lot of things I don't tell Orvyn these days."

Eleanor leaned forward, reaching for Tilly's knee, she found it and squeezed it gently. "You still haven't told him about the Valunan Guard either, have you?"

Tilly's shoulders sagged, she ran her finger along the rim of her ceramic cup. "There's no point now, those bikies gave him his patch last week. It's official."

Eleanor didn't look surprised. "That is his path child, not yours. Have you told him how you feel about them?"

"He doesn't listen anymore, he just drags me along to their clubhouse to train when he knows I hate being there."

"I think it might be time you —"

Eleanor stopped and turned her ear towards the front door. Tilly glanced at the door just as someone knocked impatiently. "Are you expecting someone?" she asked quietly.

"It's not for me."

Tilly walked over hesitantly and pulled it open. Orvyn was leaning against the door frame, glaring down at her with his cold, blue eyes. Even in this heat, he wore dark jeans and his leather jacket. Proudly showing off the silver snake winding up the sleeve, marking him as a member of the Iron Vipers. Lightly tanned and athletically built, Tilly used to find him attractive—now she didn't even like looking at him. Orvyn shoved his messy, white hair back from his face. "Are you having fun in here? I've been looking for you, let's go."

Tilly peered back at Eleanor and the untouched cake. She wasn't ready to leave yet, but there was no point arguing with him. "Thank you for the tea," she said quickly.

Eleanor nodded. Even with the blindfold on, Tilly could see the concern on her face as she closed the door behind her.

Tilly followed Orvyn down the front steps, glaring at the back of his head. She hated how rude he was to everyone. They headed back towards town with Orvyn staying uncomfortably close to her side. "What were you doing with that loony again?" he sneered. "God, you even smell like her."

Tilly felt anger spark in her chest, Eleanor was like family to her. "I was just dropping something off for Mum."

Orvyn rolled his eyes. "You shouldn't let that woman order you around."

"Oh, but it's fine for you to do it," she muttered.

"What?"

"I don't have much choice while I'm living under their roof," she lied, she would do anything for her mother and father.

Orvyn gave her a sly smile. "I've told you, you can come live with me."

Tilly's heart started racing, she forced a sweet smile. "And miss out on Mum's home-cooked meals? No way, you and I can't cook for shit," she joked.

Orvyn tried to look unimpressed, but she could see the amusement in his eyes. She looked away from him, breathing slowly to calm herself down. Moving in with him would mean living at the clubhouse. He would have complete control over her and she could never let that happen.

The streetlights came to life as the sky darkened. People

started filling the streets, dressed up for dates and dinner parties. They passed a small restaurant decorated with vines and twinkling lights. Tilly noticed an older couple eating and laughing together. She smiled at them wistfully, wondering what it would be like to be happily in love, rather than the complicated mess she had found herself in.

They walked in silence and Orvyn flung his arm over her shoulder, she tried not to flinch as he did. She peered up at him and noticed he was glaring at everyone who passed them, as if he were ready for a fight at any moment. A wave of sadness swept over her, he really wasn't the same boy who had built forts with her and helped their elderly neighbour carry groceries. Tilly missed that boy.

"Why do you always wear that shit? I swear it's like you want everyone looking at you."

"Huh?" Tilly hadn't realised he was staring back at her. She glanced down, she was wearing a black singlet with high-waisted blue jeans and her black combat boots. She never bothered trying to wear anything prettier because she knew how he would react. "I don't want anyone looking at me," she muttered. Not even you, she thought to herself. Tingles crept up Tilly's neck, she could sense her follower nearby. She tensed and looked around, this was not a good time for him to show up.

They reached the end of Tilly's street, a tidy row of grey, modest townhouses with the same shimmering, silver-leaved trees lining the footpath. Orvyn's large motorcycle was parked out the front of her house, he stopped on the sidewalk in front of it. Tilly glanced over at the house next door. Orvyn had once lived there with his mother and father, but now his mother was all alone. Tilly felt sorry for her, she knew Orvyn never bothered to visit. She noticed her peeking through the window and gave her a small wave. The curtain quickly closed.

"Well?" Orvyn said annoyed.

"Well, what?"

He shoved his white hair back. "Aren't you gonna ask why I was looking for you?"

"I'm sure you'll tell me anyway."

"We have a surprise for you."

Tilly's face shot towards him. "What kind of surprise?"

His eyes glinted in a way that made her nervous. "We want you to join the Iron Vipers, your initiation is tonight."

Tilly stared at him with wide eyes. "But, I thought we agreed I would only train with them."

Orvyn raised his eyebrows and scoffed. "You and I are the best fighters in this shit city, they've seen what you can do and they want you in."

Tilly didn't know what to say, that was the last thing she wanted.

"You're already with me most of the time," he added. "You just have to prove your loyalty—it'll be easy."

"How?" she said panicked. He had completely caught her off guard.

Orvyn smirked, he leaned down and kissed her hard on the mouth. "I'll see you at the clubhouse at midnight, don't be late or I'll be pissed." He walked over to his motorcycle and climbed onto it, revving the engine.

"How?" she yelled.

Orvyn laughed and rode off into the night.

Tilly stared after him, not believing what had just happened. "Shit."

Chapter Two

The Follower

T illy heard her mother rummaging around in the kitchen, she crept upstairs to her bedroom and quietly closed the door. Her room had forest green walls, a timber-framed, double bed, a full-length mirror and a bookshelf crammed with books. A few months ago, her mother had hung a pin-board beside her bed and wrapped fairy lights around it. She told Tilly it was for her goals and dreams. Tilly had joked that her only dream was to taste every type of cake in the realm, they had both laughed about it. The next day, Tilly had come home to find a map of Valuna pinned to her board. Since then, her mother had slowly added more to it until it was overflowing with pictures. Tilly's favourite was a photo of the Valunan Five she had cut from a magazine. They were the fiercest and most famous protectors of the realm—who she and Orvyn had always idolised. As well as incredible speed and strength, they had the ability to shapeshift into an animal form. Apart from that, they were just five incredibly good-looking men.

She glanced up at the only thing she had pinned herself, an acceptance letter to join the Valunan Guard—the defence force of the realm. It was what she and Orvyn had been dreaming of since they were children. She groaned and flopped back onto her bed, pulling her white pillow over her face. She couldn't believe he wanted her to join the Iron Vipers, which was the exact opposite.

"God, I'm such an idiot," she said, her voice muffled. She was so mad at herself, she should have ended things before it became this bad. Her heart still hadn't stopped racing, she was sure she was on the verge of a panic attack. Tilly ran through different scenarios in her head. More than likely, they would ask her to steal something or fight someone. Worst case scenario, kill someone. Her eyes widened. "I can't do that!"

There was a soft knock at the door. "Tilly dear? Do you have a friend with you?" her mother called.

Tilly jumped up and opened the door, forcing a smile. "You know I don't have any friends."

Her mother, Edith, stood in the doorway holding two cups of coffee. Edith was always neatly dressed, today in navy pants and a white blouse. She was short and fair-skinned, her curly, brown hair pulled back into a small bun. Whenever she smiled her brown eyes sparkled, reflecting her kind soul. She shook her head at Tilly dismissively, with a small smile on her lips. "You used to have friends, have you thought about calling them?"

Tilly did have a few girlfriends, but Orvyn had scared them all away. "I've tried, they don't answer."

"I'm sure they'll come around." Edith placed the coffee on the bedside table and studied Tilly's face. "Is there something wrong?"

Tilly flopped back down on her bed, staring at the ceiling. She couldn't tell her mum about her follower or the bikies, it would make her worry. "Just Orvyn issues, as usual. His moods are getting worse."

Edith sat on the bed with concern in her eyes. "I know you care about him," she said carefully. "But it's not fair for him to take everything out on you, it might be time to try and distance yourself a little."

Tilly felt tears in her eyes, that was easier said than done, she thought. "He's not that bad, he's just hurting. You know he hasn't been the same since his dad left."

Orvyn's father, Nero, was a Commander in the Valunan Guard, everyone in the city feared and respected him. As a child, Tilly would watch from her window as he trained Orvyn to fight in their backyard. One day she knocked on their door and begged him to teach her too—he had hesitantly agreed. She had never taken anything so seriously, fighting felt so natural to her. When Nero realised this, he began training them both properly. She practiced with Orvyn every day after school, and they had been best friends ever since. Around a year ago his father left without a word. She would sit with Orvyn at the city gates, day after day, waiting for him to return. He never did.

Edith laid beside Tilly, staring at the ceiling with her. "Do you really want to be with someone who's not that bad?"

"He's always been there for me," Tilly argued. "What kind of friend would I be if I turned my back on him now?"

"He doesn't see you as a friend though, does he?" Edith said. "Do you want to be his girlfriend?"

Tilly hesitated, no one had ever asked her that before—not even Orvyn. "No, he's always been like a brother to me, but I don't want to hurt him."

Edith took Tilly's hand and squeezed it. "I know you don't, but one day he might ask you for something that you don't want to give him. I think you need to tell him the truth before that happens."

Tilly knew she was right, other than kissing he had never pushed her to do anything intimate. But even joining the Vipers for him was something she wasn't willing to do.

Tilly laid on her bed for hours, thinking about everything her mum and Eleanor had said. She wondered what would happen if she just stayed there and ignored all of her problems. She groaned, Orvyn would probably show up and then her parents would get involved. She definitely didn't want that. Tilly checked her phone; it was almost ten. She had messaged Orvyn hours ago asking to meet up somewhere and talk. He still hadn't replied and he wouldn't answer her calls. She was growing restless waiting around, she needed to get out of the house.

Tilly changed into tight black pants and a dark T-shirt, before pulling out two bronze-hilted daggers from her closet. She tucked them into holsters around her thighs. To her parents' horror, Nero had given her the daggers as a gift for her sixteenth birthday—Eleanor thought it was hilarious. She pulled on her combat boots and a thin, black hooded cloak that stopped just above her knees. She left her long, black hair down in waves and checked her reflection in the mirror. Her hazel-green eyes were bloodshot from stress and lack of sleep. She wondered how everything had gone so wrong lately. "I still think you're an idiot," she told her reflection seriously.

Tilly left her room quietly and tiptoed down the stairs, not wanting to wake her parents. Her dad had been working late every day for the past week. He was the best shoemaker in the city and had his own factory downtown. One of the Lords, Lord Dalton, had personally hired him to make custom shoes for all of his upcoming social events. Tilly shuddered at the thought, she'd always found Lord Dalton terrifying.

She grabbed some honey cake on her way out and made her way towards the south gate. Silverleaf had been built in the middle of Silkwood Forest, which she visited as often as possible. The air felt too muggy for her inside the tall city walls. Tilly passed a noisy bar and pulled her hood over her head. She heard whistles and glanced back, tightening a hand around her dagger. A small group of men were stumbling out the door, watching her. She crossed the road and peeked back, they were heading in the opposite direction. She sighed with relief and walked a little faster.

As she approached the gate, one of the old guards gave her a toothy grin. "Evening Til, I've been hearing rumours that you might be one of us soon."

Tilly laughed and passed him the honey cake. His eyes lit up excitedly as he took it from her. "I've been accepted," she said. "I get my ranking next Friday after my trial."

"Well, I guarantee you won't be put on guard duty," he said through a mouthful of cake. "They aren't gonna know what's hit 'em."

Tilly grinned, feeling butterflies in her stomach at the thought. It had been a while since she'd felt excited about the future. She hoped after her trial the Guard would send her somewhere else, preferably somewhere cold. She followed the road out of the city and stopped at a small opening between the trees. Glancing around, she made sure she hadn't been followed before stepping into the overgrown forest.

The air was fresh on her face and she could smell the damp leaves beneath her feet. She walked the familiar path through the trees, watching the full moon through the branches. Tilly reached a small clearing and took off her cloak, resting it on a large rock. She sat by the creek and pulled off her boots before she dipped her feet into the cool water and closed her eyes. Tilly imagined herself sitting on a snowy mountain with a frosty breeze caressing her face. Usually it would calm her down, but tonight it was no use, she was too anxious. She jumped up and pulled her daggers out, using the clearing to practice. Her thoughts turned to Orvyn and she grew angry, how could he set her up like that when he knew how she felt about the Vipers? Tilly yelled in frustration and threw her dagger into a large oak tree. She leaned her head back and squeezed her eyes closed, holding in tears.

She took a deep breath before walking over to the tree. "I'm sorry Oaken, you didn't deserve that." She tried pulling the dagger out, but it wouldn't budge.

Leaves crunched behind her. She whirled around just as she felt tingles creeping up her neck, her heart started to race and warmth enveloped her body. A man around six feet tall stood in the darkness between the trees, his face hidden under a dark hooded coat. She could see the hilt of a sword behind his broad shoulders. "What did Oaken ever do to you?" he teased, his voice deep and playful. "It hardly seems like a fair fight."

Tilly felt anger burn in her chest, this man had been following her around, scaring her for days. Finally, he reveals himself and the first thing he does is make fun of her, she'd had enough. Without thinking, she shot towards him, ready to knock him on his arse. When she reached him, she feigned left and aimed a kick to the back of his knee—he dodged her at the last second. She tried grabbing him, but he blocked her. Each time she advanced towards him he would move at the last second, he was so fast it was infuriating. Tilly swung her fist towards his side and he knocked her arm away. She brought her other arm up and elbowed him in the side of the face. The man chuckled and grabbed her without warning, spinning her around so her back pressed against his chest. His arms wrapped around her so tight she couldn't move. Tilly's breath quickened, the warmth she had felt before was nothing compared to what she felt now. She knew she should break free, but her body didn't want to, she was drawn to him like a magnet. Her heart raced but she wasn't afraid. She leaned back against him as he trailed his nose down the side of her face, stopping at the curve of her neck. Tilly closed her eyes, lost in the moment.

"Please stop fighting me, I don't want to hurt you," he whispered. "I just want to talk."

Tilly's eyes shot open, she pulled herself free and backed away from him. Slowly he stepped into the moonlight and drew down his hood.

Her eyes went wide as she recognised him from the photo on her wall. Bronze skin with a chiselled, unshaven face and short black hair. He was the youngest of the Valunan Five and easily the most attractive man she'd ever seen. His warm, brown eyes watched her with amusement as the hint of a smile played on his full lips. "You," she whispered, unable to bring words to her mouth.

His smile widened and he extended his hand towards her. She noticed a gold ring on his finger, carved into a lion's face.

"I'm Leo, you must be Tilly."

She frowned as she placed her hand in his, she wondered how he knew her name. Leo brought her hand to his lips, kissing it softly and sending shivers up her arm. "I need to know something," he said, his eyes gleaming excitedly. "Have you named all of the trees?"

Tilly snapped back to life. "Don't be ridiculous," she said. "Only the trees I talk to." She immediately squeezed her eyes shut, realising how stupid she had sounded.

Leo laughed and quickly cleared his throat to stop himself. Tilly noticed he was still holding her hand and pulled it away nervously. "Why have you been following me? You've been freaking me out," she said annoyed. "And how do you know my name?"

He smiled sheepishly, rubbing his cheek where she had elbowed him. "Where did you learn to fight like that?"

Tilly crossed her arms over her chest. "Nero taught me, now answer my questions."

His eyebrows shot up in surprise. "Nero's a legend, no wonder you're so good."

She stared back at him, waiting for her answer.

Leo bit his bottom lip as his eyes searched hers. "I didn't mean to scare you, I just needed to make sure you were alright."

"Why wouldn't I be?"

He nodded towards the oak tree. "You tell me. You seemed quite mad at Oaken."

Tilly looked back at the dagger, feeling embarrassed that he'd seen that. "I was uh, thinking about someone else."

Leo went and pulled the dagger out with ease, he passed it back to her. "Orvyn?"

Tilly slid it back into her holster and looked up at him in

surprise. "You know Orvyn?"

She thought she saw a flicker of anger in his eyes. "I've seen him a few times," he said casually. "Drinking with his friends, always a different girl on his arm." Tilly felt her stomach drop, she glanced down at the creek, unable to meet Leo's eyes. She wasn't stupid, she knew Orvyn fooled around with other girls. A selfish part of her had hoped he would leave her for one of them, but it hadn't happened so far. Leo stepped towards her, standing only inches away. He lifted her chin with his finger, bringing her face up to his. "You knew? Why would you stay with him?"

She met his concerned eyes, she didn't understand how, but it didn't feel like she was talking to a famous brother of the Valunan Five, it felt as if she were talking to someone she had always known. "I want to leave," she whispered, "but I'm scared of how he'll react." It was the first time she'd spoken the truth out loud. She closed her eyes, turning her head as a tear ran down her cheek.

"Let me help you," he said gently. "I have to leave Silverleaf soon, you could come with me and get away from all of this."

She quickly wiped her eyes, suddenly embarrassed that she'd cried in front of a man she just met. "I can't leave with you—I don't even know you."

He gave her a sad smile. "What will you do if you stay?" he asked. "I know about the initiation, these bikies won't just let you walk away."

"Shit! The initiation!" Tilly pulled out her phone, she had five missed calls from Orvyn and ten minutes to get halfway across the city.

She pulled on her boots and grabbed her cloak as Leo followed along behind her. "You can't seriously be thinking of going through with this? It's a life sentence," he said. Tilly fastened her cloak and pulled on her hood. Leo placed his hand on her shoulder to stop her. "I can help you."

She met his pleading eyes, already hating herself for what she was about to say. "No one can help me." She turned and ran through the forest as fast as she could.

"Tilly, please!" he called after her. Her body ached to run back to him, but she couldn't let him get involved. This wasn't his problem to fix—it was hers.

Chapter Three

The Iron Vipers

Tilly raced down the road at full speed, passing through the city gates so fast that she startled the guards. "Sorry!" she yelled, watching them shake their heads. Her heart was pounding, she couldn't believe Leo had been the one following her, she'd never seen one of the Five in person before. She wondered how she was able to sense him and how he had known so much about her. She cringed as she recalled the hurt in his eyes when she ran from him, he hadn't deserved that. Once she had cleaned up this mess, she would need to find a way to apologise to him.

Tilly kept running until she reached the industrial area of the city. During the day, trucks travelled in and out and smoke filled the air from the factories. At night, it was eerily quiet, with not a single person in sight—which made it the perfect place for the Iron Viper's clubhouse. She turned a corner and saw their warehouse up ahead. It was a decrepit, grey building with blackened windows and graffiti down one side. Anyone would think it had been abandoned. She noticed a small crowd gathered out the front, wearing a lot of black leather and surrounded by a cloud of smoke. Their rowdy banter carried through the air. She stopped in front of a small warehouse and rested her hand against the wall as she tried to catch her breath.

Orvyn left the crowd and staggered towards her angrily, a half-empty bottle swinging in his hand. "You're fucking late, why are you so hopeless?"

Tilly winced. "I need to talk to you," she said breathlessly.

He stopped at her feet, his bloodshot eyes boring into hers. "Everyone's been waiting for you. Whatever it is, it can wait."

Her body trembled, but she raised her chin defiantly. "No Orvyn, I won't do this."

Without warning, Orvyn swiftly pushed her against the wall, smashing his bottle beside her head. Tilly cowered away from him in shock, he had never touched her like that before. "What do you mean you won't do this?" he seethed. His face was so close she could almost taste the alcohol on his breath. "You already made us wait, you're not gonna embarrass me more."

Tilly squeezed her eyes shut and clenched her fists. "I won't be a bikie. I've never wanted this."

Orvyn sneered and let go of her. "What are you gonna do? Join the Guard? They would never want you."

She glared back at him as tears burned her eyes. "You're wrong, I've already been accepted."

Orvyn's face turned furious. "That's too fucking bad, you have no idea what I've done to get you into the Vipers. If you don't do this, I'm dead." He grabbed her arm and dragged her towards the clubhouse.

"What do you mean?" Tilly said desperately. "Orvyn! What did you do?"

Orvyn swung his arm around her shoulder as they drew closer to the crowd. "Bloody girls, she fell asleep," he lied.

Most of them laughed, but one of the older men did not look amused. He nodded towards the warehouse. "Mav's waiting for you both."

Orvyn led her inside to a decaying office that reeked of mould—she knew the room well. There were no other doors, only a trapdoor hidden behind a large corner desk. He shoved her ahead and she carefully climbed down the ladder, shaking so badly she was scared she would fall.

The inside of the clubhouse was sleek and modern. They walked through a spacious training room full of burly men and a handful of women. They were working out on gym equipment and grappling on a large black mat. Orvyn had once told her that Mav found most of his members on the streets. He took them in and they would sleep during the day and work during the night—wreaking havoc wherever they went. Orvyn gripped her arm, leaning close to her ear. "Stop shaking."

Tilly held back tears, she wished she had stayed in the forest. She wondered if Leo had already left the city—her heart ached at the thought. Orvyn led her down a dark, winding corridor to a set of glossy, black doors. He knocked twice and the doors opened. A brawny man with lip piercings and a snake tattoo gave them a once-over. He stepped back and nodded for them to go inside. The room was dimly lit and full of smoke. In the centre was a large oval table with older club members seated around it, drinking and smoking. Small tables lined the outside of the room, full of younger, rowdier bikies.

Orvyn dragged her to the head of the table where Mav was waiting. Mav's sharp eyes followed her every move. Tilly hadn't met him before, but he was easy to place. Dark, greasy, slicked-back hair and a heavy gold chain gleaming under his leather jacket. His elbow rested on the table, with his claw-like hand covering his mouth. Mav stood abruptly as they reached him, making her flinch. He lifted a heavy eyebrow and she shuddered under his gaze. She wasn't sure what he was, but she knew he wasn't entirely human. He tilted his head to the side. "I was surprised when I heard you wanted to join us, sweetheart."

Tilly jerked her head towards Orvyn, but his expression didn't change. "So was I," she said honestly.

Orvyn quickly laughed. "She's kidding, she's been nagging me for weeks."

Mav grabbed her shoulders, digging his sharp nails into her skin. He gave her a twisted smile, she noticed some of his teeth had been replaced with gold fangs. "Hmm, you're too pretty—isn't she pretty gents?" Laughter and whistles filled the room. Tilly had a sudden urge to punch him in the face, but she knew that would not go well for her.

"I'll admit though, she knows how to fight," he said, he gave a raspy laugh. "I reckon she could give some of you lot a run for your money." He flung his arm around her shoulder, pulling her close to his side. Tilly held her breath, he stunk of sweat and smoke. "You'll be useful to us sweetheart. You're a quick little thing, good for those hard-to-reach places." There were more laughs around the room, everyone other than her seemed to be enjoying Mav's comments.

He took his arm off her and stalked around the table slowly. "You should know though, we have rules around here." His expression hardened. "If you betray us, you die. If you try to leave, you die. But, if you prove yourself useful, we'll take good care of you." The men cheered and raised their bottles. Tilly felt like she was going to be sick. Mav studied her face. "Are you ready for this?"

Tilly opened her mouth as Orvyn threw his arm back around her. "She's ready, she won't let you down." She felt anger burn in her chest, she'd never felt so humiliated and angry.

"If you want in, you need to do something for me," Mav said, he glanced at Orvyn and smirked. "I've been told you're a little afraid of Lord Dalton."

Tilly's face shot towards Orvyn, but he wouldn't meet her eye. Mav nodded towards the door. "Time to face your fears, sweetheart, bring me one of his ridiculously large amulets. Take a few of the boys with you and go have some fun."

She felt too numb to even speak, Lord Dalton was the last person in Valuna she wanted to see.

Tilly and Orvyn rode through the dark city on his motorbike. She tightened her grip around his waist, she didn't mind the bike, but it scared her that he'd been drinking all night. She stared at the moon as tears streaked down her face, she wished more than anything she had accepted Leo's offer and left with him.

Two other bikies, Zado and Jep, trailed behind on their motorbikes. She was glad it was them who came along. She had trained with them both before and they'd always been respectful towards her. They rode towards the heart of the city. The houses grew larger and grander as they went. They decided to park a few streets away from Lord Dalton's mansion and continue on foot.

Zado was practically bouncing with excitement, he was a Fenx, with tanned skin and bright green eyes. His pointed ears were the colour of honey, the same as his long hair which was tied in a knot on top of his head. He hadn't stopped talking since they got off their bikes. Jep was human and quieter, dark-skinned, with scraggly brown hair and a lanky body that towered over the others. He watched the streets vigilantly as they walked. Each of the guys wore an Iron Viper jacket—Tilly couldn't even imagine herself in one and she didn't want to. She zoned out as they walked, she'd heard enough of Zado's stories. Her head was spinning and she felt nauseous thinking about what she had to do.

"Are you even listening?" Orvyn said annoyed.

She glanced at Orvyn. "What?"

"I said, we'll distract the guards and meet you back at the bikes."

"Can't wait," she muttered.

Orvyn stared at her with disbelief. "You better take this seriously."

Zado stopped beside Orvyn and smiled. "Don't worry Tilly, this will be quick and easy."

Jep checked his phone before placing it back in his pocket. "He's right, Lord Dalton's at some fundraiser tonight. One of the guys saw him earlier."

Tilly felt slightly relieved, but she was still furious. Zado and Jep hurried ahead and she turned to Orvyn angrily. "How could you do this to me? And why would you tell Mav about Lord Dalton?"

Orvyn scoffed, she thought she saw a hint of guilt in his eyes, but maybe she had imagined it. "It's not a big deal. You'll be fine, he's not even there."

"Not a big deal?" she hissed. "This is my life Orvyn, I wanted to protect people, not steal from them."

"We're here," Zado whispered back excitedly. "Good luck Tilly." She glanced at Lord Dalton's mansion, only two guards stood outside the gate.

They stayed close to the fence, walking in the shadows. Orvyn pulled her aside and shoved his white hair out of his face in exasperation. "I owe Mav money alright, this was the deal we made—you and the amulet. Just get it or we'll be screwed."

She looked into his cold, blue eyes, shaking her head with disgust. "I swear I don't even know you anymore."

Orvyn gave her one last hard look before running off towards the guards, the other two followed, leaving her behind. She stared after them, trying to calm the fury in her chest. She would get the amulet to pay his debt, but after that, she was done. Tilly watched Orvyn knock down a guard while Zado and Jep circled the other. She climbed the fence and jumped over, her boots landed on the soft grass. She ducked behind the hedges and followed them up towards the white mansion, staying as low as she could. As she drew closer, she saw more guards run out towards the front gate. She glanced around before racing to the door, quickly pulling it open and slipping inside. Tilly instantly began shaking. She wrapped her arms around herself and hurried up the sweeping staircase, she wanted to get out of there as fast as possible.

Inside was just as she had remembered it—white marble floors and beige walls adorned with an intricate gold pattern. The furniture was made of polished wood and large works of art hung on every wall. Her dad had brought her here a few years ago when he was delivering shoes. Lord Dalton had his eyes on her the entire time, they kept wandering down her body. She shuddered at the memory, she was only sixteen at the time and it had completely creeped her out. Orvyn was the only person she had ever told.

Tilly reached the top of the staircase and heard footsteps. She ducked into the first room and held her breath. The footsteps passed and she peeked her head out as a cleaner hurried down the stairs. Tilly sighed and crept out slowly. She checked each room down the long corridor and started to panic, she'd been there for too long. She reached the last door and looked inside. Her eyes widened in shock, she had found Lord Dalton's bedroom. Her knees went weak as she stepped inside the room. Hung around his walls were large, horrific photos of women. Reluctantly, Tilly looked at the closest photo. It was a barely dressed, young brunette woman with her hands bound. The sheer terror in her eyes told Tilly the woman had not wanted to be there. "You sick bastard," Tilly whispered. She felt tears burn her eyes, these poor women. She bent down and rested her hands on her thighs, taking deep breaths. No wonder she'd felt so terrified of him.

She searched the room as quickly as she could. It had plush white carpet, high ceilings and a full-length window overlooking the city. She ran past his four-poster bed towards the walk-in wardrobe, her hands were shaking badly. She found a glass cabinet full of jewels and cried out in relief. At the very centre was a ruby amulet the size of her palm. Tilly carefully opened the cabinet and pulled the amulet out, she wrapped the chain around her wrist and hurried out of the room.

Tilly froze. Lord Dalton was blocking the bedroom door—his red face puffed with excitement. His crystal blue eyes widened when he saw her. He flattened his thinning, grey hair with his hand. "You have no idea how happy I am to see you again." Tilly gripped the door frame as fear took over her body. Lord Dalton grinned and took a slow step towards her. His pinstriped suit was so tight over his heavy body that she could hear the fabric protest as he moved.

"Stop! The Iron Vipers will come after you if you touch me," she lied.

His eyes gleamed wickedly. "Who do you think told me you were here?" Realisation dawned on her face. "Stupid girl," he said. "Mav told me you were coming. He knew I'd pay a handsome price for you."

"No," she whispered, she didn't trust them, but she had never expected to be set up.

He looked up at his photos fondly. "Since the moment I met you, I knew I'd have you on my wall one day." He tapped his finger on his lip thoughtfully. "My, my, what would your daddy think? You've broken into my home and stolen from me. I could have you arrested for this."

She tried to move, but her legs turned to jelly beneath her. "I'm sorry," she whispered. "I didn't want to steal from you."

He stalked towards her and his eyes flicked to the amulet in her hand. "Perhaps we can come to an arrangement. If you play nice, I'll forget this whole thing ever happened. I'll even let you wear that for your photo."

He was inches away from her. She'd never felt so terrified, he was a Lord who had caught her red-handed. She would spend her life locked away for stealing from him. Her head spun and her heart pounded, she felt like she was about to collapse. His hand reached out towards her face.

Your daggers! Do not let him touch you.

A regal, female voice entered her mind, snapping her to life. She felt a warmth build in her chest, it spread through her body, giving her strength. In one swift move, Tilly pulled her dagger free and swiped it across Lord Dalton's cheek. He shrieked and brought his hands to his face as she kicked him hard in the chest. She didn't waste any time as he stumbled back, she shot towards the door and pulled at the handle—it was locked. She pulled at it again. "No!"

"You bitch!" he screamed. She turned around and Lord Dalton was running towards her, covered in blood. He tried to grab her, but she swerved under his arm and hit him hard in the side. He dropped to the ground as the door burst open. Six guards entered the room, all armed with swords.

"Shit," she cried, backing away from them.

The closest guard noticed the amulet in her hand. "You little thief!"

"Get her now," Lord Dalton spat. The guard lunged towards her, she dodged him easily and knocked him down. He fell beside her and grunted angrily. The others circled her and her heart sank, she didn't think she could take all of them. A guard to her left sprang towards her, she whirled around him as the rest of them followed. She ducked between them before spotting an opening and running towards the door. She had almost reached it when the closest guard threw his whole body towards her and grabbed her foot. Tilly cried out as she fell to the ground. The guards gripped her arms and pulled her up. Lord Dalton stormed over and slapped her hard across the face. "I'll kill you for this," he seethed.

"What should we do with her, my Lord?"

Lord Dalton held his cheek where she had cut him, he was still bleeding. "Tie her to my bed and put that amulet around her neck—nobody touches her until I return." They snickered and dragged her towards the bed. Lord Dalton hurried out the door with two guards following behind. "I need a doctor immediately!"

Tilly thrashed around as they pulled her towards the bed. "Stop moving or we'll knock you out."

Her shoulders sagged. They stood her against a bedpost and bound her wrists and feet to it. A guard placed the ruby amulet around her neck and then reached down to cut her holsters off. He held up her dagger and sneered. "What do you think she uses these for? Are they cheese knives?" The others laughed as he tossed them across the room.

Tilly turned her face away from them. She was so angry, angry at herself, angry at Orvyn. She felt so stupid for trying to help him after everything he'd done to her. Now she would pay for her stupidity with her life.

Chapter Four

This is Goodbye

Tilly scanned the room desperately, looking for anything that could help her escape. One of the guards yawned, looking bored. If she could catch them by surprise, she might have a chance to save herself. She pulled at her ropes, but they wouldn't budge. Suddenly, a warmth crept over her body and tingles ran up her neck—Leo was close by. The feeling had scared her in the past, now it filled her with excitement and relief. Without warning the window shattered. Leo landed on the carpet, surrounded by broken glass. Tilly could see him more clearly now under the light. He wore green military pants and combat boots, his black T-shirt hugged his torso and his large sword rested between his shoulder blades. He flicked glass out of his black hair and glanced towards her. The playful man she had met in the forest was gone. His brown eyes blazed with fury as he saw her bound wrists. Leo looked back at the shocked guards. "Untie her," he growled.

The guard who had taunted Tilly approached him with

confusion. "This woman is a thief. We're just having a little fun and then we'll hand her—"

Leo didn't allow him to finish his sentence, he booted him in the chest, sending him flying across the room. The other guards drew their swords and charged towards him. Leo didn't even bother reaching for his. He swatted them away effortlessly, moving so fast they barely had time to react before they were all knocked to the ground. He stood over them with a menacing look on his face. "Leave."

The guards stared at him fearfully as they scrambled out of the room. Leo rushed over to Tilly and untied the ropes. She fell forward and he grabbed her arms to steady her. "I'm so sorry," she cried. "I can't believe you came back for me."

"I tried getting here sooner but I was held up, are you hurt?"

She shook her head. "No, I'm okay."

His eyes narrowed as he noticed where Lord Dalton had slapped her. He reached up and stroked her cheek with his thumb. "What happened?"

"I was set up. Lord Dalton tried to—"

She squeezed her eyes shut, she couldn't bring the words to her mouth. "I shouldn't have come here."

Leo's expression softened. "Why did you go through with it?" he asked gently.

She bowed her head, feeling so ashamed of herself. "I tried to say no—I was too weak."

"No, Til." Without hesitation, Leo pulled her into his arms, he smelt just like the forest after it rained. Tilly was surprised by how her body welcomed the embrace. "I've seen the person you are, weak is the last thing I would call you," he said. She rested her head against his chest, listening to his steady heartbeat. "Let's get you out of here."

Tilly looked up into his warm eyes. "You said you were leaving Silverleaf, can I still go with you?"

He gave her a small smile. "Of course, are you sure you want to leave?"

Tilly knew she didn't have a choice. Lord Dalton wanted her dead, Mav had set her up and Orvyn had traded her life for his debt. "I have to, it's not safe here anymore."

Leo nodded in understanding. "I promise you'll be safe with me—I'd never let anything happen to you." His body tensed, he tilted his head towards the door. "Footsteps." Leo hurried her over to the window. "I'll buy you some time. Go say your goodbyes and head to the west gate when you're ready—I'll find you."

She carefully climbed over the windowsill, avoiding the jagged glass. "Thank you, I don't know why you're helping me, but I owe you my life."

"You don't owe me anything."

She watched him head towards the door. "Will you be okay?" she blurted out.

He glanced back and grinned, his eyes sparkled mischievously. "Don't you worry about me."

Tilly was dumbfounded, he had the most breathtaking smile she'd ever seen, and it completely caught her off guard. She held onto the windowsill, staring at him like an idiot. He tried to hide his smile. "You should probably get going."

Tilly moved too fast and her arm slipped. Leo tried not to laugh as she gave him an embarrassed smile and quickly climbed down the side of the mansion. She reached the lower floor and heard a loud growl above. She jumped onto the grass and checked for guards—there were none in sight. Tilly ran out the gate and back through the city.

The sun had started to rise and the air was already warm. Tilly had never felt more grateful to breathe it in. She was dreading saying goodbye to her parents, but she'd never been so anxious to leave Silverleaf. More guards were patrolling the streets than usual, she kept her head down, hoping none of them would recognise her. She was only a few blocks away from home when she turned a corner and ran straight into Orvyn.

"Tilly!" He grabbed her shoulders and eyed her down. He had a black eye and a cut across his forehead. Zado and Jep stood behind him—looking even worse. None of them were wearing their Iron Viper jackets. "What happened?" he asked. "We've been looking everywhere for you."

Tilly glared at him furiously. "Everywhere except the mansion. Mav set me up, Lord Dalton was expecting me."

Orvyn looked at her in shock. "Mav wouldn't do that."

Tilly stared at him in disbelief. "Are you serious? He's a criminal Orvyn, of course he would."

Orvyn scoffed angrily and threw his arm around her shoulder. "It doesn't matter now, the Valunan Guard raided the warehouse and one of the Five was with them." He glanced around nervously. "They've taken Mav, we have to get off the streets."

She shoved his arm away. "I'm not going anywhere with you. Lord Dalton said he would kill me for what I did. If Leo hadn't shown up, I'd probably be dead already."

Orvyn stepped towards her angrily. "Who the fuck is Leo?"

"Are you even listening?" she yelled. "Lord Dalton wants me dead, I have to get out of the city."

He looked at her incredulously. "You're not going anywhere, you're one of us now."

Tilly felt anger build in her chest. "I don't give a shit about your stupid club. I didn't even finish the initiation."

Orvyn grabbed the amulet around her neck and pulled it from her. "What the fuck is this then? You're not leaving me—I'll hide you if I have to."

Her eyes narrowed. "No. You and I are done."

Orvyn clenched his fist and stood over her. Tilly tried stepping around him, but he blocked her path, holding the necklace in her face. "You're one of us. If you want to leave you can fight your way out like everyone else."

"You can't be serious," Tilly hissed. "I'm not fighting you."

Orvyn glanced behind him. "Don't let her go, she's coming with us."

Zado shook his head at Orvyn. "It's not safe for her to stay."

Tilly nodded at him gratefully. Jep gave her a small smile. Orvyn looked back at her desperately. "You took the amulet so you're one of us."

She eyed Orvyn with disgust, the pity she'd felt for him before was gone. "Goodbye Orvyn."

She tried to step past him again, but he reached out to grab her. Tilly ducked and spun around to face him. Orvyn gritted his teeth and swung his fist towards her, she dodged and he tried again. Tilly watched him with disbelief as he kept trying to hit her. They had trained together for almost their whole lives, she knew his every move. He had always been the strongest, but she had always been the fastest. "Stop being stupid," she said angrily.

Orvyn started growing mad. He threw his whole body towards her and Tilly fell back onto the sidewalk. He pinned her down and brought his face to hers. "You're so weak, why won't you fight me?" he cried.

Her eyes burned with hatred. She didn't want to hurt him,

she just wanted to get out of there.

Stop holding back, show him who you are.

She heard the same regal voice she had heard when Lord Dalton tried to touch her. She felt a warmth build in her chest, filling her body with feral rage. "I am not weak," she snarled, "and you'll never touch me again."

Orvyn's eyes widened in surprise. She pulled her arm free and punched him hard in the nose—her own strength surprising her. He fell back and she pounced on top of him, punching him again and again. Zado and Jep backed away in shock. Orvyn tried to grab her hands, but she shoved him away.

"Tilly, stop," Zado pleaded.

She looked down at Orvyn's bleeding face, not believing what she had just done. "Please don't leave," Orvyn whimpered. "I love you, I can't lose you too."

She stared into his blue eyes. This was the first time he'd ever said he loved her. "No, you don't," she said. "This isn't love."

His expression turned pained, he closed his eyes and Tilly watched a tear run down his face. She climbed off him and ran home without looking back, promising herself she would never let anyone treat her that way again.

Tilly bolted inside and slammed the door shut. She slid down against it, breathing heavily as she stared at her bloodied hands. She couldn't believe what she had done. Whose voice had she heard? Maybe all of the stress was driving her crazy.

"Tilly, are you okay?" her mother asked softly.

Tilly's face shot up, she hadn't even noticed her parents and Eleanor sitting around the dining table, watching her. Her parents were both in pyjamas and Eleanor was wearing one of her colourful sundresses and a matching blindfold. She could smell the fresh coffee coming from the steaming jug in front of them. Tilly glanced between them with tears in her eyes, how could she ever say goodbye?

Her mother and father rushed over and dropped to the floor, pulling her into their arms. Tilly let out a loud sob. "We've been so worried," her father said. She noticed his usually neat, dark blonde hair sticking out all over the place. "What happened?"

Tilly stared into his worried, green eyes, she felt awful for scaring them. Her parents had always been there for her no matter what. She decided she didn't want to lie to them anymore. Tilly told them everything that had happened and they listened quietly. When she reached the part about Lord Dalton and Orvyn they both looked horrified. "I'm so sorry," Tilly whispered into her hands. "Neither of you deserved this."

"You didn't deserve it either Til," her father said, she could see the anger in his eyes.

"Orvyn's behaviour was unacceptable," Edith said. "As for Lord Dalton, we'll send an anonymous tip to the Guard about the photos after you leave."

Tilly nodded. "That's a good idea, I don't want anyone else getting hurt."

Edith cupped her cheek. "We do need to get you out of here though. He is not known for being merciful."

"Will you be okay?" Tilly asked, looking between her parents. "What if he comes here looking for me?"

"We'll be fine dear, he can't do anything to us," Edith said.

Tilly noticed they were all awfully calm. "You don't seem worried that I'm leaving."

Her mother raised her eyebrows. "Of course we're worried, but, we did know this was coming. Eleanor saw you leaving around your nineteenth birthday. We just weren't sure when." Tilly had almost forgotten it was her birthday in two days.

Her father took her hand, holding it in both of his. "Before you leave, there's something we need to tell you."

Her parents glanced at Eleanor, Tilly followed their gaze with confusion. Eleanor sighed and slowly walked over to them. She knelt in front of Tilly and untied her blindfold, letting it fall to the floor.

Tilly gasped. "Your eyes. Eleanor, you have eyes! They're beautiful."

Eleanor chuckled sadly, her piercing golden eyes stared fondly at Tilly. "I told you I had eyes child, but my name is not Eleanor, it's Celia. Eleanor is my twin sister."

Tilly stared between them all. Her mother began to sob as her father squeezed her hand. "And we aren't your biological parents Til," he said gently, "but we have loved you, since the moment we saw you and you will always be our daughter."

Tilly's heart sank in her chest. "I don't understand," she whispered.

Celia placed her finger under Tilly's chin. "Do you remember my stories of Panthera?"

"The fallen kingdom?" Tilly asked. Celia had told her many stories of Panthera, it had been the greatest city in Valuna and home to the royal family. They were part of the last magical race called Spirids and had ruled peacefully for centuries. Almost two decades ago, Panthera had been destroyed and the Spirids all hunted down to extinction. Celia had told her that all of Valuna went into mourning over the loss. Now Panthera was gone and it had become the most dangerous place in the realm. It was forbidden to travel there and no one spoke of Panthera anymore.

Tears filled Celia's eyes, she nodded slowly. "You are a child of Panthera. The last of your kind."

"How is that possible?" Tilly asked, her head was spinning.

"Nineteen years ago, I helped deliver you into this world—the very day Panthera was attacked," Celia said. "Your real mother, Alwyn, was my dearest friend. She asked me to take you away and keep you hidden. She knew if she left she would be hunted down, so she stayed behind to keep you safe." Celia cried into her hands. "Leaving her was the hardest thing I've ever done."

Tilly's heart ached for Celia and for the mother she had never known. "I'm so sorry Celia."

Celia held Tilly's arm and squeezed it gently. "I had seen Jack and Edith in my dreams," she said, sniffing. "I didn't know who they were, so I brought you here to my sister Eleanor, not knowing that she had spent the day with Edith."

Tilly glanced at her mother. "Eleanor was a friend of ours," Edith said. She took a long breath. "I had given birth that day, to a sleeping angel. Jack and I were heartbroken and Eleanor had been helping us through our grief."

Tilly looked between the three people she loved most in the realm, her heart breaking for each of them. "You've all lost so much," she whispered.

Jack took Edith's hand and kissed it, his eyes full of tears. "Eleanor and Celia showed up in the middle of the night, with a beautiful baby girl," he said. "They asked if we would take you in as our own and never tell a soul. You were a dream come true."

"We didn't want to draw any suspicion," Celia added. "So

Eleanor left the city that night and I stayed in her place to watch over you. The only problem was that Eleanor is blind."

Tilly looked at her incredulously. "So, you've been pretending to be blind for nineteen years? That's insane."

Celia chuckled. "It was worth it to keep you safe. Besides, I could always see through the blindfolds somewhat. I actually enjoyed it—you see a lot when people think you can't see at all."

"That actually explains so much," Tilly muttered, thinking about the coffee table.

Jack stood up and looked out the window. "As much as I don't want you to leave, we need to get you out of here."

"How can I leave you?" Tilly whispered. "You've all done so much for me, I don't know how I can ever thank you."

Edith took her hands. "You don't have to dear, you've been a blessing."

Jack held Tilly's cheeks in his hands and smiled. "A complete smart-arse, but still a blessing. We've loved raising you." Tears streamed down Tilly's face. "This is your dream," Jack said, wrapping his arm around her. "You've always wanted to travel. Go and do it—don't let anyone hold you back."

Edith hurried out of the room and returned with a small box. "This was meant to be for your birthday, but I want to see you open it." Tilly took the box and pulled off the lid, inside was a dainty gold bracelet with three, small, coloured beads on it. The beads were in the shape of a cake, a shoe and an eyeball. Her mother took it out and fastened it around Tilly's wrist. "Something to remember each of us by and to remind you that this will always be your home," she said.

Tilly held each of the tiny beads between her fingers, she looked at the eyeball and glanced up at Celia. "I thought it would be funny," Celia said with a grin.

Tilly laughed through her tears. "It's perfect, thank you all, it means so much to me."

Jack passed her a new pair of black leather combat boots. Tilly noticed they each had a gold, crescent moon charm on the bottom row of laces. "Yours were looking a little old, your Mum added the charms," he said.

Tilly thanked him and pulled on the boots before she hugged her parents goodbye, telling them how much she loved them. "I'm going to miss you both so much."

Celia picked up a brown leather backpack and opened the front door, she glanced out nervously before putting her blindfold back on. "Come child." Tilly followed her out. She stopped on the sidewalk and looked back at her parents one last time.

Edith smiled sadly. "It's just goodbye for now dear."

Tilly could see the love in their eyes as they stood in the doorway, waving goodbye.

Chapter Five

The Journey

Tilly and Celia hurried through the city. They passed two energetic joggers who gave them startled looks. "You're still covered in blood," Celia muttered.

Tilly cringed, everything had happened so fast, she wished she'd had time to shower before they left. Celia took off the leather backpack and handed it to her, the two buckles were tarnished as if she'd had it for a very long time. "Put this on," she said quickly. "Edith packed you food and there's enough money to get you by for a few months. Most importantly, there's a box from Alwyn. Do not open it until you are safe and alone."

Tilly pulled the backpack on and thanked Celia, she had so many questions running through her mind. "If you came from Panthera, does that mean you're a Spirid too? Is that why you dream about the future?"

Celia chuckled and shook her head. "No, I'm a Spirling—a half-blood. My mother was a Spirid and my father was human. Spirlings don't inherit magic or have a guardian, but we are born with our own gift."

Tilly stopped on the sidewalk, staring at Celia with confusion, she'd never heard any of this before. "If I'm a Spirid, why don't I have magic?"

Celia lowered her voice. "Alwyn hid your magic to protect you, Spirid children are easy to recognise."

"What was she like?" Tilly whispered.

"She was the bravest woman I ever knew, she was strong and kind. You remind me so much of her. Except for your sense of humour, Alwyn's jokes were always terrible."

Tilly laughed sadly as she tried to imagine Alwyn. "What about my father?"

Celia hesitated for a moment and continued walking. Tilly fell into step beside her. "Namir, he died in the battle just before you were born. He was a quiet and serious man, but he was fiercely loyal. He and Alwyn shared a beautiful bond, he was so happy when she fell pregnant."

Tilly squeezed her eyes shut and held back tears. When she glanced up, she noticed two burly guards heading towards them in the distance—they seemed to be in a hurry. She quickly pulled Celia into an alleyway and they hid behind a stack of crates until the guards passed. Tilly rested her head against the wall, wondering if her heartbeat would ever return to normal. She hoped Leo was okay, they were only two blocks away from the west gate.

Celia pushed her blindfold up, eyeing Tilly with concern. "Try not to worry child. Lord Dalton may not have told the Guard what happened. I doubt he'd want them to know what you saw."

"I was actually thinking about Leo," she admitted. "I thought he would have found us by now."

Before she finished speaking, she sensed him close by. She glanced down the alleyway as he strolled towards them with warmth in his eyes and a grin on his face. "Did I just hear you were thinking about me?" he said. Tilly laughed, she felt relieved to see him. His face dropped as he drew closer. "Whose blood is that?"

"It's not mine," she said. "It's a long story." She looked at Celia who was staring wide-eyed at Leo. Tilly gently jabbed her with her elbow.

"He's even better than my dreams," Celia muttered.

Leo tilted his head, looking confused. He held his hand out towards Celia. "Thank you, I think? I'm Leopold of the Valunan Five." Celia shook his hand. "I'll take good care of Tilly, you have my word."

Celia's eyes flashed with amusement. "Oh, I know you will."

Tilly looked at her incredulously as a faint smile crossed Leo's face. "Unbelievable," Tilly murmured. She hugged Celia goodbye, not wanting to let go. "I'm going to miss you—I might even miss your tea."

Celia chuckled as she squeezed Tilly tight. "I have a feeling I'll see you again one day."

Tilly smiled at her tearfully and turned to Leo, his eyes softened as they met hers. "Ready to go?" he asked.

She looked down the alleyway towards the city, watching the cars pass and the silver-leaved trees glitter under the sunlight. She turned back to Celia, she was studying Tilly with her knowing, golden eyes. Celia smiled and gave a small nod. Silverleaf City was all Tilly had ever known, but she knew it was time to move on. "I'm ready," she said.

Leo started pulling off his boots, he placed them in a bag on his back. "What are you doing?" she asked.

Leo laughed at the look on her face. "You might want to stand back."

She stepped back and watched in awe as he leaned down on all fours and changed before her eyes. Gold fur sprouted from his skin, shining under the sun. His clothes ripped as his body grew larger. His hands and feet turned to paws. Leo's black hair lengthened into a mane, his teeth sharpened and a tail flicked around behind him. Dark wings grew from his sides, resting against his body. A winged lion now stood before her, he had changed in seconds, and now he barely fit into the alleyway.

He stalked towards Tilly, bringing his face inches to hers. She stared into his familiar brown eyes and reached up to stroke the soft fur above his nose. He closed his eyes at her touch.

"He's magnificent," Celia whispered.

Tilly stepped around him, running her hand along his wing. "So, this is why I could never see you." She felt his body quiver, she could tell he was laughing. He crouched down and Tilly carefully climbed onto his back. She noticed he was still wearing the sword and backpack, she sat between them and wrapped her arms around his neck. "Am I holding you too tight? I've never done this before."

She felt him shake with laughter, he shook his head and bowed to Celia before turning and sprinting down the alleyway. Tilly tightened her grip just as he reached the open street and pushed off the ground, spreading his strong wings. The wind rushed past Tilly's face as they soared above the city. She glanced back at Celia, watching her wave goodbye. Silverleaf slowly faded into the distance. Tilly smiled to herself—she was free.

Tilly's body ached from holding Leo so tight, but it was worth it. Valuna was even more beautiful than she imagined. She saw vast forests and farms, winding rivers and rocky mountains. She'd seen more in the past few hours than she had in her entire life. Leo gradually flew closer to the ground. He landed beside a creek full of mossy rocks and shaded by tall trees and ferns. He leaned down and she climbed off. She stretched her arms and legs as Leo wandered off behind a tree trunk, stepping out a moment later wearing only pants. Tilly couldn't pull her eyes away, his smooth, bronze torso was toned to perfection. His arms flexed as he pulled on a white T-shirt. "My face is up here you know," he said, grinning.

She glanced up with eyes full of guilt. "I was just thinking you must go through a lot of clothes," she said quickly.

He shrugged. "It comes with the occupation. I usually only shift if I have to."

They sat down beside the creek, dipping their feet in the water and sharing sandwiches that Edith had packed. Tilly peeked over at Leo whenever she thought he wasn't looking, even sitting near him she could feel a strong pull towards him, she didn't understand it. Leo watched with amusement as she finished her third sandwich. "You must be hungry—you've hardly said a word. I thought you'd be full of questions."

She thought for a moment, then met his eyes. "Your name is Leopold?"

He let out a surprised laugh. "After everything that's happened, that's what you want to talk about?"

"Don't worry, I have plenty of follow-up questions."

He shook his head, trying to keep a straight face. "Yes, my name is Leopold, but I hate it. Everyone just calls me Leo."

"I think Leopold suits you," Tilly said seriously.

He elbowed her playfully. "What about you, are you just Tilly?"

Her smile dropped. She glanced down at the creek, her reflection was distorted by the ripples in the water. "I don't know who I am anymore. I just found out my parents aren't my real parents."

He looked at her in surprise. "I'm sorry, that must have been really hard to hear."

"It was unexpected," she said, she wasn't ready to talk about it yet. She glanced back up at him, there was something still bothering her. "You never told me why you were really following me. How did you know who I was?"

Leo looked away, he picked up a stone and threw it. They both watched it skip across the water. He stared off into the distance, his eyes lost in thought. "The Silverleaf Guard kept sending us reports of growing bikie activity, it's been getting out of hand. I was sent to Silverleaf to track down members of the clubs and lead the raids. That's why I was following Orvyn." Tilly's face fell, she hated that she'd had anything to do with the Iron Vipers. Leo's eyes met hers with an intensity she hadn't seen before. "I can't really explain it," he said. "I'd been there for a few days when I flew out of the city one night to clear my head. That's when I first sensed you. I found you sitting alone in the forest and my whole being was drawn to you." Tilly's heart pounded, she couldn't believe he'd felt it too. He looked back at the creek. "I couldn't stop thinking about you," he said. "I kept telling myself to leave you alone, but once I saw you were with Orvyn it made me worry. I couldn't help checking in on you to make sure you were safe. Then one night I heard them laughing in the pub about your initiation and knew I had to do something about it."

Lord Dalton's face flashed in her mind. She squeezed her eyes shut, trying to push the image away. "I should have listened to you," she said. "I never wanted anything to do with the Vipers."

"Will you tell me what happened?"

Tilly wrapped her arms around her legs, drawing her knees to her chest. She told Leo everything that had happened after she left him in the forest, he listened silently with a clenched jaw. "I should have gone with you," he said. "After you left, I went straight to the Guard to start the raid on the warehouse. I planned to get you out of there myself, but you were already gone."

She could tell he was upset with himself and she hated it, none of it had been his fault. She nudged him gently with her shoulder. "Hey, you can't fight all of my battles—you have no idea how many enemies I have."

Leo laughed loudly, shaking his head. "You're too adorable to have enemies, they would just fall at your feet in surrender."

She scoffed in disbelief, trying to ignore the fluttering in her stomach. No one had ever called her that before. "Was my elbow in your face adorable?" she joked.

He leaned towards her and grinned. "You have no idea." He was so close she could feel the warmth radiating from his body. He leaned closer and stopped. Tilly noticed his eyes lingering on her lips and the feel of his arm pressed against hers.

Suddenly, Leo stood up and pulled off his shirt. He reached his hand down towards her. "Come for a swim?" Tilly looked at the creek, then back at Leo. He gave her a puzzled look. "You can swim, can't you?"

"Of course I can, it's just, what if there are eels?" she said nervously.

Leo tilted his head to the side, his eyes sparkling. "So, you took on one of the Five without a second thought, but you're scared of eels?"

"Who isn't scared of eels?" Tilly said seriously. With incredible speed, he scooped her into his arms and stepped into the water. "Leo! What are you doing?" she laughed.

"Protecting you from eels." She held onto his neck as he swam into the creek, stopping when the water reached their shoulders. Tilly tried not to think about his bare chest pressed against her side. "This should wash some of the blood off you at least," he said.

She gave him a shy smile. "Thanks."

His expression softened. "You've been through hell, are you really okay?"

Her smile faded. "I don't think I've had time to process it yet," she said honestly. Something slimy brushed against her foot. "What the hell was that!" She wrapped her arms and legs around Leo, holding onto him for dear life. Leo reached into the water and pulled out a handful of seaweed—they both burst out laughing as he tossed it back into the water.

She glanced down, only just realising she'd wrapped her legs around his waist, she went to pull away when she noticed his eyes blazing with longing. His fingers tightened around her thighs as he pulled her closer. They fit together perfectly. She wound her fingers up through his dark hair as his hand snaked up the back of her shirt, gliding against her bare skin. Her body answered eagerly, she arched her back as he trailed his nose up her neck, stopping just as he reached her lips. Leo sighed and closed his eyes, resting his forehead against hers. "You have no idea how scared I was when I found you in that mansion," he whispered.

Tilly closed her eyes, trying to calm her racing heart. "You have no idea how happy I was when you smashed through that window," she said honestly. "It was very subtle."

Leo laughed, she thought he looked slightly embarrassed. "It's called making an entrance," he said, splashing her. "They teach you all about it when you join the Five."

Tilly grinned. "You'll have to teach me sometime."

They left the water and packed up their belongings. Tilly untied her long hair and checked the backpack for a change of clothes—no luck—at least she would dry quickly in this heat. "Where are we going exactly?" she asked.

"Everorb City," Leo said smiling. "But we'll stop at one of the safe houses tonight. It's closer and we could both use a good night's sleep." Tilly's face lit up excitedly as she pictured Celia's snow globe, Celia had loved Everorb City. It was known as the most advanced and wealthiest city in Valuna. The Orbarians who lived there were famous for their precious gems and mining abilities, she couldn't wait to see it.

As they hiked through the forest, Tilly asked Leo every question she could think of. She wanted to know everything about him. He asked just as many questions about her own life. Tilly glanced sideways at him as the sun gleamed on his face. They'd walked a fair distance already and he'd hardly broken a sweat. "I'm surprised you didn't want to fly the rest of the way," she said.

He smiled and reached over to pull a leaf from her hair. "I'm in no rush to get back, I like the fresh air. You'll understand when we get to Everorb."

"Do the brothers get to choose which flying animal they shift into?"

His eyes flashed with amusement. "No, we don't know what we'll be until we turn sixteen and shift for the first time."

"How did you become one of the Five?" Tilly asked curiously.

Leo glanced ahead thoughtfully. "I was chosen as a child after I was almost kidnapped. I managed to escape and save the other kids who were with me. Not long after, four of the brothers showed up on our doorstep. Their brother Torben had abandoned them and they asked me to take his place."

"How old were you?" Tilly asked.

"Five."

She looked at him in shock. "That's so young."

He shrugged. "The Valunan Five are almost always chosen as children. We need to be trained up so we're physically and mentally ready to shift for the first time."

"And your mum and dad were okay with you leaving?"

"My parents told me it was a great honour, so I did what I was told," he said. She thought she sensed a slight bitterness in his voice. "I'm sure I would have ended up in the Guard anyway," he added. "I've always felt the need to protect the people around me. It's just, being one of the Five is a little different, we have so many obligations and so little free will, it's not the life I would have chosen."

She watched him sadly, knowing exactly how it felt to be trapped in a situation you never asked for. "There must be some perks to being one of the Five," she said lightly.

The corner of his mouth lifted. "It's not always as glamorous as it sounds. I tended an elderly woman's garden once, just because I felt too bad to say no."

"You actually did it?"

"Of course I did," he said proudly. "She had the best-looking garden in the street by the time I was done." He hesitated.

53

"Then I realised she was just trying to get me into her bed, my brothers have never let me forget it."

Tilly burst out laughing. "Well, at least you left knowing you did a good job," she teased.

Leo gave her a sly smile. "And I got her phone number."

They both laughed. Tilly couldn't wipe the smile off her face as they walked. Even without the strange pull she felt towards him, she loved being around him. Tilly gasped as they reached a hillside, the sun had started to set behind fields of pastel-coloured flowers, they grew in every direction. The colours reminded her of ice cream and her stomach growled loudly. She peeked at Leo from the corner of her eye, wondering if he'd heard. He was biting his lip to hide his smile. "Damn your excellent hearing," she muttered.

He laughed and picked a purple flower from the ground before passing it to her. "Are you always hungry?"

She took the flower and grinned. "Mostly yes, I just really like food."

"What's your favourite?"

"Cake," she said a little too quickly. "What's yours?"

Leo looked thoughtful. "A really good steak."

"Huh," Tilly said. "I figured you'd just maul a deer or something if you were hungry."

He shook his head, trying to keep a straight face. "That's disgusting Tilly, I do have standards you know." She held back a laugh as he smiled down at her, his gaze was so intense she had to look away. No one had ever looked at her the way he did.

They reached the other side of the hill and the trees grew thicker. Night fell and the woods came to life, Tilly could hear owls hooting and insects chirping. Leo stopped in front of her and held out his arm. "We're not alone," he said quietly. "I think I'll fly us the rest of the way—we've both been in enough fights today." He looked around quickly before he started taking off his clothes. She tried not to watch but she couldn't help it. He stood in front of her in his dark, cotton boxers and smirked at her expression—at least he didn't seem to mind.

"I'm sorry," she sulked. "You're very distracting."

Leo chuckled and leaned down on all fours, shifting before her eyes. Tilly watched him just as entranced as she had been the first time. She climbed onto his back and he pushed off the ground, beating his wings. He flew close to the treetops, the only light coming from the full moon above. Tilly admired the night sky—she couldn't remember ever seeing so many stars. They landed in an overgrown area of the woods and Leo crouched down. Tilly climbed off and looked around, there was nothing but trees in every direction. Leo stopped at her side as he pulled on his shirt. "Where is the safe house?" she asked curiously.

"They're hidden differently depending on the landscape," he said, pointing west. "There's a cliffside just behind those trees, this house is underground."

"How is that possible?"

He took her hand and led her through the darkness. "The Valunan Five were created by Spirids as a gift to Valuna. Since we travel around so much, the Spirids built us safe houses all over the realm, so we always have a place to call home."

Her heart quickened, it was the first time she'd heard anyone other than Celia speak of Spirids. Leo walked ahead, stopping in front of an old tree with a wide trunk. He pressed his lion ring into a small groove. The trunk glowed under his fist and the outline of a doorway appeared. He moved his hand away and a handle grew out of the trunk. Tilly couldn't believe her eyes—she had never seen magic before. Leo turned the handle and pulled the door open for her. She peeked inside, a winding staircase led underground with thousands of glowing, jagged crystals wrapped around the inside of the trunk, lighting the way to the bottom. Leo placed his hand on the small of her back. "It's safe, you can go inside."

She stepped into the tree and slowly walked down the stairs, looking around in awe. She reached the bottom and couldn't believe her eyes, the safe house looked as if it were made in another time. The interior was masculine and modern, the outer walls made of rugged rock and the floors dark, polished stone. The high ceiling was covered in the same glowing crystals as the staircase. Leo touched a single crystal on the wall and they all grew brighter, lighting the entire house. It had a spacious kitchen to the left and the entire far side had angular sofas arranged around the back wall, which Tilly realised wasn't a wall at all, it was a window. She ran over to it, it was nightfall, but she could see Everorb City in the distance, it looked just like Celia's snow globe. "Incredible," Tilly whispered. Everorb was a huge, brightly lit city covered in a glass dome. It had been built on an island just off the coastline, with one bridge in and out. Waves crashed around the rocks at the base of the city. Celia once told her that the Orbarians had lived underground by the ocean. Over a century ago they were attacked by greedy humans. The Spirids saved them and helped them build a city protected by an indestructible dome. This allowed them to survive above ground and control the light and climate around them.

Leo yawned beside her. "I guess it is pretty impressive when you see it for the first time."

Tilly looked at him with raised eyebrows. "It makes Silverleaf look like a dump."

He laughed. "Silverleaf's not that bad—I did find you there after all."

She glanced back out the window. "Wouldn't someone be able to see the safe house from the outside?"

Leo shook his head. "It looks the same as the rest of the cliffside, I think there's an illusion over it or something."

He showed her around the house. There was a dining room near the kitchen with a solid stone table, a laundry, a gym, a large study and a long corridor with five bedrooms. Leo took her into the first bedroom, it had a king-size bed and a full-length window with an armchair beside it. "You can have this room, I'll be in the one next door if you need me," he said softly.

Tilly turned to him, noticing for the first time how tired he looked. "Thank you, Leo, for everything," she said earnestly.

He smiled at her. "Goodnight Til." He placed his hand on a glowing crystal, waiting as they all dimmed to a soft glow before he left the room.

Tilly sat on the bed and opened her backpack. She eyed the box from Alwyn. She was dying to open it, but she was too tired tonight. She grabbed her phone to call her parents—it was flat—she threw it back into the bag and made her way into the bathroom.

The ensuite was made of dark polished stone with a raw timber vanity, she washed her clothes in it and hung them on the towel rack to dry. She ran a hot shower and sighed happily as the water ran down her body. Tilly washed her hair and scrubbed her skin before drying off and climbing into bed. She started thinking about Leo in the room next to her, wondering if he was sleeping naked too. "Don't think things like that, you'll never fall asleep," she said, scolding herself. She heard Leo laugh loudly and squeezed her eyes shut, she'd forgotten about his heightened hearing. She turned onto her side and looked out towards the dome city, exhaustion soon took over her body and she drifted off to sleep.

Chapter Six

The Safe House

Tilly woke to a knock at the door. "I'm awake Mum." She yawned, not opening her eyes. It felt like she had only just fallen asleep.

The door opened and Leo walked into the room, smirking. "Can't say I've ever been called—"

He stopped and his eyes widened. Tilly remembered where she was and squealed, pulling the blanket up over her head. She heard Leo backing towards the door. "Sorry, I swear I didn't see anything," he said. "There's a closet full of clothes in here, help yourself. Breakfast is ready."

The door closed and Tilly pulled the covers down, her face flushed with embarrassment. The blanket had been twisted around her, so she was sure he really hadn't seen anything. She squeezed her eyes closed and groaned—she couldn't believe she had just called him her mother.

Tilly got out of bed and stretched, her body felt surprisingly achy. She found the closet next to the ensuite and pulled it open. It was full of T-shirts and military pants—she held up a pair. The Five must all be tall and broad like Leo, there was no way they would fit her. She grabbed a black T-shirt and pulled it on. It was so big it stopped at her thighs, but it would have to do for now. She tied her long hair into a ponytail and searched the ensuite drawers. They were well stocked. She sprayed on some deodorant and brushed her teeth.

Leo was setting food down on the table, he paused as she walked in, his eyes lingering on her bare legs. "And you called me distracting," he said playfully, he motioned towards the food. "I hope this is okay. I wasn't sure what you liked."

The smell of coffee wafted through the air, she went and sat down excitedly. Neatly arranged on the table were oddly shaped crystal plates filled with fruit salad, pancakes, eggs, bacon and pastries. "It looks incredible," she said. "Where did you get all of this?"

Leo took the seat opposite her and poured her a mug of coffee, she took it gratefully. "Spirid magic," he said. "When I put my ring in the tree the house sort of—came to life. The lights came on and the kitchen filled with food. The Spirids wanted to make sure we were well taken care of."

Tilly looked around the room, it really was extraordinary. She started wondering what else their magic could do and then she realised something. "If the Spirids are all gone," she said slowly. "What will happen to the Five?"

Leo's expression dimmed. "I'll be the last one."

Tilly's heart sank. The Valunan Five had always protected the realm, it would be a huge loss if they were gone. "How exactly did the Spirids turn you into a shapeshifter?"

Leo picked at his food. "After I was chosen my brothers took me to Panthera for my ceremony, it was tradition to be blessed by the Queen. She awakened my spirit animal."

He absentmindedly placed his hand on his left shoulder. "I'll never forget the feeling of her magic running through my body. Once we have it, it stays with us for life."

Tilly ate quietly, hanging on to Leo's every word. "What was Panthera like?"

His eyes lit up. "Like nothing you've ever seen before. The city is built into the mountains and is almost always covered in snow. Everyone who lived there had a place and a purpose—there was a happiness in the air I've never experienced anywhere else." His smile faded. "I was only six when it fell, but my brothers still carry the burden of the loss."

Tilly's heart started to race. "Do you know what happened?"

He sighed and sat back in his chair, nursing a cup of coffee. "Only what Conrad and the others have told me, I was training in Everorb City at the time," he said. "There were random attacks all over the realm. Spirids were being hunted down and the Five were all separated and sent to help. That's when Panthera was attacked by Calvarian Assassins. It was well planned. It happened so fast that no one was prepared and none of the brothers were close by. Faris was the first one to reach them and he barely made it out alive." Leo sipped his coffee, staring out the window. "The entire city was taken over by the Calvarians. Everyone thought they were a myth."

Tilly felt anger burn in her chest. "Why didn't the Five and the Guard try to take it back?"

Leo's jaw clenched. "Trust me—they all wanted to. Conrad kept sending scouts to gather intel but none of them ever returned. The Historians declared Panthera too dangerous and cut it off from the rest of the realm."

The Historians, Tilly had learned about them in school. They were a group of scholars who took control when the attacks happened and brought order back to the realm. Now they ruled Valuna. "Is Conrad one of the Five?"

"No, he's a Historian who specialises in military operations. He's in charge of the Guard as well as the Five now." Leo smiled at her. "He would actually be the person to talk to about your trial."

Tilly's eyebrows rose. "How do you know about that?"

He leaned forward, his eyes twinkling. "I may have read your file at Silverleaf—it was very impressive."

She feigned shock. "How dare you, that's private."

Leo chuckled. "Not to me, we work very closely with the Guard. We could probably arrange your trial in Everorb if you wanted to."

She felt excitement build in her stomach, joining the Guard would be a dream come true. She stood up and walked over to the window, looking out towards Everorb City. Now that it was day, she could see the ocean and rocky mountains surrounding the dome. Leo came and stood beside her. "We'll leave tomorrow, we could both use another day to rest." His eyes turned playful, he took her hand and stroked it gently, making her heart race. "So, are you going to tell me what you were thinking about last night?" Tilly gave him an embarrassed smile. He chuckled and stepped behind her. "Was it that bad?" he whispered in her ear.

She squirmed, the warmth from his body and the closeness of his lips were almost too much to bear. "Scary stuff," she lied. "Things you shouldn't think about before bed."

"Is that right?" he said seriously. "Do you need me to check for monsters before you go to sleep?"

"That's definitely a good idea," Tilly replied sarcastically.

He rubbed his nose against her cheek. "If you're that scared,

I could always stay in there with you—just to keep you safe."

Her mouth dropped. She knew he was still teasing her, but the thought made her heart race even more. "That depends," she said softly. "Do you growl in your sleep?"

Leo laughed and nipped her neck. "Only if you want me to." She looked back at him and grinned. His phone suddenly buzzed from his pocket, he pulled it out and frowned. "I better take this, it's Conrad." He glanced at her apologetically as he retreated to his room. Tilly cleared the table before returning to hers, closing the door behind her.

With shaky hands, she took out the velvet box from her backpack and sat on the bed, staring at it. She slowly opened the lid and a folded envelope fell out, stamped with a wax crest. The crest showed a leopard wrapped around a crescent moon. She carefully opened the envelope and pulled out a handwritten letter.

Dear Matilda,

My sweet Tilly, there is so much I wish to tell you and so little time. As I write this you are fast asleep in my arms. I need you to know that giving you away is the hardest decision I've ever made. It fills me with sorrow knowing I'll never get to know the woman you become, but it fills me with strength knowing you will have Celia and your guardian to guide you.

I hope you can forgive me for taking your magic, please know that I did it only for your protection. I've asked Celia to return it to you when the time is right.

There is so much more I wish I could say, but it would not be safe if this was to fall into the wrong hands.

I love you Matilda, be happy and be brave my sweet girl.

Love always, Mum

Tilly re-read the letter with tears running down her cheeks, it had raised more questions than it answered. She touched the elegant handwriting. Her name was Matilda, she hadn't known that. Her heart longed for this mother she would never know.

Something shiny caught her eye. She reached for the box, inside was a delicate gold chain with an oval-shaped, moonstone amulet encased in gold. It had the same crest on it as the wax stamp. She leaned closer and noticed the moonstone was shimmering. As she touched it, her body flew back onto the bed, her eyes glowed white and she felt warmth and energy flowing through her. She tried to scream, but nothing came out. The feeling stopped almost as quickly as it had started. Tilly was left breathless and shaking. She looked at her hands, she felt different somehow, she felt whole.

Finally.

Tilly heard a woman's voice in her head and jumped. "Who's there?" she said quietly, not wanting Leo to hear.

I'm your guardian, my name is Annora.

Tilly recognised her voice. "You helped me when I was getting attacked."

Yes, our connection was dulled when Alwyn took your magic. I could only reach you when you were highly emotional and not in full control, but I have always been here with you.

"Magic," Tilly whispered, she looked at her hands again. She could feel it pulsing through her body.

It was hidden in the necklace. You can put it on now, it won't hurt you.

Tilly poked the necklace quickly before she pulled it out of the box and clasped it around her neck. She admired the moonstone before hiding it under her shirt. "If you're my guardian," she whispered excitedly. "Do you have a physical body? Can I meet you?"

It's best if I stay hidden for now. It's not safe for anyone to know who you are.

Tilly's excitement dropped and then came back. "Do I really have magic now?"

Of course, you can feel it.

"Will you show me?" she asked, she needed to see for herself.

I can't show you, but I can guide you. Spirid magic comes from the heart and runs through your blood, you need to feel it and guide it with your thoughts. Think about something you really want.

She thought about Leo.

Not someone. Something.

Tilly flinched at her stern voice. She thought about the honey cake her mum always made.

Good, think hard about what it looks like, feels like and tastes like. Now feel the magic build in your chest, imagine it as light.

Tilly thought about the honey cake. She focused on the warmth in her chest, picturing it as a bright golden light. She felt it grow stronger.

Hold on to that feeling. Now place your left hand out and wave your right hand down in front of it. Think about the cake and feel the light move through your hand.

She did as Annora said and waved her right hand downwards, her fingertips began to glow and a honey cake appeared in her left hand.

Tilly was so startled she let out a small scream.

Within seconds, Leo burst into the room with his sword, stopping when he saw her. He looked around in confusion. "Why did you scream?" he asked.

Tilly panicked and held the cake out towards him. "I forgot

I had this—cake," she said, trying to sound convincing. "I just got so excited when I saw it—it's my birthday tomorrow." Her face dropped and she lowered the cake. She had forgotten about her birthday. She glanced at her charm bracelet sadly, she had never celebrated it without her parents before.

Leo sat on the bed beside her, still looking confused. "Have you been carrying that this whole time?"

Tilly tried to keep a straight face. "Mum must have packed it." She nodded towards his sword. "Do you think you could cut the cake with that?"

His expression turned amused. "No way," he said. "Wait here a minute." He grabbed the cake from her and hurried out of the room.

Annora started to laugh.

"You could have warned me," Tilly whispered.

It was more fun this way. You'll get the hang of it. Your magic is like a muscle, the more you use it the stronger it will get.

Tilly noticed she did feel a little drained, she couldn't wait to learn more. Leo returned holding two plates in one hand and the other hidden behind his back. He sat beside her and presented the cake. He'd decorated the top with ten, thin, glowing crystals, they almost looked like candles. Her heart swelled in her chest. "Thank you," she said softly.

"Happy almost birthday—now make a wish," he ordered playfully.

She beamed and closed her eyes, thinking hard about her wish. When she opened them, Leo was smiling at her, his eyes full of love. Tilly was mesmerised, she felt as if her body was being called to his. She ached to move closer. Leo leaned towards her, just as entranced as she was. He placed the cake aside and laced his fingers through her hair, gently bringing his lips to hers. Without breaking the kiss, Tilly climbed onto his lap, gliding her hands through his stubble. He gripped her waist, pulling her closer as the kiss deepened. Leo trailed kisses down her neck and Tilly sighed happily, it felt like the first time she had ever really been kissed. Leo rested his forehead against hers with a small smile on his lips. "What did you wish for?" he asked.

"You just gave it to me," she breathed.

"Is that all?" he said. "I'd give you the world if you asked for it."

She opened her mouth to make a joke and stopped. Meeting his steady gaze, she realised he meant it.

After night fell, Tilly showered and got ready for bed, thinking about the day she'd had with Leo. Laughing with him and sharing the cake, as well as that unforgettable kiss. She stood in front of the bathroom mirror wearing a towel and a ridiculous grin on her face. She never thought she'd want a boyfriend after Orvyn. Leo had been completely unexpected. She knew things were moving fast, but everything about him just felt right.

After the cake disaster, she was excited to try her magic again. She held her hand out and closed her eyes, building the magic in her chest and conjuring an emerald green, silk nightgown. It had thin straps, a lace bodice and stopped at the top of her thighs. She held it out in front of her and her face lit up, it was softer and prettier than any clothing she had ever owned. She put it on and pulled her hair down. It fell in soft waves around her, stopping just above her waist. Tilly hopped into bed and laid there restlessly, her mind began to wander and the weight of everything that had happened came crashing down on her. She was furious she had to leave her family so quickly. She was devastated that her real mother and father had been killed. She was mad at Orvyn for everything he'd done and furious at herself for going into Lord Dalton's mansion.

Don't be so hard on yourself Matilda.

Annora's voice was gentle, but it was all too much. Tilly's eyes began to tear up, she couldn't hold it in any longer. She dropped her face into her pillow and sobbed. She was exhausted, physically and mentally. She cried until she couldn't cry anymore.

There was a small knock at the door, Tilly wiped her eyes and sat up. "Come in."

Leo walked into the room wearing cotton boxer shorts, his hands covered his eyes. "Are you decent?"

She let out a small laugh. "Yes, I'm decent."

He dropped his hands and sat on her bed, watching her with concern. "Are you okay?"

Tilly pulled her knees up and hugged them to her chest. "I'm just overwhelmed."

"Do you want to talk about it?"

"I..." Her mind flashed to Lord Dalton stalking towards her. She dropped her face onto her knees, sobbing again.

"Come here Til." Leo pulled her into his arms and laid back on the bed, holding her while she cried. "You've been so strong," he said, kissing her head. "But you've been through so much, anyone would be overwhelmed." He held her quietly and stroked her arm as she cried herself to sleep.

Tilly woke the next morning from the most peaceful sleep she'd ever had, she opened her eyes and noticed Leo's arm around her. She turned carefully so she didn't wake him and studied his peaceful face, he was too good to be true. He opened his eyes and glanced around the room. "Sorry," he said sleepily. "I didn't mean to fall asleep in here."

Tilly's heart quickened. "I don't mind, I had the best sleep I've had in a long time."

His eyes turned warm. "So did I actually. How are you feeling?"

"Much better," she said, smiling. "I'm sorry for crying all over you."

He laughed. "You can cry on me anytime."

"I'd rather not make that a habit," she joked. She looked around the room wistfully. "It's a shame we have to leave today." Leo's smile faded, he glanced at the crystal ceiling, lost in thought. Tilly's heart sank. "Is everything okay?" she asked.

He gave her a reassuring smile. "Better than okay. I'm just not looking forward to going back."

She returned his smile, but she felt like there was something he wasn't telling her, it made her feel uneasy. She got out of bed and stood by the window, glancing out towards Everorb City. She was anxious about leaving today, she wondered what would happen when they arrived, so much was unknown. Leo came and stood behind her, gliding his hands across her stomach. The feeling of his fingers on the silk sent tingles down her body. "I like this," he said. "It's almost as nice as what you slept in yesterday."

She laughed as he buried his face in her neck. She closed her eyes, wishing they could stay like that forever. "I need to ask you something," he said seriously. "I told you at the creek that I felt drawn to you, but it's more than that. I think you're the most beautiful thing in the world, inside and out." She could feel his heartbeat racing against her back. "I know we haven't known each other for very long, but I've never felt like this before. You feel like home to me and that's something I've never had. I have to know if you feel the same."

She glanced up and met his eyes. "I do," she said. "I love everything about you. My body aches just to be near you."

He rested his head against hers. "The more I get to know you, the harder I fall."

"I feel exactly the same." She leaned up and kissed him. She felt his hand glide lower and moaned softly against his lips.

"Do you want me to keep going?"

"Yes," she breathed, she wanted more. Leo pushed her hair to the side and kissed her neck. His hand slowly slid down the silk, stopping between her legs. His fingers moved in delicate circles as his other hand stroked the lace over her breasts. She pressed herself against him, arching her body into his hands. He slipped his hand under her nightgown, gliding it up her thigh before stroking her gently. She gasped as he pushed his finger in, teasing her slowly before moving faster, leaving her completely breathless. He kissed and bit her neck as she cried out in pleasure, feeling a blissful release. Tilly looked up into his eyes, she could see the hunger in them. Suddenly she felt nervous, she'd never done anything like this before.

Leo's eyes softened. "We don't have to do anything you aren't ready for," he said gently. He kissed her lips. "Happy birthday Til."

She gave him a shy smile. "That was the best birthday present ever."

His eyes lit up as he laughed. "It wasn't what I planned to give you, but I'm glad you liked it." He hugged her tight and sighed. "I'm definitely going to miss this place."

"Me too," Tilly said sadly.

Me three.

Tilly's eyes widened. She had completely forgotten about Annora—who had just witnessed all of that.

It's fine Matilda, it's your life and Leo's your soulmate. You won't hear me complaining.

Her soulmate. She wondered how that was possible.

Spirids can sense them. Your souls call to each other, it's the reason you can feel when he's close by. He can only feel it too because he's been blessed by Spirid magic, otherwise, only you would know. He's your match in every way—it's incredibly rare to find them.

She heard Annora sigh happily. She glanced up at Leo, unable to wipe the smile from her face. Annora was right, he was her match in every way.

Spirids would often marry within a week of finding their soulmate. He will show you passion and dedication like no other.

Tilly tried not to scoff, she wanted a husband and family one day, but she had always planned to travel and serve the Guard first.

They ate breakfast together and slowly got ready to leave. She could tell he wanted to stay as much as she did. Tilly packed her things and glanced at the bedroom mournfully. She closed the door before following Leo up the steps and out of the safe house. Together they watched the doorway disappear into the trunk. Now the tree looked just like all of the others, yet it was full of so many memories.

Chapter Seven

Everorb City

Tilly held onto Leo as he flew down the cliffside towards Everorb. Rugged mountains formed a cove around the dome city and the ocean glittered under the sunshine. She breathed in the salty air as the wind rushed past her face. Leo veered towards a waterfall flowing down the mountainside, flying close enough for the droplets to spray them as they passed.

This is extraordinary. I've never seen Moonee Cove like this.

Tilly wondered how Annora had been there before.

Before I was sent to the spirit realm, I was a Spirid too. This is how I'm able to guide you, from my own experiences in life.

Tilly tried to imagine what the spirit realm would have been like—she pictured a city of clouds. Annora chuckled.

Not quite, it is a happy place though.

Why would you want to leave? Tilly thought.

I've never been one to turn down an adventure.

Tilly laughed, she liked having Annora with her. Before she'd left Silverleaf City she had felt so alone sometimes—it was why she had made friends with the trees.

Leo landed near the bridge that led to the city. She turned to give him privacy as he shifted and pulled on his clothes. Before they had left the safe house, she had managed to conjure some dark grey, high-waisted tweed pants and a black tank top. She glanced down at her combat boots fondly, admiring the little moon charms. She wondered how her mum and dad were doing, she couldn't wait to tell them where she was.

Tilly stared up at the bubble filling the sky, Everorb was like nothing she'd ever seen before. The dome was tinted but she could still see the tall towers inside, covered in greenery. Leo had told her that the Orbarians needed a dark and humid atmosphere after living deep underground for so long. He came and stood beside her, he was back in his military green pants and white T-shirt. He laced his fingers through hers. "Nervous?"

She grinned at him. "Yes, but mostly excited."

He kissed the back of her hand and led her towards the floating bridge. It was enclosed with a tinted glass tunnel and went straight from the cliffside to the city, with only the turquoise ocean beneath it. Leo turned to her with a glint in his eyes. "Have you ever seen an Orbarian?"

"Only in photos," she admitted.

He gave a half-smile. "It can be a bit of a shock the first time, just keep eye contact when they speak to you and you'll be fine."

The tunnel doors opened automatically. They entered an elegant foyer—the temperature was instantly warmer than outside. Someone sat behind a large desk made of raw emerald, their face hidden behind a newspaper. All that was visible was dark green, combed-back hair peeking from above. Leo cleared his throat and the man tossed the paper aside. "My apologies," he said. "There's much excitement in the paper today." His silver eyes widened as he saw Leo, and he quickly scrambled to his feet. "Leo, you're back." The man placed his hand over his heart and bowed to him.

Leo looked embarrassed. "Nice to see you, Gera, please, I've told you there's no need to bow."

Tilly tried to keep her face neutral as she took in Gera's appearance. He looked human but his skin was translucent with a green hue. She could see the veins and muscles in his neck and face as well as the small bones in his fingers. Gera straightened his uniform—a black coat with emerald buttons running from his left shoulder to his navel. "Would you like me to inform Conrad you've arrived?" Gera asked.

"That would be great, thank you." Leo placed his arm around Tilly's waist. "This is Tilly Norris. Would you please arrange a suite for her, she'll be staying in Everorb indefinitely."

Gera studied her curiously and smiled, showing perfect white teeth. "A pleasure to meet you, Tilly." He glanced back at Leo. "I'll set her up in the Sapphire Tower, Sir."

Leo nodded appreciatively. Gera grabbed a tablet from the desk and busied himself for a moment before passing it to Tilly. "I just need some details from you." She filled it out and handed it back.

Gera took out two ice-blue bands from his drawer and passed them to Leo. Tilly looked at them curiously as Leo pulled open the smaller band and clamped it around her wrist. It was smooth and made of some kind of quartz, it felt cool against her skin. He clamped the other band around his wrist and smiled at her expression. "These keep our body temperature down."

"That's everything. Now follow me," Gera said cheerfully. He strolled towards the back of the foyer and another set of doors opened. They entered a small train station with detached carriages lined up on a track. Gera led them to the front carriage—it was black and sleek with crystal-clear glass windows. He pushed a button and the door opened. Inside were rows of black leather seats and a separate driver's compartment at the front. They sat in the first row and Gera disappeared into the compartment. After a moment, the carriage shot forward.

Tilly glanced out the window, admiring the city ahead. It looked like something from a fairy tale. Leo took her hand in his. "What are you thinking?"

She turned to him and blushed. "I was wondering what kind of cakes they'll have."

Leo laughed, his brown eyes shining fondly. "I should have guessed you'd say something like that."

"What are you thinking about?" she asked.

He glanced ahead. "I'm probably about to get a lecture from Conrad. He wanted me back as soon as I was done with the Vipers."

Tilly's face dimmed. "I'm sorry, I hope you won't be in trouble because of me."

He stroked a lock of hair back from her face. "I was the one who didn't want to rush back. I'll take the lecture—it was worth it."

She leaned up and gave him a small kiss. "Thank you for letting me come with you."

"It wasn't completely unselfish," he admitted. "I'd probably still be in Silverleaf if you'd stayed. Then I really would be in trouble."

Tilly laughed as Gera brought the carriage to a stop. He opened the doors and offered her his hand. "Watch your step."

She smiled gratefully and took his hand, trying not to stare at the bones in his fingers. "Thank you, Gera," she said kindly. They stepped out onto a platform just outside of the dome.

"Can I take you on a tour while Tilly's room is prepared?" Gera asked hopefully.

Leo looked at him apologetically. "Sorry Gera, I have a few errands to run. Would you give Tilly a tour and then show her to her suite?" He gave Gera one of his dazzling smiles. "There's no one I trust more than you to take care of her for me."

Gera looked like he was about to faint from Leo's praise, he puffed his chest out proudly. "Of course Sir, it would be an honour." Tilly had become so used to being around Leo, she'd almost forgotten how famous the Five were. People worshipped them. They had songs and stories dedicated to them.

Leo turned to her, his expression softened when he saw the excitement in her eyes. He gave her a quick kiss on the forehead. "I'll find you when I'm done." He hurried off towards the city, glancing back to give her one last smile.

Gera straightened his posture and led her inside the dome. "Come, Gera will take good care of you." He threw his arms up in the air as they stepped inside. "Welcome to the great Everorb City," he announced grandly.

Tilly looked up in awe. The towers were made of winding, black metal and shimmering crystals, the pattern reminded her of snakeskin. Vines and moss twisted up around them and glass bridges joined one tower to another. Mist fell through the air, and what little light reflected through the dome created a rainbow across the city. The ground was elegantly paved, surrounded by gardens with soft tufts of purple grass and mushrooms in different hues of orange. "It's breathtaking," Tilly whispered.

It looks almost as I remember it.

Gera's eyes shone proudly. "Yes, the greatest city there ever was if I may say so myself."

"Do you all live in the towers?" she asked curiously.

Gera's expression dulled. "No, the towers are occupied by the high-ranking Orbarians. The ruling families live at the top, followed by the wealthy. The workers who directly serve the city—such as myself—reside in the lower floors." He pointed to different towers. "You can find almost anything you need in the towers. Shopping, entertainment, health retreats, sports facilities you name it." He strolled over to a staircase which led underground. "We also have a subway, though it is expensive to use."

"Why is it expensive?" Tilly asked.

"To keep certain classes from using it. The ruling families do not like to mingle," he said bitterly.

Tilly wiped the sweat from her forehead as Gera led her through the city. He motioned towards the dome. "During the daylight, the dome is tinted to protect us from the sun. At night it clears so we can admire the stars. Since moving above ground we have become fascinated by them." Tilly smiled, feeling as if she could relate. She couldn't explain her own fascination with the moon.

I can, Spirids worshipped the moon. We believed it was the source of our magic.

She felt a warmth in her chest at Annora's words. Gera stopped in front of an impressive water fountain, an eight-point star perched in the centre. "This is the star of Everorb City, cut from a single diamond. It is the sigil of our people." Tilly was amazed they could keep something so precious out in the open, if they were in Silverleaf City, it would have been stolen within a week.

They made their way towards the back of the city. Small huts and underground caves were built into the rock beneath the dome wall. Tilly watched the Orbarians with interest. Their translucent skin varied in shades of purple and green, now that the surprise had worn off, she could appreciate their beauty. A few children ran past and a small boy accidentally bumped into her legs. He was adorable with his silver eyes and wild, white hair. He looked up at her and screamed before running off to his mother. Tilly laughed as Gera shook his head, unimpressed. "This is where the common folk live," he said sadly. "In their own filth."

Tilly looked closer at the people around her. They were poorly dressed and she could sense a deep sadness in the air. *This is certainly new.*

Annora sounded angry. "Why do they live like this?" Tilly asked. "Isn't Everorb the wealthiest city in Valuna?"

Gera stopped by a makeshift school. The children sat on the ground, using their fingers to draw numbers in the dirt. "We have seven families who govern our great city. The eldest of each family is part of a Council who make all decisions regarding Everorb." Gera gestured towards a bustling marketplace. "These people are malnourished, overworked and underpaid, they receive less than adequate health care and don't have access to basic facilities. They live short and sad lives." He motioned towards the towers. "On the other hand, our rich are so well taken care of, they often live very long lives. The Councillors are very old, their laws and beliefs are outdated and they keep most of the riches to themselves. This is a great city, yet it could be so much greater," he said passionately.

Tilly could see the determination in his eyes. "I think you should be one of the Councillors," she said honestly.

Gera chortled—it sounded like he was gasping for air. It took every ounce of Tilly's self-control not to laugh too.

Is he choking?

He patted her cheek fondly. "That's very sweet of you, if only it were possible." He wiped a tear from his eye, still smiling. "Although, there was some exciting news in the paper this morning. One of the Councillors died a few days ago, leaving an only child and no other family. Lady Jaini Zirk—only thirty years young. She's been causing quite a stir with some of her ideas. These Orbarians are livelier and more hopeful than they've been in decades."

Tilly looked around at the Orbarians—they didn't seem very lively to her—she had a sudden urge to conjure food for them.

You can't Matilda, there are too many people around.

Tilly knew she was right. "Gera, would you mind if I grabbed some things from the markets?"

Gera regarded her fondly and showed her through rows of market stalls, some were made of cardboard boxes and wooden crates. She stopped at a table of old, second-hand electronics and bought herself a phone charger. Gera took her to a stall run by a mother and her small daughter. They sold beautiful, palm-sized crystals with delicate paintings on them. The small girl had purple-tinted skin and shining black hair plaited down her back. Tilly smiled at her and she smiled back shyly. "These are amazing," Tilly said honestly. The mother beamed and bowed her head. The girl picked up a smooth amethyst stone and passed it to Tilly. Painted on the surface was a lion sitting under a full moon. Tilly's smile widened as she admired it.

"For protection," the mother said quietly. Tilly passed her some money and thanked them both. They stopped at a few more stalls. The Orbarians were friendly and grateful each time she bought something. Gera seemed to be enjoying all the attention they received.

He showed her the rest of the city. She saw the entrances to the mines, which he said went for miles underground. They passed the Everorb Guard Headquarters—a wide, modern building around six stories high. Gera told her they housed a decent-sized army and had a large underground arena.

Once the tour was over, he led her to the Sapphire Tower. Two guards opened the doors for them and they entered an extravagant foyer. There was a large desk made of raw sapphire crystal, a matching chandelier and a plush gold and blue sitting area. An Orbarian woman with dark blue hair stood behind the desk, wearing the same uniform as Gera. As they approached her, Gera noticed Tilly admiring the desk. "We supply the finest gems to Valuna," he said. "Though we keep the best for ourselves."

He spoke to the woman and passed Tilly a key card. "Room four eleven on the fifty-fourth floor." He walked her over to the lift. "If you need anything at all, just ask for Gera." He placed his hand over his heart and bowed to her. She thanked him for the tour and he smiled before he strolled out of the tower.

Tilly stood speechless inside her suite—surely this was a

mistake. It was larger than her home in Silverleaf City and lavishly decorated. She stood at the end of the long entryway, it had two steps leading down to an impressive open living area. The far side of the suite had diamond-shaped windows that took up the entire wall. Near the windows, eight chairs were arranged around a large, timber dining table with a polished opal top. In the living room was a matching opal coffee table with stylish, white sofas around it. To her left was a spacious kitchen with white cabinets. It had a fully stocked bar beside it with crystal bottles displayed on shelves. Tilly found a tablet on the wall showing it was two thirty in the afternoon. She swiped the screen and found the temperature controls. It was already set to a cool twenty-four degrees.

Tilly explored the rest of the suite, she found a large bedroom with a bed big enough to sleep four adults. It had an opal headboard encased in gold and bedding made of white satin. A closet and bathroom were attached to the room, the closet was as big as her bedroom at home. She stepped into the bathroom. It had an entire wall made of raw, white crystal. It flowed down and had a bath carved out at the bottom. She walked back into the bedroom and looked around—she had never seen so much luxury. Tilly shook her head, thinking about the Orbarians living in huts and caves. "This doesn't feel right."

I agree, the Orbarians thrived in my time. There was no poverty back then, they shared what they had.

Tilly unpacked her bag and plugged her phone in to charge. She placed the amethyst crystal on the bedside table, smiling at it fondly. Her skin felt sticky from walking around under the dome, she eyed the crystal bathtub and filled it with warm water. She poured in some bath oil she found on the vanity and sank into the tub, sighing happily. She had loved every minute with Leo, but it felt nice to have a moment to herself. When she got out, she found a white fluffy robe on the back of the door and pulled it on. She unplugged her phone and sat on the bed to call her mum, her stomach fluttered excitedly as it rang.

"Tilly! Happy birthday honey! Hold on, I'll put you on speaker," Edith said.

Tilly laughed, it felt so nice to hear her voice. "Hi, Mum."

"Til! Are you safe? Where are you? We've been so worried," Jack said.

She told them where she was and about the journey they had taken to get there—leaving out the intimate moments she'd had with Leo.

"One of the Five," Edith said breathlessly. "Can you send us a photo?"

"I am right here Edith, calm yourself," Jack said.

Tilly burst out laughing. "I'll send photos whenever I can. I miss you both so much."

"We miss you too Tillio. Keep in touch, we love you."

Tilly got off the phone and felt a weight off her chest, she'd been anxious to speak to them. She tried calling Celia, but there was no answer.

She raided the kitchen and found it had already been stocked with food. She made sandwiches and sat at the huge table, devouring them. When she was done, she cleaned up and laid on the couch, glancing out the diamond-shaped window towards Everorb City.

"Will you teach me something else Annora?" she asked.

Hmm, I always found invisibility handy.

"Invisibility?" Tilly said with surprise. "Was there anything Spirids couldn't do?"

Annora laughed softly.

Of course, we can't fly like the Five do, we don't shapeshift, and we cannot alter free will. There is plenty we can't do.

"That seems fair," Tilly said with amusement. "How do I use invisibility?"

Build your magic up like I showed you before and run your finger down your forehead. Focus on what you want the magic to do. Think of yourself as weightless.

Tilly reached up and placed a finger on her forehead, expanding her magic and running her finger down. She felt a sensation creep down her body, making her feel lighter than air. She held her hands out in front of her—they were gone. "This is great," she said excitedly.

It wears off after a while or you can undo it yourself, the stronger your magic gets the longer it will last.

There was a knock at the door. Tilly reached up and ran her finger up her forehead, pulling the magic away. She felt the sensation vanish.

You're a natural.

She smiled to herself and went to answer the door, already sensing Leo behind it. He stood in the doorway in a black training outfit and combat boots, holding a large paper bag. He eyed her down with amusement. "I see you've made yourself at home."

Tilly looked down—she was still wearing the fluffy robe. She hugged it around herself happily. "It's like wearing a cloud."

Leo laughed. "As much as I love the cloud, you might want to change before we go to Headquarters."

Her face shot to his. "You're taking me to Headquarters?"

she asked excitedly.

He stepped inside and kissed her on the forehead. "Conrad's expecting us soon."

Tilly closed the door and followed him to the bedroom. Leo started taking clothes out of the bag and placing them at the end of the bed. "I know you didn't have much time when you left home, so I asked one of the female soldiers to help me grab a few things."

He'd brought her mostly gym clothes as well as tank tops and shorts. Tilly held up a sports bra and some underwear. Now that she had her magic, she hadn't even thought to worry about clothes, though Leo didn't know that. "Thank you," she said with a shy smile. "For looking after me."

Leo pulled her hand up and kissed the back of it, his eyes lingering on hers. "I will always look after you."

Her heart raced at his words. He sat on the bed and pulled her down beside him, handing her a package wrapped in green and gold paper. "This is what I actually planned to get you for your birthday," he said.

Tilly unwrapped the gift, inside was a drawstring bag made of green velvet. She glanced at Leo curiously. He kept a straight face, giving nothing away. She opened the bag and pulled out two matching daggers. At first, she thought the blades were silver, but as she studied them closer she saw pinks, purples and blues reflecting off them under the light. The hilts had a star-shaped moonstone with an intricate gold design swirled around them, the design reminded her of a tree. She looked up at Leo with tears in her eyes, he had no idea how much this meant to her. She hadn't felt like herself since losing Nero's daggers. "They're the most beautiful daggers I've ever seen," she whispered.

Leo looked relieved. He shook his head, smiling. "I've never met a woman who gets teary over weapons," he teased.

She laughed and leaned over to kiss him. "They're perfect."

"You're perfect," he whispered against her lips. He climbed on top of her and pushed her back onto the soft bed. She loved the feeling of his body on hers. He trailed kisses down her neck to the top of her robe. He began untying it and stopped, nuzzling his face into her neck. "I can't believe I'm saying this, but we really should be going," he said. "If we go any further, I'm not sure I could stop."

"I don't want you to stop," Tilly said breathlessly.

"That's not helping," Leo laughed.

She grinned and sighed dramatically. "Fine, I'll go change."

Tilly climbed off the bed and headed for the closet—she was feeling brave. Just before she reached the doorway, she dropped her robe. She peeked back and Leo was frozen on the bed with his mouth open in shock. She laughed and stepped into the closet, feeling on top of the world.

Then she realised she'd left the clothes on her bed. "Shit!" she yelled. Now she just felt stupid.

She heard Leo burst out laughing. His hand appeared in the doorway, holding the clothes. "Forgetting something?" he asked. Tilly took the clothes and laughed sheepishly. She got dressed and tied her black hair into a high ponytail—even tied up it was down past her shoulders. She tucked her necklace under her shirt and looked at her reflection. She felt like she was glowing. Her eyes were shining and she couldn't remember the last time she felt so happy and free. This was only the beginning of her adventure, and she was ready for it.

Chapter Eight

The Valunan Guard

Tilly and Leo walked along the ornate pavement between the towers. Even with the crystal band on her wrist, she felt like she was in a sauna. She peeked over at Leo, he'd hardly said a word since they'd left her suite. "How did everything go with Conrad?" she asked casually.

He raked his fingers through his dark hair. "He's not happy with me. There's a lot going on right now with Councillor Zirk dying and Jaini taking his seat." Leo's expression softened. "Which reminds me— Jaini wants to meet you."

Tilly glanced at him in surprise. "Me? Why?"

Leo chuckled. "I mostly grew up here in Everorb. Jaini isn't much older than I am, she's like a sister to me," he said fondly. "She's invited us to dinner tomorrow and she's very hard to say no to."

"Why is she hard to say no to?" Tilly asked, amused.

Leo grinned. "Because she's so annoying. She'll pester me until I take you there."

Tilly laughed. "Well, now I can't wait to meet her." She

glanced at the Headquarters building up ahead. "Are all of the Five in Everorb?" she asked curiously.

"No, Conrad likes having at least two brothers close by, there are three of us here right now. Myself, Alerio and Faris."

Tilly noticed his eyes harden. "You aren't a fan of Faris?"

"He's my least favourite brother. He's a massive show off and acts like everyone is beneath him." Leo frowned. "Really he's just an arsehole."

Tilly laughed loudly. "I don't think I've ever heard you swear before."

"Yeah well, you'll understand when you meet him."

"Faris is a horse, right?"

Leo rolled his eyes. "A flying horse, he thinks it practically makes him a god."

"I'd pick a lion over a horse any day," Tilly said seriously.

Leo's eyes flashed with amusement. They reached Headquarters and took a few steps up to the main entrance. Tilly could still see the tension in Leo's jaw—it was making her nervous. The Everorb Headquarters was nothing like the Silverleaf Headquarters. This foyer was brightly lit with dark polished floors, a large black desk and a crystal feature wall with water flowing down it. There were long corridors running down each side of the room with the longest rug she had ever seen, trailing from one end to the other. In the entryway, there were headshots of all the soldiers, with photos of the Five at the very top. Tilly peered at Leo and grinned. "How much of your job involves modelling?" she asked.

Leo shook his head and steered her away from the photos. "More than I would like."

His hands dropped to his sides as a well-dressed man strolled towards them. He looked out of place in a crisp white shirt, navy tailored slacks and brown leather shoes. His dark grey vest had a golden shield pinned to it, with a chain running to the top button. "Ah, Leopold! Right on time," he said excitedly, rubbing his delicate hands together. His inquisitive, blue eyes wandered over Tilly. The man was sharp-faced, fair-skinned and lean, his black hair was peppered with grey and pulled into a small ponytail. An attractive human woman with short, tousled red hair, followed behind him holding a tablet.

Leo smiled at the man, but it didn't reach his eyes. He gestured towards Tilly. "Conrad, this is my friend Tilly Norris, Til this is Conrad Golding."

Tilly forced a smile, she didn't know what her and Leo were yet, but it was definitely more than friendship. "It's lovely to meet you, Sir, thank you for seeing me."

Conrad took her hand, kissing the top of it while studying her face. "My, my, my, she is divine Leopold, it's no wonder you couldn't leave this friend behind. Please, Tilly, call me Conrad."

Tilly shifted uncomfortably—she wanted her hand back. Leo cleared his throat. "She was already accepted into the Silverleaf Guard, I think she'd be a great asset to us."

"Fascinating, how old are you Tilly?"

"I just turned nineteen."

Conrad placed his finger over his mouth and circled her. "You don't look like much of a fighter. Where would you place her Leopold?"

Would he like us to demonstrate on him?

Tilly pressed her lips together to stop herself from laughing.

"Special forces," Leo said instantly. "I've never met a human as fast as she is."

Tilly heard the woman behind Conrad huff. Conrad's

eyebrows shot up. "Special forces? You'd send her straight to the top?"

Leo nodded. "She was trained by Commander Nero Wileman."

Tilly didn't think Conrad's eyebrows could get any higher. "Nero?" he said, looking at Tilly. "When was the last time you saw him?"

"Over a year ago now," Tilly said. "But he started training me when I was a child."

Conrad tapped his bottom lip thoughtfully. "She can complete her trial first thing tomorrow. I want to see how she fares against the other two." He gave a dismissive wave. "It's an unfair match of course, but it's the quickest way to gauge her skill level."

Tilly tried keeping a straight face, on the inside she was panicking. "Thank you, Conrad, I appreciate the opportunity." She glanced at Leo and noticed he looked troubled.

Conrad held out his arm. "Come, let me show you our facility." She hesitantly took his arm and he led them down the corridor. A few soldiers passed them, eyeing her curiously and saluting Leo and Conrad. Conrad showed her the barracks that housed the soldiers, as well as the cafeteria. He explained that he and the Five had private housing on the other side of the building. They passed the operations room full of soldiers sitting behind screens, a large screen on the wall showed a blueprint of a building. "Tell me about your family Tilly, is your father a soldier?" Conrad asked.

Tilly laughed, imagining her quiet and quirky father trying to fight. "No, he makes shoes and my mother is a chef."

He gave her a tight smile. "You are fortunate to have them." They walked down a large set of stairs to an underground training area. Tilly was excited to see that there were almost as many female soldiers as there were male. Conrad noticed her expression. "We take the best, we don't discriminate." She had a feeling she was going to like it here. He escorted her to a tall set of open doors at the back of the room. "And this," Conrad said dramatically, "is where all the fun happens."

Her eyes widened as they entered a modern arena, with a boxing ring in the centre and enough seating for thousands of people. Only a handful of soldiers were seated, watching a tall, bulky man in the ring, fighting three soldiers at once. He was brutal. He kicked one of them in the back, sending him flying across the stage. The man jumped and half shifted the top of his body into a horse, stomping on one of the soldiers before shifting back in the blink of an eye. He grabbed the last one by the shirt and punched him hard in the jaw.

Conrad approached the ring. "Ah, Faris, excellent timing. There's someone here I'd like you to meet."

Faris was breathing heavily, his dark blonde hair dripping with sweat. His shirt had ripped off when he'd shifted, showing his bulging muscles. He had an attractive, yet arrogant face and it was obvious his nose had been broken many times. He glanced between Leo and Tilly and his lips set in a hard line. "You and your bloody damsels in distress Leo. You know you're not meant to bring them here." Faris motioned towards a soldier to bring him water.

Well, isn't he delightful.

Leo opened his mouth, but Conrad held out a hand to stop him. "Tilly will actually be joining you in the ring tomorrow," he said.

Faris gave Tilly a pathetic look and laughed. "You're joking. You're gonna put that little thing up against me? I'd be afraid of killing her."

"That's funny," Tilly said sarcastically. "I didn't think a unicorn would be afraid of anything."

The soldiers all went quiet. Leo snickered while Conrad stood there in surprise. Faris was furious. "I am not a fucking unicorn!" he bellowed, jumping over the ring towards her.

Leo stepped in front of Tilly as Conrad stepped in front of Faris, letting out a cheerful laugh. "It's settled then. You will see Tilly tomorrow."

Faris stopped and glared as Conrad steered her out of the arena. Leo beamed at her. "That was priceless," he said, laughing.

Conrad shook his head, but he looked amused. "That was either very stupid or very brave. He will make you pay for that."

"Someone needs to knock him off that pedestal," Leo said bitterly.

Conrad smoothed down his vest. "He may not be for everyone, but he protects our realm just as you do," he said. "Now, I have places to be." He waved over the red-haired woman. "Piper, please have Tilly's file transferred from Silverleaf and ensure she has everything she needs." He glanced back at Tilly. "I look forward to seeing you first thing in the morning." His eyes lingered on her face before he swiftly walked away. Piper asked her a few questions and eyed Leo before storming off.

Leo showed Tilly around the armoury before they headed back to the cafeteria to grab dinner. She noticed he drew a lot of attention wherever he went, it was obvious the soldiers held a lot of respect for him. They grabbed a tray of food each and sat in a quiet corner. Tilly leaned towards him and lowered her voice. "Does Conrad usually put new recruits up against the brothers?"

Leo rubbed his temple, looking uncomfortable. "No, I think that might be my fault. He probably wants to see if you're as good as I say you are." He noticed the worry on her face. "You don't actually have to beat them, you just have to stay in the ring and stay conscious."

Tilly wondered if she had a chance, she'd never had a proper fight before and had never really seen what she could do. "Do you think I can do it?"

Leo looked at her thoughtfully. "I do, Nero was one of our best and he trained you almost your whole life, that's no small feat. And learning from those bikies has made you unpredictable, it actually gives you an advantage." He stabbed a chip with his fork. "You're also very fast, no one has seen how fast you are."

And now you have your magic, this is going to be fun.

She couldn't use her magic, she thought, everyone would know what she was.

Spirid magic makes you stronger and faster than humans, even with your magic dulled you were fast, now you'll be even quicker.

Tilly could feel Annora's excitement, she was excited too. As they ate dinner, she noticed a female Orbarian soldier sitting on her own. She was beautiful, with purple-tinted skin and long white hair. She caught Tilly looking at her and Tilly gave her a small smile, the woman smiled back and kept eating.

Leo walked Tilly back to her suite, as they reached the door, he wrapped his arms around her and leaned down to give her a kiss. "Goodnight Til," he whispered.

"You don't want to stay?" she asked surprised.

He swiftly picked her up and carried her inside, closing the door with his foot. "I was hoping you'd say that."

Tilly laughed. "Well, who else is going to check for monsters?"

Leo chuckled and threw her onto the bed playfully. "And here I thought you only wanted me for my body."

She eyed the way his T-shirt hugged his sculpted torso and tried to look insulted. "That's not even one of the reasons," she said seriously.

"No?" He slowly pulled his shirt over his head and threw it at her. Tilly's face flushed instantly. Leo bit his lip, holding back a laugh. "Hmm," he said. "That's not the impression I get."

She pulled him onto the bed and climbed on top of him, laughing. "Okay yes, but it's definitely not the main reason."

"What's the main reason?" he asked curiously.

She met his gaze. "I love who you are on the inside and I love the way you make me feel," she said honestly.

He sat up, bringing his face to hers. "Sounds like you might be falling in love with me."

Her heart fluttered. "It's hard not to."

Leo nodded. "Do you know what tipped me off?" He grabbed the amethyst crystal from the bedside table and showed her the lion. "The shrine you started in my honour," he said proudly.

Tilly laughed and grabbed the crystal, hugging it defensively. "One of the little girls at the market picked it for me."

Leo grinned. "You don't have to explain yourself." He leaned over and kissed her. "I'm falling in love with you too."

Chapter Nine

The Trial

Tilly woke the next morning to Leo kissing her neck. She sighed happily, not opening her eyes. She could definitely get used to this.

"In case you're wondering," Leo whispered. "It's not your mother."

Her eyes shot open and she started to laugh. "Gross Leo!" She was so embarrassed she had called him that, she pulled the pillow over her head, hiding under it.

He laughed loudly. "Come back, I was teasing."

"No thank you."

"Today's your big day, you'll have to come out eventually," he said playfully. Her trial, she had butterflies in her stomach at the thought. She felt Leo get out of bed. Suddenly he yanked the blankets off. "Come on, out you get."

She stayed under the pillow, trying not to giggle.

"If that's how you want to play," he threatened. He grabbed her ankles and pulled her down towards him. She cried out in surprise as her nightgown slid up to her stomach. Leo lifted her leg and kissed her ankle, making his way up to her knee before he stopped. "If you don't come out, I'll keep going."

Tilly threw the pillow off and leaned up on her elbows, studying his face. He was no longer being playful, he was staring at her like he was about to devour her. "Keep going," she whispered.

Without taking his eyes off hers, Leo trailed kisses up the inside of her leg until he reached the top of her thigh and stopped. Tilly was already breathless, she wanted him to keep going. "I better do the other leg too, just to be fair," he said seriously.

Tilly groaned and threw her head back—he was messing with her. She felt him laugh against her skin as he slowly kissed her other leg, from her ankle to her thigh. Only this time, he didn't stop. He reached the top and kept going, moving his tongue over her slowly. She closed her eyes and moaned, the pleasure was intense.

He held her thighs down and she grabbed his hair with one hand, the other squeezing the pillow behind her. She looked down at Leo between her legs, his dark eyes were still on hers. He slid his finger in and moved it in rhythm with his tongue, gliding it up and down. She could feel the pleasure building. He started going faster and she couldn't hold on any longer. She felt euphoric, she cried out loudly as her body shuddered from the sensation. Leo crawled up over her and kissed her on the mouth. His lips moved down her neck and over her breasts, teasing her nipples with his tongue over the lace. She moaned softly and slid her hand into his boxers. She wanted to make him feel as good as he made her feel. Leo watched as she wrapped her fingers around him and stroked him. Tilly pushed him down onto the bed and pulled down his shorts. His eyes turned to fire as she bent down, kissing him and gliding her tongue around his tip. She took him into her mouth and he groaned happily. She moved back and forth, using her hands as she went. When she peeked up at Leo, his eyes darkened. "Careful Til," he said softly. She moved faster and a low moan escaped his lips as he finished.

"You know you didn't have to do that," he said breathlessly.

"I know," she said with a small smile, "but I wanted to."

He pulled her to his chest and hugged her tight. "I could get used to waking up with you every morning," he said softly.

Her eyes shone happily. "So could I, but now all I can think about is your tongue, when I should be worrying about my trial," she teased.

Leo laughed. "I'm not sorry about that."

Tilly stood in front of the mirror, checking her reflection. Leo had grabbed her some dark green military pants from Headquarters, they were loose fitting around her backside and hugged her legs at the bottom. She hid her necklace under her black T-shirt and pulled on her combat boots. She was ready.

This suits you, Matilda.

When she walked into the kitchen, Leo's face confirmed it. "You look like someone who should not be messed with."

"That's the sweetest thing you've ever said to me," she said seriously. He smirked and passed her a plate of scrambled eggs on toast. They sat at the table and ate silently, she was growing more nervous by the minute.

"How are you feeling?" Leo asked.

"I'm starting to panic a little."

He gave her a small smile. "You've been training for this

your whole life. Just remember what I said, you're faster than they are. That's your advantage, don't let them get a hold of you."

"I wasn't fast enough to beat you," she pointed out.

"You elbowed me in the face before I could stop you and not to brag, but I'm faster than the other two as well. I'm a lot younger than they are."

Tilly pushed the eggs around her plate with her fork. "I feel like I know what to expect from Faris, but I've even met Alerio. Will he shift during the fight too?"

"No, Alerio is very honourable. He'll fight you fairly and he'll be curious to see what you can do. He's not about showing off." Leo reached over and put his hand over hers. "I wouldn't have let Conrad go ahead with this if I didn't think you could do it."

Tilly smiled at him, he really believed in her and now she just needed to believe in herself.

They reached Headquarters and made their way through the training room. It was surprisingly quiet, with not a single soldier in sight. Tilly thought they would go straight to the arena, but Leo led her to a small room off to the side and pointed to a set of doors. "They lead out to the stage. Someone will come and get you when it's time."

"Where will you be?" she asked.

"Sitting with Conrad." He wrapped his arms around her and kissed her forehead. "You can do this Til, just don't hold back." He left through the arena doors and she started to panic. Fighting other soldiers she would have been prepared for, but this felt out of her league.

Calm down. I can help, but you need to focus.

Tilly closed her eyes, taking deep breaths and visualising herself on a snowy mountain with icy-cold air caressing her face. She felt her heart slow.

Beautiful, you dream of your homeland.

She felt the sorrow in Annora's voice. "It's always made me feel at peace," Tilly whispered.

You would have loved it there. Now, focus on your magic, feel it grow as I've shown you.

She kept her eyes closed, feeling the familiar warmth build in her chest.

Direct it through your body—feel it strengthen every part of you.

Tilly expanded her magic, she stretched it and spread it through her body until she felt like she was made of it. She wasn't afraid anymore, she was burning with energy.

This is how a Spirid warrior prepares for battle, now go and make your people proud.

Tilly paced around the room restlessly, she tied her hair into a high ponytail and started stretching and warming up. A soldier pushed the door open, it was the white-haired Orbarian woman she had noticed yesterday. She had purple-tinted skin and light silver eyes. "Um, Tilly?" she said nervously. "They're ready for you."

"Thank you…"

"Cali," she replied.

"Cali." Tilly smiled at her. "It's nice to meet you."

Cali smiled back and glanced down. "Hey I love your shoes, those moon charms are so cute." Cali held the door open for her. Tilly thanked her and walked out towards the ring. "Good luck," Cali whispered.

Tilly's eyes went wide as she looked around—the entire arena was packed. The crowd fell silent as she came into view. Conrad stood in the middle of the ring in a light grey suit, his shield badge glimmered on his chest.

Keep walking Matilda.

She hadn't realised she'd stopped, she kept walking towards the stage, glancing around nervously. She spotted Leo seated in the front row—he gave her an encouraging smile. Faris and Alerio sat beside him. Behind them were rows of extravagantly dressed Orbarians. She could see sparkling gems glittering around their hands and necks, she guessed they were some of the ruling families. Every other seat was taken by soldiers—this wasn't what she had expected at all.

Looks like Conrad enjoys putting on a show.

She stepped up into the ring towards Conrad. He motioned for her to stand beside him. "Are you ready for this?" he asked quietly. "There's no shame in backing down."

She felt the magic burning through her body. "I'm ready."

Me too.

Annora growled, making Tilly smile.

"That's our girl," Conrad said beaming. He looked over the crowd and lifted a microphone to his mouth. "Welcome everyone. Thank you for joining us on this exciting morning." He gestured towards Tilly. "Tilly Norris has been nominated by Leopold of the Valunan Five, he believes her capable of joining our Special Forces Unit." Conrad paused dramatically. Tilly noticed looks of surprise throughout the crowd. "But first, she must prove herself. She will undertake her trial against two of the Five. Alerio, would you please join us in the ring."

The crowd cheered as Alerio stood from his seat and made his way towards the stage.

Conrad leaned towards Tilly. "Just make it to three minutes, good luck." He walked off the stage, nodding to Alerio as he passed. Alerio was as tall as Leo, dark-skinned with wise, brown eyes and full lips, his shaved head shone under the stage lights. Tight-fitting gym pants and a singlet hugged his muscular physique.

He is gorgeous.

Now is not the time, Tilly thought with amusement. She had to admit though, he had a certain calmness about him that she couldn't help admiring. He studied her curiously. She thought she saw a slight twitch of his lip. Conrad took his seat next to Leo. "Are you both ready?"

Tilly and Alerio nodded.

Don't hold back.

Conrad hit a button and a siren sounded. "Your time starts now."

Alerio and Tilly circled each other, waiting to see who would make the first move. He struck first. She dodged easily, stepping out of his way as he tried again. He reached out to grab her and she slipped under his arm, elbowing him in the side with more force than she expected. He stepped back in surprise. Tilly had a feeling he was going easy on her. His expression suddenly changed from curious to excited.

Here we go.

Alerio shot towards her with impressive speed. She dodged a fist and jumped onto his leg, twisting herself up onto his shoulders. She wrapped her legs around his neck and pulled him down, surprising herself with her strength. He rolled them both over and knocked her off. She fell back and quickly sprang to her feet. Alerio didn't waste any time, he tried swiping her legs from under her, but she spun out of the way, bringing her foot up to the side of his face. He staggered back and she kept advancing on him, giving him everything she had. He tried to grab her around the waist and she gripped his shoulders, pushing them down and bringing her knee up to his chin. Alerio pulled himself free and straightened up. He feigned left and kicked her in the side, catching her by surprise and sending her flying across the stage. Tilly fell to the ground. She felt her magic start to fade and she built it up again, sending it through her body even stronger than before. She crouched down as Alerio's foot came flying towards her face. Tilly grabbed onto it, ducking between his legs and pulling his foot along with her, bringing him to the ground. She jumped onto his back. Alerio swung his elbow up towards her and she shot out of the way.

The siren sounded. "Time!" Conrad said.

The crowd went wild. Alerio stood up and glanced over at her, he looked impressed. "You've got talent little one." He placed his hand over his heart and bowed to her.

"Thanks, Alerio, it was an honour to fight you," she said, bowing in return. He gave her an approving smile and left the stage.

Well done Matilda.

She could feel the pride in Annora's voice. Conrad returned to the stage and held up the microphone. "What a delightful surprise," he said. He pointed to Leo. "You were not wrong Leopold."

Leo gave him a small nod, then smiled at Tilly with eyes full of love. Conrad threw his arm around her shoulder. "That was really something, how do you feel? Do you need a quick break?"

Tilly glanced at Faris, he was already glaring at her, she felt her magic flare. "No, I'm ready for him," she said.

"Ah," Conrad said laughing. "She is a fighter. Faris, come on down."

Alerio had returned to his seat. Tilly saw him whisper something to Leo, they looked down towards her, both smiling. Faris stomped up the steps, his arrogant face looking down at her. There were hushed voices in the crowd.

Bring it on pony boy.

Tilly accidentally let out a laugh. A vein bulged in Faris' forehead, he looked murderous.

"Uh oh, I better get out of the way," Conrad joked. The crowd laughed as he strolled back to his seat.

Faris pulled his shirt off and threw it out of the ring. He moved his head from side to side, cracking his neck. "I'll try not to break you," he said obnoxiously.

"You'll have to catch me first," Tilly taunted.

His lips pursed.

Get ready, he's not going to stop.

Faris pulled his fists up and stepped one leg back.

"Are you ready?" Conrad called from his chair. They both nodded, not breaking eye contact. The siren went off. "Your time starts now."

Faris lunged towards her, his foot flew to her chest. She ducked and he shot towards her again and again. She dodged and spun out of the way. Each time he missed he grew angrier.

You're embarrassing him, keep going.

His fists kept flying towards her, but he couldn't touch her. He yelled in frustration and rammed his shoulder into her side. She fell to the edge of the stage. Faris jumped towards her excitedly. Tilly grabbed onto the ring and kicked backwards, her foot made contact with his chest and sent him stumbling back. She shot towards him, building up her magic and pushing him to the ground.

There were gasps from the crowd.

Tilly knelt on top of him as his hand shot up and wrapped around her throat.

"Tilly!" Leo cried, jumping from his seat.

Faris' grip was strong. She grabbed at his hand, but he wouldn't let go. His face looked triumphant as he pulled her towards him, smiling gleefully. "It's nap time you little bitch."

Tilly pulled her magic to the top of her body, using all her strength to headbutt him hard in the nose.

There was a loud crack.

Faris cried out, dropping Tilly and grabbing his bleeding nose. She coughed and crawled away from him.

Faris stood and stormed towards her, he pounced and started to half-shift. He was going to stomp on her and there was no way she would recover from that.

Move Matilda!

Tilly turned onto her back as his hooves came towards her, she slid down just as he stomped the stage above her head. Tilly burned with rage. Without thinking, she directed her magic to her legs, kicking him with both of her feet as hard as she could. The impact was so great that he went flying across the stage.

Conrad stood up and gripped the railing in front of him.

Faris shifted back just before his head hit the ground. The crowd went completely silent as a medic ran over to inspect him. "He's been knocked unconscious," he confirmed, glancing towards Tilly.

The soldiers jumped from their seats, cheering and whistling. Tilly sat up and rubbed her throat. "Damn you Faris, that's gonna leave a mark," she muttered. She glanced over at his motionless body. What had she done? She didn't mean to kick him that hard.

Your instincts took over, your magic is a part of you as much as your arm or leg. One day you won't even need to direct it, it will just happen. Don't feel bad Matilda—you earned this.

Tilly felt relief wash over her, it was finally over. Conrad and Leo ran across the stage as Faris was carried off on a stretcher. Leo held his hand out and pulled her to her feet. "That was amazing, you were too quick for them, they could barely touch you," he said excitedly, his eyes shining with pride.

"I think I'm in shock," she said truthfully.

"Aren't we all," Conrad agreed, his blue eyes studying hers. "How did you kick him like that? Are you part Gribbin?"

She held her throat. "I have no idea. I just saw what he did to that soldier yesterday and I panicked, I had to get him away from me."

Conrad plastered a smile on his face. "Well, it was highly entertaining." He took Tilly's hand and raised it into the air. "Ladies and gentlemen, please welcome our newest recruit!"

Leo beamed at her as the crowd cheered. "I knew you could do it," he said quietly. "So did Alerio, he knew you'd beat Faris. I'm so proud of you, you should be too."

Tilly looked back at him, grinning. For the first time in her life, she really was proud of herself.

Chapter Ten

Lady Jaini Zirk

Tilly sat in her crystal bathtub, replaying the day in her mind. They'd spent the whole day at Headquarters, everyone had wanted to meet and congratulate her. Conrad loved the attention and introduced her to many of the ruling family members. Leo told her that Faris woke up after the fight and locked himself in his room. She worried about what the consequences would be for beating him. Her body was already making her pay for it—she ached from using so much magic.

It will get easier. The more you use it, the less it will affect you.

Tilly climbed out of the tub and wrapped herself in her fluffy white robe. She'd been so worried about her trial that she'd forgotten Leo had planned dinner with Jaini. She still needed to conjure something to wear. Tilly entered her closet and stood in front of the full-length mirror—her mind went blank. "Help me, Annora," she said in a panic.

Matilda, this is not the kind of thing I'm here to help with.

Annora sounded amused. "I have no idea what to wear to

dinner with a Lady," Tilly said.

Well, you definitely can't wear pants.

Really helpful she thought, she had already guessed that much.

Nothing black either.

"Why not black?" she asked, it was her favourite colour.

You aren't going to a funeral.

Annora was scolding her now. Tilly glanced at her green nightdress. "Green it is then."

She placed her left hand out and pictured herself in a deep green, satin dress. It had small petal sleeves, a sweetheart neckline and a gauzy, flowing skirt. Her fingers glowed as the dress appeared in her hand. She put it on and pulled her hair down, hiding some of the marks Faris had left around her neck.

That's quite lovely.

She could sense Annora's approval. Tilly felt extremely uncomfortable, she reached down and hid her moonstone daggers around her thighs. That's better she thought, now she felt a little more herself. She conjured some simple black heels and went into the living room to wait for Leo. Tilly glanced out a diamond-shaped window, the dome had cleared showing off a brilliant star-filled sky. A week ago, she never would have imagined herself here, so much had happened in such a short period of time.

She felt Leo's presence and turned as he entered the room. He wore a black suit with a green shirt underneath, his black hair still wet from the shower. She was sure no one had ever looked so good in a suit. He froze as soon as he saw her. "Til, you look—"

"Ridiculous?" she said nervously.

He stalked towards her and pulled her into his arms. "Like a goddess," he said softly. Tilly scoffed, she felt her cheeks turning red. He took her hand, bringing it to his lips. "I mean it, you are breathtaking."

"So are you," she said shyly.

He chuckled as his eyes trailed down her body, stopping at her thighs. "Are you wearing your daggers?" he asked with delight.

She glanced down at her dress sheepishly. "I didn't think you'd be able to see them."

Leo laughed loudly. "There's my Tilly," he said affectionately. "You can't see them—I was just guessing."

She grinned up at him. "You know me too well."

They took the lift to the penthouse and Tilly couldn't stop fidgeting. "She lives in this tower?"

"Yes, it's why Gera chose this one for you." Leo squeezed her hand. "Don't be nervous, I know she'll love you." he looked ahead with a small smile. "Probably too much," he added quietly.

The lift stopped and they stepped into a spacious foyer. Two guards stood on either side of a tall set of golden doors, they bowed and pushed them open. Tilly and Leo thanked them as they stepped inside. Jaini had the entire floor to herself, the ceiling was high and sweeping and the floors were made of white opal. White furnishings and golden statues were expertly placed around the home and flowering plants trailed down the windows like botanical waterfalls. Tilly glanced around in awe as Leo led her to the living area. He sat down on one of the white, curved couches, that could easily seat ten people. She sat beside him and examined the golden willow tree with glittering, crystal leaves placed in the corner of the room. Leo laughed at her expression. "It's a bit much, isn't it?"

"Leo!" An Orbarian woman strolled into the room excitedly, a long-sleeved burgundy dress twisted down her body, flowing to the floor.

Leo stood up and kissed her on the cheek before he motioned towards Tilly. "Jaini, this is Tilly."

Jaini turned and beamed at her. She had to be the most beautiful Orbarian Tilly had seen. Green-tinted skin, purple shining hair in an elegant bun and long dark eyelashes framing her bright, silver eyes. Her purple lipstick matched the shade of her hair and large jewels glittered around her neck and fingers.

Jaini gave Tilly a tight hug. "I am so excited to meet you, you're all everyone has been talking about—let me look at you." She held Tilly's shoulders and focused on her face.

"Um, it's lovely to meet you too Jaini," Tilly said amused.

"My god, you are stunning. No wonder Leo brought you home." She glanced back at Leo. "Did you two match your outfits?"

"No," Leo said laughing. "Not on purpose."

"I wasn't allowed to wear black," Tilly said without thinking.

Jaini looked at Leo accusingly, he lifted his hands in the air. "I didn't say she couldn't wear black—I know it's her favourite colour."

"You do?" Tilly asked.

"Of course I do."

She smiled at him and Leo smiled back. Jaini stood there looking between them with a huge grin on her face. "Come, let's eat, I want to know everything about you, Tilly." She turned and they followed her to the dining table, her dress gliding along the floor behind her.

The dining area was intimately decorated, with candles and colourful flowers running down the long white table. Leo pulled Tilly's chair out for her before taking the seat beside her. Jaini sat opposite them and reached for her wine glass.

"How's the preparation going for the Ceremony?" Leo asked.

Jaini rolled her eyes. "We're getting there. I have a vision, but it's been difficult getting everyone else on board."

"I was sorry to hear about the passing of Councillor Zirk," Tilly said gently.

Jaini waved her hand dismissively. "Don't be. He was an old fool who made me feel inadequate every day of my life." Jaini glanced between them with interest. "Now tell me, how long have you two known each other?"

Leo smirked. "Almost a week."

Jaini's purple eyebrows rose. "And how did you meet?"

Tilly and Leo looked at each other. "Leo was following me around," Tilly teased. "And then he saved my life."

Jaini looked confused. "So, you followed him back here? Even though you just met and he had been stalking you?"

Leo shook his head with disbelief. "It's a little more complicated than that Jaini."

Servers arrived with crystal trays of food and placed them around the table. Roast meats and vegetables, salads and bread. Tilly's stomach growled and Leo coughed to hide his laugh. She excitedly filled her plate with some of everything, while Leo and Jaini spoke about the other Councillors.

"You've got quite the appetite, Tilly," Jaini said approvingly.

Tilly felt her face flush. "I usually eat more after I fight," she said quickly.

"She also just loves food more than anything else," Leo said.

There was a glimmer of amusement in Jaini's eyes. "You sure do know a lot about each other already."

Servers entered the room as they finished dinner, replacing the dishes with an array of desserts. They placed a honey cake in front of Tilly. She had a flashback of Leo running into her room with his sword and couldn't stop herself from laughing. Leo noticed the cake and grinned at her.

Jaini watched them both fondly. "You must tell me Tilly, how did it feel knocking Faris out this morning? He's a bit of a bastard that one."

Tilly laughed. "I think Leo enjoyed it more than I did." She rubbed her neck and Leo's eyes darkened. "I'd probably feel bad if he hadn't tried choking me," she admitted.

Jaini's expression turned angry. "I heard about that—he must have panicked."

"I was surprised Conrad allowed it to be honest," Leo muttered. His pocket started buzzing, he pulled out his phone and frowned. "I'm really sorry ladies, Conrad's looking for me, he said it's urgent." He sighed and squeezed Tilly's hand. "I'll come and see you when I'm done." He stood from his seat and nodded to Jaini. "Thanks for dinner, you were full of well-prepared questions, as always."

Jaini grinned. "It was good to see you too."

They watched Leo leave and Jaini sighed loudly. "Poor Leo, it's such a shame isn't it, you two really are perfect for each other."

"I'm sorry, what's a shame?" Tilly asked politely.

Jaini gave her a confused look. "That the Five can never marry or commit themselves. Hasn't he told you that?"

Tilly's heart sank in her chest. "He's not allowed to be with anyone? Why?"

Jaini's expression softened. "When they take their oath, they pledge their lives to the realm, their whole lives. They commit themselves only to their brothers and are stripped of their family name so they can never pass it on. Could you imagine the Five married or having kids? Their priority would not be the safety of Valuna."

Tilly was lost for words, Leo had never told her any of this.

Jaini lifted her wine glass and took a long sip before she spoke. "It's both an honour and a burden being one of the Five, Leo has never been allowed a life of his own."

I'm so sorry, Matilda.

"I can't believe he didn't tell you," Jaini said annoyed.

Tilly's head was spinning. "Why hasn't anyone said anything about us always being together?" She thought back to each time they'd been at Headquarters, she realised Leo hadn't touched her around Conrad or the others.

Jaini looked embarrassed. "Ah, people are definitely talking about Leo arriving with a beautiful human and um, staying in her suite at night."

"Even though he isn't allowed?" Tilly asked confused.

Jaini looked very uncomfortable. "They're allowed casual… night time companions," she said awkwardly.

"Oh my god." Tilly dropped her face into her hands, she felt so hurt and ashamed. She thought he loved her, but she was his plaything and everybody else knew except for her.

Jaini rushed over and sat beside her, placing her arm over Tilly's shoulders. "I am so, incredibly sorry, I had no idea you didn't know."

"Does Leo do this all the time? Bring women back here?" She remembered what Faris had said about the damsels in distress, at the time, she thought he was just being obnoxious but maybe he was telling the truth.

"No Tilly, do you think I'd invite you here if that were the case? He may not be allowed to be with you, but I knew there was something special about you. That's why I wanted to meet so badly."

"From the moment we met we've had a connection—I thought it was love," Tilly whispered.

Jaini took her hand. "He said the same thing about you and I saw it tonight with my own eyes. It's like you were made for each other, I've never seen him this happy before."

Tilly felt lost and confused, she looked up at Jaini and cleared her throat. "I'm so sorry Jaini, I didn't mean to ruin your dinner." She had so many questions, but she needed to ask Leo himself.

"Please, I ruined it with my big mouth. Leo really should have told you though, I'm quite disappointed in him."

"Have you two ever?" Tilly stopped, she couldn't believe she was about to ask Jaini that when they had just met.

"Gross no," Jaini laughed. "He's my annoying and sarcastic brother. Besides, I'm not interested in uh, men." Jaini picked at one of the flowers on the table, not meeting Tilly's eyes.

"Oh," Tilly said in surprise. "Do you have a special lady in your life?"

"No," Jaini replied sadly. "I'm so busy I barely have time for myself."

"I met some of your people when we arrived," Tilly said. "You've given them hope."

"I won't let them down. For too long we've ruled from the top of our towers, keeping far away from our people so we can pretend there's nothing wrong with this city."

I like this one.

"You're going to do incredible things," Tilly said. "You have a lot of devoted people down there waiting for you to take your place."

They smiled at each other. Jaini glanced down at her hand still holding Tilly's. "Are you sure you like Leo?" She sighed. "I could do with someone like you in my life."

Tilly laughed. "I could do with a friend," she suggested.

Jaini smirked. "Hmm, that will have to do for now. Leo told me you had to leave your home quite quickly, do you have everything you need?"

"I think so, the suite is full of food and Leo brought me some clothes from Headquarters. I'll be getting a uniform as well," Tilly remembered.

Jaini's face turned to disgust. "I can just imagine the ugly clothes Leo brought you." She patted Tilly's hand. "Don't worry, I'll look after you."

"You don't have to do that," Tilly said quickly.

"I really do, will you join me again soon? I'd love to get to know you more."

Tilly smiled. "I'd love that."

Jaini walked her out to the lift, giving her a tight hug goodbye and making her promise to keep in touch. Tilly thanked her for dinner and promised she would. She entered the lift and her face dropped— what was she going to do about Leo?

Tilly paced around her bedroom, it had been hours since she left Jaini's and she still had no idea what to do. She didn't know how long it would be until Leo returned.

You need to calm down and just talk to him.

"And then what?" Tilly said angrily. "Happily be his toy?" For months she had felt like she was Orvyn's possession, she never wanted to feel like that again, she promised herself she wouldn't. She really thought Leo was different.

He is different, he is nothing like Orvyn and you know that.

Tilly let out a frustrated sigh and flopped back on the bed, she was exhausted but there was no way she could sleep right now. She dragged the blanket off the bed and took it to the couch, she laid down and wrapped it around herself. "Did you know? That he couldn't be with me?" she whispered.

Annora sighed.

Yes.

"Why didn't you tell me?"

Because he's your soulmate and that's more powerful than any oath.

Tilly woke to a small knock at the door, she must have accidentally fallen asleep. She went to open it with the blanket still wrapped around her. Leo stood there with a strange look on his face. "Sorry I took so long, I hope I didn't wake you."

"Come in." She closed the door behind him, trying to hold in tears. She was going to be strong. She led Leo to the couch, he looked confused, but he took the seat opposite her. "We need to talk."

Leo studied her face and ran his fingers through his hair. "Jaini told you—I shouldn't be surprised."

"So it's true?" she asked. "You can never be with me?"

She saw the pain in his eyes. "Yes, it's true. I'm so sorry, I never wanted to hurt you."

Her heart was racing. "What did you plan on doing then? Keeping me around until we had sex and then getting rid of me?" she asked accusingly.

Leo looked taken aback. "Of course not. After everything

we've been through, do you honestly think all I wanted was sex?"

"No," Tilly said quietly, then she asked a question she had been dreading. "Have there been a lot of other women?"

Leo hesitated. "Yes, but that was years ago, it was purely for fun and they knew that."

"I see," she said, not knowing what else to say. How could she know for certain she wasn't just like those other women?

Leo looked at her seriously. "Everyone has a past. It's not always one we're proud of, but it doesn't define who we are now. I thought you of all people would understand that."

Tilly thought about her own past, when Leo met her, she had a horrible boyfriend and was involved with bikies—she definitely wasn't proud of that. "You're right," she said. "I can't hold your past against you, mine isn't great either. Why didn't you tell me about the oath though?"

"The same reason you didn't want my help with the Vipers, it was my problem to fix," Leo said quietly. "I never wanted you to feel the way you do right now."

She tightened the blanket around herself. "You should have told me, maybe we could have worked it out together," she said. "Now I find out I can never be with you, and the whole city knows I'm your casual night time companion. I feel so stupid."

He tried to keep a straight face. "My what?"

"Never mind, you know what I mean," she said embarrassed.

Leo knelt on the floor at her feet, he took her hands and stared into her eyes. "You have to understand, I grew up knowing I'd never be allowed to fall in love or have a family. I never expected to find you, you've changed everything." He took a deep breath. "I love you Til, I love you, body and soul.

When you told me yesterday you felt the same, I knew nothing would stop me from being with you, not even a damn oath."

Tilly held back tears, she could feel it was true, she always could and she knew she loved him too. "Did you talk to Conrad about it?"

Leo closed his eyes. "I did, it's why he called me in tonight. He's not happy that I called out to you when Faris choked you, he said I'm getting too attached and need to stop whatever we have immediately. We'll just have to be more careful."

She frowned. "What would happen if you stayed with me and he found out?"

Leo hesitated. "I'd be stripped of my title and banished, I would be a disgrace and we wouldn't be welcome anywhere we went."

Tilly slowly shook her head. "I want to be with you more than anything, but not like that. I'd never forgive myself if you were sentenced to that life."

"I'd take the risk if it meant I could be with you," he said honestly. "I told you I never asked for this life. I would have loved a wife and family of my own one day. I want that with you."

Tilly's heart felt like it was breaking into a million pieces, she wanted this life with him too, more than anything. "I'm sorry, I won't sneak around with you and risk you losing everything."

Leo's eyes searched hers. "Please don't do this. I swear I'll find a way for us to be together."

"I know you will," she said. She climbed onto his lap and took his hands. "And I'll be missing you every moment until that day comes."

He closed his eyes and pressed his forehead against hers. "I know this is the right thing to do," he whispered, "but it feels like the biggest mistake of my life."

A tear slid down her cheek. "Mine too."

He leaned forward and kissed her. "I love you Til."

Tilly squeezed her eyes shut. "I love you too."

They held each other, neither of them wanting to let go. Leo sighed and gave her one last kiss on the forehead before getting up and heading to the door. He stopped and glanced back with eyes full of regret. "I promise we'll be together again."

He left and Tilly burst into tears, she climbed back onto the couch and cocooned herself in the blanket.

I know it doesn't feel like it, but you did the right thing.

Chapter Eleven

The Recruit

Tilly opened her eyes—something didn't feel right. A heaviness filled her chest as the memories from last night flooded back to her. She tightened the blanket around herself and held back tears—she had no idea how to deal with a broken heart.

Just take it one day at a time.

"How can I face everyone?" she whispered. Today was her first day as a recruit and she was already dreading leaving the safety of her couch.

You can't let this hold you back. Look at what you did yesterday, you have nothing to prove to anyone.

Tilly felt Annora sharing her strength, warmth filled her chest, easing the crushing pain from her aching heart.

Now, let's go and remind everyone why you're here.

Tilly smiled, feeling a sense of purpose. She would focus on training and finding her place in Everorb City.

That's my girl.

She showered and got ready before stopping at the door and

taking a deep breath. "I am strong. I can do this." She didn't feel strong, but maybe if she said it enough, it would be true.

Tilly walked through the city towards Headquarters. The dome was dark and the humidity seemed worse than usual—or maybe it was just her mood. She took the steps up to the entrance as two guards placed their hands over their hearts and bowed to her. She smiled uncomfortably. That was strange, she thought.

They respect you.

An Orbarian soldier approached her as she entered the foyer. He was tall with a shaved head and purple-tinted skin. His silver eyes widened excitedly as he shook her hand. "Tilly, welcome. I'm Vona one of Conrad's assistants, it's such a privilege to meet you in person."

She smiled politely. "Thanks, Vona, it's nice to meet you too. I hope I haven't kept you waiting."

"Not at all, please follow me. Conrad's expecting you." He turned right and strolled down the corridor. Tilly followed behind him. She hadn't seen this part of Headquarters before, she started wondering where Leo's room was and stopped herself.

"We're so excited to have you join us," Vona said eagerly. "Everyone was surprised at your trial, we thought you were just getting special treatment."

"Why did you think I was getting special treatment?" she asked with confusion.

He chuckled. "You know, because of you and Leo."

Tilly felt her magic flare in her chest.

Breathe Matilda.

She took a deep breath, it was time to start standing up for herself. "Actually, I was already accepted into the Silverleaf Guard, before I came here." She frowned at Vona. "Leo's nothing more than a friend and I don't appreciate those rumours," she said firmly, acting as if saying his name out loud didn't hurt her heart.

Very good.

She watched Vona's face drop. "Yeah, of course. I'm so—I'm so sorry, I shouldn't have said that."

Tilly gave him a hard stare, it felt out of character for her, but she wanted to make it clear she didn't find his opinion amusing. Vona quickly walked ahead. "Conrad's office is just through here." He opened the door for her, unable to meet her eye. "I'm sorry if I offended you, I hope you can forgive me," he said nervously.

She gave him a curt nod before stepping into Conrad's office. She glanced around, 'office' felt like the wrong word for it, it looked more like a library mixed with a gentleman's club. The walls were hidden behind overflowing bookshelves and the wooden floor was decorated with large patterned rugs. To the left was an impressive bar, with hundreds of bottles displayed in glass cabinets. Small tables were scattered throughout the room, encircled by brown leather armchairs. Conrad sat at the back of the office behind a large oak desk. Today his vest was navy and his shoulder-length, black hair was down and tidy around his face. Tilly approached him slowly, she noticed a gold-framed painting behind him—a city built into snow-capped mountains.

Panthera.

Conrad looked up at her with his sharp blue eyes. "Good morning my dear, please take a seat." She sat in the armchair opposite him and he gave her a sad smile. "I spoke to Leopold this morning, I'm sure you're quite upset with me today."

Tilly forced a smile. "No, not at all, if I had known about the oath it never would have happened. I'm sorry if I caused any trouble."

Truthfully, she had no idea what would have happened if she'd known from the start. Her bond with Leo was hard to ignore. Conrad grinned at her. "Ah, you are wise as you are beautiful, I'm very impressed. I'm sure we can forget this whole thing ever happened." She nodded gratefully, her eyes flicked to the painting again and Conrad followed her gaze. "Panthera, have you seen this before?"

"No, I've just heard stories."

He nodded sadly and stood to look at the painting. "I keep it here as a reminder of why our job is so important and why I keep the Valunan Five on such a tight rein."

Tilly tilted her head in confusion. "But, it wasn't the Five's fault it fell, they couldn't have known what the Calvarians were planning. Leo said the attacks came out of nowhere."

Conrad pursed his lips and tapped them thoughtfully. "Did Leopold tell you who was leading them?" Tilly shook her head. Conrad paced across the room and sighed heavily. "It was Torben, the brother who abandoned them before Leo joined. He was the one who led the army."

Annora snarled. "Why would he do that?" Tilly said quickly.

Conrad frowned. "We believe he was angry at the Spirids for placing such a burden on him. He wanted his freedom back. The brothers thought he'd simply given up his place and gone into hiding, but they were wrong, he came back for revenge." Tilly felt a shiver down her spine. Conrad waved his hand dismissively. "It's all in the past now of course, but we Historians never forget. The Valunan Five are a dangerous asset, they need to be kept under control." He sat on the desk beside her, watching her carefully. "Torben's actions are not common knowledge, if this was to get out it would tarnish the reputation of the Five. I trust you will keep this discussion to yourself."

Tilly nodded. "Of course."

Conrad smiled and pointed to a pile of folded clothing. "Your uniform. You've been assigned to our Special Forces team. However, before you join them and get your badge, you need to undergo formal training." He handed her a sheet of paper. "As part of that team, you will work directly under the Valunan Five, so your schedule will be slightly different from the others."

She glanced down at the schedule. As well as the expected strength training, combat classes and study periods, she also had defence classes with Faris and two specialised classes each week with Leo and Alerio. "Training with Leopold won't be an issue, will it?" Conrad asked.

She tried to keep a straight face. "It won't be an issue, I would never risk this opportunity."

"Good. Faris took some convincing to allow you to join his sessions, I ask that you don't cause any trouble."

"I'll be on my best behaviour," Tilly said, already knowing that would be difficult around Faris.

"Excellent. Lastly, your sleeping arrangements. You're entitled to a shared room here, but Leopold mentioned you'd pre-paid for your suite for the time being, would you prefer to stay there?"

"Yes, thank you for the offer though." She liked her privacy, especially if she wanted to practice magic with Annora.

"Very well, while you're here, you'll report directly to me.

Faris is second in charge in my absence. If there's anything you need or wish to discuss, please come and find me." Conrad motioned towards the door.

Tilly stood up and grabbed her uniform. "Thank you again, Conrad."

He gave her a small nod. She turned to leave and as she reached the door, he called out again. "Oh, and Tilly, I thought you should know. Commander Nero handed his resignation in a year ago. We haven't heard from him since."

Tilly's brow furrowed, that was news to her. She wondered if anyone had told Orvyn or his mother. She thanked Conrad for letting her know and walked out to find Vona waiting for her. He still looked nervous, he passed her a key and escorted her to the women's locker room. "There's a locker number on the key, you'll need to change into your uniform before you start. If you need directions, ask any of the guards." She thanked him and he gave her an awkward bow before he hurried away.

Tilly found her locker and changed into her uniform—dark grey fitted cargo pants and a matching button-up shirt. She tied her hair up and placed her daggers around her thighs. As she walked out of the room she caught her reflection in the mirror. A feeling of pride welled in her chest, this was a moment she had been dreaming of since she was a child.

Tilly glanced over her schedule, she had a session with Alerio and then group combat with Faris—she cringed at the thought. She found a guard and he directed her to the stairs leading to the underground training area. When she reached the bottom, she was met with hushed voices and glances from the soldiers. She held her head high as she walked to Alerio's training room and knocked on the door. There was no answer. She slowly turned the handle and peeked into the room. Her mouth dropped and she walked inside. All around her were tall trees and plants, the ground was covered in fake grass and the air was fresh. It was breathtaking, it reminded her of the forest back home. She was so mesmerised that she didn't notice the large harpy eagle perched on the branch above her, it swooped down and landed at her feet. Tilly fell back in shock. "Ah!"

The eagle was taller than she was, with brown eyes and dark feathers. It tilted its head before disappearing behind a tree. A moment later, Alerio walked out in nothing but linen pants and a necklace—laughing at her.

"Alerio, you scared me!"

He chuckled. "I didn't mean to little one," he said, helping her up.

"Is that how you welcome all of your recruits?" Tilly asked.

"No." He paused, looking thoughtful. "But I think I will from now on."

She laughed. "This place is amazing—it reminds me of home."

He looked around fondly. "It helps me focus, I don't like being stuck inside for too long. Being in this dome can be difficult sometimes."

"I thought it might be something you get used to after a while," Tilly said.

Alerio considered. "Maybe if you aren't part animal." He gestured towards a clearing in the middle of the room. "Let's begin, I was studying you during your trial yesterday. Your speed and agility are beyond anything I've seen in a human, but your technique is a little sloppy."

Well, that was half a compliment.

"Thank you?" she said uncertainly.

"You're very welcome," he said seriously. "Leo mentioned you trained with bikies for a while, which would explain that. I'm going to help you use that agility to move more fluidly, you'll be even more untouchable than you are now."

She watched eagerly as Alerio showed her some techniques, they then practiced them together. Alerio was a patient and observant teacher, by the end of the lesson Tilly had already felt a huge improvement. Alerio was impressed too. "You could have been one of the Five," he said approvingly.

Tilly looked at him in surprise. "Do they allow women? I thought it was always men."

"It has been in the past, but if it were up to me, I'd sign you up in a heartbeat," he said.

He is my kind of man.

"I know Leo would too," Alerio added. Her face dimmed at the mention of Leo's name. Alerio squeezed her shoulder gently. "I'm sorry, I was in the meeting with Conrad last night too. It's very brave of you to be here today."

"I didn't mean for him to get into trouble."

Alerio sat on the grass and motioned for Tilly to sit beside him. "Let me tell you something. Leo would never admit this, but he's always been the perfect soldier, trained to do as he's told, like we all are." Alerio smiled kindly at her, the corners of his eyes crinkled. "The Leo who came back with you is not the same one who left. In only a few days you've made him re-evaluate everything."

"And that's a good thing? I thought you'd be mad at him too."

Alerio laughed softly. "I'm not mad, I find it refreshing. I've never seen him so focused and sure of what he wants."

"He seemed like he'd always been that way," Tilly said

honestly.

"No, you've made him stronger. You're a good match for him."

"But, it's not allowed?"

"He'll find a way," Alerio said quietly. "Don't give up on him."

Tilly gave him a sad smile. "Never."

Look at his necklace.

Tilly noticed the gold medallion hanging on a leather band around his neck, it showed the same crest as her mother's necklace. Alerio glanced down and clutched it between his fingers. "The crest of Panthera. You'd probably be too young to remember."

"Why do you wear it?" she asked curiously.

His eyes turned distant. "I lived there for most of my life, some of the Spirids were like family to me. I wear it for them."

"I'm so sorry," she said gently.

Alerio's brown eyes met hers. "We all blame ourselves for what happened, especially Faris."

Tilly thought back to what Leo had told her. "Leo said Faris barely made it out alive."

"Then I'm sure Leo also told you about Torben, he and Faris were as close as real brothers. When Faris found him in Panthera it broke him, he tried to face him on his own and failed."

"Poor Faris," she whispered.

"He's never forgiven himself for what happened, it's why he tries so hard to be the best and why we put so much time into training our soldiers—have you ever seen a Calvarian before?" Tilly shook her head. Alerio ran his hand over his smooth head. "They wear the skull of their greatest kill as a mask and move like nothing you've ever seen before. Fighting one is like fighting four men at once." Tilly shuddered at the thought. "We believe a day will come when Panthera isn't enough for them anymore. We all need to be ready for that day."

Her magic flared in her chest, she gave him a slight nod. "We'll be ready for them."

He smiled and glanced at the clock near the door. "You should get going, Faris will be overjoyed if you're late and he can scold you."

"I could always knock him out again," Tilly joked.

Alerio gave a hearty laugh. "I'd advise against it, that man can hold a grudge."

She thanked him for the lesson and headed for the door, as she reached it, she glanced back. Alerio was watching her thoughtfully, a small smile on his face. He placed a hand over his heart and bowed his head.

Tilly made it to Faris' class just in time. He had a spacious training room with black padded mats on the floor. The walls were covered in graffiti-style art, with a winged horse spray-painted in the very centre. Piper was leaning against the wall, holding a tablet. When she saw Tilly, she looked down her nose at her. Tilly ignored her and went to join the dozen soldiers waiting in line. She recognised Cali at the end, with her white hair tied in a messy bun. Tilly smiled and took the place beside her. Cali watched her with surprise—the other soldiers seemed surprised too.

Faris entered the room in the same uniform as theirs, his nose looked badly bruised. He checked over the soldiers, not making eye contact with Tilly. Relief washed over her, she would happily be ignored for the entire lesson.

"Pair up," Faris spat.

Everyone moved to face their partner, Cali looked grateful when Tilly turned to her.

"Right, I'm going to show you an offensive move and then a few defences you can use to counter it, you will practice these in your pairs." That sounded pretty straightforward, Tilly thought. "Tilly, please join me to demonstrate," he said coldly.

"Shit," Tilly muttered without thinking.

A few of the soldiers snickered and Cali accidentally snorted. Faris' face turned red. "I will not tolerate your disrespect in my class, I am your superior." His face looked as if it were about to burst.

"Yes Sir, sorry Sir," Tilly said as respectfully as she could.

We are not off to a good start.

Faris pointed to the spot next to him. Tilly went and stood beside him. First, he showed everyone the offensive move, knocking Tilly to the ground. After that he instructed her to use the offensive move, while he demonstrated the counter moves, knocking her down each time. Piper snickered each time she hit the mat. She could tell Faris was enjoying himself.

"Now take turns with your partners." He glared at Tilly and stalked off.

She went back to Cali who was watching her with sympathy. "He's such an arsehole," Cali whispered. "I usually have to partner with him."

Tilly shook her head, rubbing her back where she had fallen each time. "That sounds horrible."

Cali smiled, lost in thought. "I think I cheered a little too loudly when you broke his nose yesterday." Tilly bit her lip so she didn't laugh.

They took turns practicing the moves. Cali was good, but

Tilly could see she didn't have a lot of confidence in herself. Faris walked past them and rolled his eyes. "Pathetic Cali, it's like you're not even trying."

Cali's face dropped and her technique got slower. So that's why she has no confidence, Tilly thought. Orvyn used to make her feel like that too. She leaned close to Cali's ear. "You are not pathetic, you're actually really good and he knows it. Do the first defensive move on me, lift your arm a little more and move as fast as you can," Tilly said quietly.

Cali didn't look sure about it.

"Trust me," Tilly whispered.

She went to attack Cali. Cali did as she said and quickly moved, knocking Tilly to the ground. Everyone stopped to watch.

"That was amazing, Cali," Tilly said. Cali's silver eyes shone happily. Faris huffed and stayed away from them for the rest of the lesson.

Cali kept getting better and better, she had a huge smile on her face by the time they left. "That was the best lesson I've ever had," she said excitedly. She pulled her long white hair out of the bun and it fell around her face.

She is adorable.

Tilly smiled, she agreed with Annora. "Does Faris always speak to you that way?" she asked curiously. They stopped at the cafeteria and piled food onto their plates.

"Yes," Cali said annoyed. "And when I'm partnered with him, he never lets me practice properly."

They sat down at a table in the corner. "That's awful Cali, he shouldn't treat you like that."

Cali gave her a sly smile. "Not all of us can knock him on his arse like you did, most of us are terrified of him."

Tilly laughed as Piper walked past and whispered something to an Orbarian soldier. They both glanced over and laughed loudly. Tilly cringed. "I have a feeling Piper doesn't like me very much."

Cali looked at Piper and frowned. "Piper's a bitch. Everyone knows it's her life mission to sleep with one of the Five. She's probably jealous that you showed up here with Leo."

Tilly glanced at Piper. "That's a shame, I wasn't looking to make enemies on my first day." She looked back at Cali and smiled. "You're a good fighter, what made you want to be in the Guard?"

Cali finished her drink. "I wanted to help support my dad and brother, this is one of the highest-paying jobs in the city."

"They must be so proud of you."

Tilly sensed Leo nearby and her face dropped. She peeked up and saw him walking through the cafeteria with Alerio. He was already looking at her. He waved and she smiled back sadly.

Cali glanced between them. "Are you okay?" she whispered. "I will be."

They both looked back at Leo. Piper was now talking to him. Tilly noticed her hand touching his arm. Annora growled as Tilly felt her magic spark. Leo seemed irritated, but Piper didn't seem to notice, she leaned up and whispered something in his ear. Alerio stood beside him, now looking visibly angry.

Leo jerked away, glaring down at Piper. "Get the fuck away from me Piper. Unless it's work-related do not speak to me," he growled.

Everyone in the cafeteria went silent. Piper cowered back in fear as Leo stormed off with Alerio at his heel.

Tilly fought the urge to chase after him, she hoped he was

okay. Cali leaned towards her and lowered her voice. "I've never seen him angry before, he's quite terrifying."

They watched Piper look around with embarrassment before she hurried off in the opposite direction. Tilly turned back to Cali, trying not to think about Leo. "I know I'm only new here, but I'd be happy to train with you if you wanted to practice without Faris around."

Cali looked shocked. "Me? Are you sure? You're a legend around here, you could train with anyone."

Tilly laughed, feeling a flush creep up her cheeks. "I'd love to train with you."

Cali's face lit up. "That would be the best!" she said excitedly. "Do you have plans Friday? I'd love to buy you a drink to thank you for today."

Tilly agreed to the drink and Cali squealed excitedly—startling some of the soldiers nearby. Cali was very animated for the rest of lunch, she spoke about the club she wanted to go to and Tilly was surprised to admit, even she felt excited. She listened to Cali with a small smile on her face. It felt good to have a friend again.

I like her too.

Chapter Twelve

Annora

Tilly felt exhausted. It was late in the afternoon when she returned to her suite, ready to crash on the couch. As she approached her door, she noticed a group of Orbarians waiting for her. They were all dressed in black clothing and had brightly coloured hair. "Are you Tilly?" the closest blue-haired woman asked.

"Um...Yes?"

The woman smiled and held up shopping bags. "Lady Zirk asked us to deliver these to you, would you mind if we came in?"

Tilly opened the door hesitantly. They showed themselves to her closet as she made her way to the kitchen. Her phone buzzed and Jaini's name flashed on the screen.

"Hey, Jai—"

"Have they arrived yet? What do you think?" Jaini asked excitedly.

Tilly laughed. "They're in my closet right now."

"Oh good. I wanted to ask you something. I'm hosting a

dinner party Saturday night, will you be my guest of honour?"

"I'd love to," Tilly said, already feeling nervous about it.

"Great, see you at six."

They said goodbye and Tilly waited in the kitchen, unsure of what to do. The Orbarians walked out of her closet with empty bags and boxes, nodding to her as they left. "Ah, thank you?" Tilly said awkwardly.

She stepped into the closet and her mouth dropped. "Oh my god, Jaini." It was overflowing with clothes, handbags and shoes. A large make-up case and a stand of jewellery had been set up beside the mirror. Tilly opened one of the closet drawers, it was full of lacy bras and underwear. "Ah!" she yelled, slamming the drawer closed. Annora chuckled.

Calm down Matilda, they're just panties.

"I barely know Jaini!" Tilly said in shock.

Annora laughed harder.

She's just trying to help, she knows you didn't bring anything with you.

Tilly glanced at some of the hanging clothes. She pulled out a pink, jewelled mini-dress and shook her head, putting it back quickly. She backed out of the room and shut the door. "You enjoyed that way too much Annora," Tilly said annoyed, she could feel Annora's amusement.

You're quite entertaining, I'm glad I chose you.

Tilly laid back on the couch. "What do you mean you chose me?" she asked curiously.

When a new Spirid is born, we in the spirit realm can sense it. If we feel drawn to that soul, we can claim it as ours and attach ourselves to it.

"I didn't know that," Tilly whispered. "Why do you think you were drawn to me?"

Because I am your ancestor, your great Grandmother to be exact. You are my blood and I wanted to protect you.

Tilly sat up straight. "Why haven't you told me this?"

We haven't had a lot of time to ourselves. Would you like to meet now?

Tilly's face lit up. "More than anything."

Annora chuckled.

This may be difficult, as we have been one for so long. First, you need to move everything out of the way, we'll need some space.

Tilly jumped up and pushed the couches and coffee table to the side of the room. She pressed a button on the tablet and the windows went dark.

Close your eyes and focus. You'll need to find me, think about where my voice is coming from.

She sat on the rug and closed her eyes, listening closely. She could hear Annora in her mind, but she could feel her near her heart. She'd never noticed it before as it had always felt like a part of her.

Good, stay focused. Now you need to call me out, think of me being pulled from your body.

Tilly was a little confused, but she focused on Annora, calling her from her chest the same way she moved her magic. Very slowly she felt her move. Tilly pulled harder and felt Annora being ripped from her body. She opened her eyes as Annora shot from her chest. Tilly dropped to her hands, gasping as Annora turned and stalked towards her, slowly materialising into a solid form. Annora was a snow leopard, with white spotted fur and light blue eyes, on all fours she was almost as tall as Tilly was standing. Annora stopped and leaned down in front of her, sniffing Tilly before pressing her forehead against hers. Tilly closed her eyes, her fur was soft and warm. "You're beautiful," Tilly said. "I wish I didn't have to hide you."

So do I, but it's not safe for anyone to know who you are. You are more important than you realise.

Tilly frowned. "What do you mean?"

Annora hesitated.

I've wanted to tell you since you got your magic back, but it's not an easy thing to hear.

"You can tell me anything."

Annora laid in front of her, placing her paw over Tilly's hand.

Your real name is Matilda Astara Hazelwood. Your mother and father were King Namir and Queen Alwyn Hazelwood. You are not just a Spirid, you are royalty.

Tilly scrambled to her feet. "What?"

Alwyn was Queen of Valuna. Just as I was, just as you should have been next.

"That can't be right," Tilly said panicking. "Why wouldn't Celia have told me?"

I think she wanted you to find out in your own time, you had enough to deal with already.

Tilly sat on the rug against the couch, staring ahead in shock. She couldn't believe it, there was no way she was royalty. Annora nudged her with her nose. Tilly ran her fingers through her fur, while she tried to understand what Annora was saying.

There's something else—the day Panthera was attacked was the same day you were born. Alwyn didn't believe it was a coincidence, she believed they were after you.

Tilly dropped her face into her hands as anger and guilt flooded through her body. Her mother and father, the people of Panthera, they had all died because of her. "Why? Why did they want me?"

It was not your fault Matilda, you cannot blame yourself for the choices of others. I don't know why they wanted you, we need to learn more about Torben.

"I feel terrible," she said. Magic sparked in her chest. "And angry."

Hold that anger, we might need it.

Annora curled up beside her. Tilly could feel her sorrow, it felt like her own.

For what it's worth, I think you would have made an excellent Queen.

Tilly felt like she was on autopilot for the rest of the week. She attended her classes and spent lunchtimes with Cali, occasionally passing Leo throughout the day and sharing longing glances. By the time Friday came along she still wasn't in the mood to go clubbing.

You have to live Matilda, try to have some fun. Your problems will still be there for you tomorrow.

Cali arrived right on time. Tilly forced a smile as she answered the door. Cali wore a simple blue mini-dress, white heels, silver eye shadow and pink lipstick. Her white hair was down and straight. She gave Tilly a strange look. "You aren't planning to wear that are you?" she tried saying politely.

Tilly looked down, she'd showered earlier and forgot she was wearing her fluffy robe. "Uh, no. I wasn't really sure what to wear, I've never been clubbing."

Cali's face brightened. "I can help with that." Tilly led her inside and Cali gasped. "This place is amazing," she said, she noticed all the furniture pushed to the side of the room. "Have you been training in here?"

Tilly nodded quickly, she'd actually left it that way to practice calling Annora out. "I like the privacy, I'm not used to all of the attention I've been getting lately," she said. It was mostly true.

Cali looked embarrassed. "I have heard a lot of rumours about you."

"That I was with Leo?"

Cali nodded.

"It's complicated, but I'm not with him," Tilly said. "I didn't know about their oath."

Cali gave her a sad smile. "It's such a stupid rule, you'd think they would be even more dedicated if they had loved ones to protect." Tilly looked at her with surprise, she hadn't thought of it that way. Cali didn't ask her any questions after that, and she was grateful for it. "Show me where your clothes are, let's go and have some fun—it sounds like you need it," Cali said.

Tilly smiled at her, even with everything going on, it was impossible not to feel happy around Cali. She took Cali to her closet and stopped. "I have to warn you, this was all given to me by a friend," Tilly said seriously.

She opened the door and Cali squealed, she ran in and scanned over everything before she pulled out the pink, jewelled mini-dress. "Your friend has amazing taste, you have to wear this, it would look so good on you," Cali said excitedly.

Tilly noticed her looking longingly at the dress. "Hey, how about you wear that? If you want to. I don't really wear pink, but I think it would look perfect on you."

Cali bit her lip, staring at the dress. "I couldn't do that."

Tilly laughed and steered her towards the bathroom. "Just go try it on, I can tell you want to," she teased. Cali grinned and ran off to try it on. Tilly looked through the clothes. Jaini had put a surprising amount of black and green in there. She found a pair of tight, black leather pants, they were definitely more her. Cali came back in and Tilly's mouth dropped. "You look incredibly hot Cali, you have to wear it," she said honestly.

Cali's eyes shone with happiness, she looked so confident. Cali spotted the leather pants in her hands. "Do you ever not wear pants?"

"Only if I'm forced to," Tilly replied.

Cali laughed, she looked through the clothes and grabbed a black mini-skirt, a glittering gold top with thin sleeves and black heels with gold spikes all over them. She passed them all to Tilly. "Your turn, it's even hotter in the club than it is in the dome—I promise you don't want to wear pants."

Cali stepped out and closed the door. Tilly changed into the outfit and stared back at the girl in the mirror, she hardly recognised herself. She clutched her mother's moonstone necklace. Her mother, the Queen—she was still in disbelief.

You look just like her, only her hair was auburn.

Tilly squeezed her eyes shut, she didn't know if she could do this.

Your mother wanted you to be happy, do it for her.

"Can I come in?" Cali asked.

Tilly opened the door and Cali brought her hand up over her mouth. Tilly looked at her nervously. "Is it bad? I've never worn anything like this before."

"You look ridiculously sexy," Cali said approvingly.

Tilly's eyes widened. "Should I change?"

Cali laughed. "No way, hang on." She pulled out the make-up case and gave Tilly smoky eyes and glossy lips. "Perfect, let's go," she said excitedly. She grabbed Tilly's arm and pulled her out the door.

Tilly glanced up at the crescent moon as they walked through the city. The dome had cleared giving them a breathtaking view of the night sky. Cali took her to the Ruby Tower, but instead of going through the front doors, she led her around the back. There was a line of people waiting under a neon sign that read 'NEVERORB', Tilly had never noticed it before. The guards saw them heading towards the line and motioned for them to go inside. Cali grabbed Tilly's hand excitedly and led her down the stairs. "That has never happened to me before."

The music was so loud Tilly could feel it pulsing through her body. The club was dimly lit, with most of the light coming from a small stage with a live band. An Orbarian woman with green hair and black lipstick was singing, her voice was eerily beautiful and the beat was fast and hypnotic. The club was packed with glowing silver eyes everywhere she looked and Cali was right, it was very hot. Tilly felt tingles up her neck—Leo was here—her heart started racing, she looked around, but she couldn't see him.

"Let's get a drink," Cali said loudly. She pulled Tilly towards the bar.

As they got closer Tilly glanced to her left, Leo and Alerio were sitting together at a small booth, watching them. Leo beamed at her and Alerio waved. Tilly smiled back at them, her body ached at the distance between her and Leo.

They sat at the bar and Cali ordered drinks. The bartender grabbed two crystal glasses, the inside of each glass was shaped like a jagged star. He filled the stars with different liquids, the drinks fizzed and turned purple. He slid them across the bar as Cali passed him some coins. "Thanks, Zan."

The song finished and everyone began cheering. The singer curtsied dramatically before starting the next song. "She has a really unique voice," Tilly said. "I've never heard anything like it."

Cali sighed, bringing her drink to her lips. "I used to date her." She took a long sip. Tilly glanced over at her in surprise, but Cali didn't look up from her drink. "It's not completely accepted around here—I lost a lot of friends because of it," Cali said sadly.

"I'm sorry, they mustn't have been good friends."

Cali gave her a small smile. "It's not always great being Orbarian, we are so advanced in many ways and so behind in others." Her eyes lit up and she lifted her arm, looking at it. "It is useful when we break a bone in training though."

Annora chuckled. Tilly looked at Cali's translucent arm and laughed. "Did you just make a joke?"

Cali grinned. "I think you're starting to rub off on me." They both laughed. Cali had to be the sweetest person she had ever met. Tilly felt a tap on her shoulder, she turned around and three Orbarian men were standing there looking nervous. She glanced over at Leo, he was watching curiously with a small smile on his face.

The guy with curly, blue hair spoke first. "Um hi—Tilly, I'm Zio, this is Rin and Vorb, we were wondering if you wanted to dance?"

"With—who?" Tilly said confused.

They all looked embarrassed. "With, any of us?"

Tilly blinked, she didn't know what to say. Cali jumped in and saved her. "Sorry boys, she's mine tonight. I'm showing her around."

Zio's face dropped. "That's okay, maybe another time."

Tilly smiled at them awkwardly before they walked off. "Thanks, Cali, I'm honestly not used to this." She took a sip of her drink—it was fruity and fizzy. She took a longer sip.

"Are you serious?" Cali said in disbelief. "You mean you didn't have every guy chasing you before you came here?"

Tilly recalled what it was like being with Orvyn, that felt like a lifetime ago now. "No, it's complicated, but I had a very possessive boyfriend," she said honestly.

Cali nodded in understanding. "You know, Leo has been staring at you non-stop since we got here," she said with a sly smile.

"Very funny—it can't happen."

Cali laughed. "Then why is he coming over here?"

Tilly turned her head and Leo was standing right there. "Hi," she said nervously.

He tried to hide his smile. "Hi. Hello Cali." He nodded towards her.

"Hey Leo, we were just talking about you," Cali said kindly.

Tilly's eyes widened at her. "No we weren't," Cali said quickly. She finished her drink and fixed her eyes on the stage.

Leo watched Tilly and chuckled. "Is that right? Alerio's just gone to the bathroom, can I buy you both a drink?"

Tilly opened her mouth to answer.

"Yes please," Cali said innocently, giving Tilly a wink which wasn't subtle at all. Tilly burst out laughing. Cali was too much.

Leo ordered four drinks and Alerio returned as he was passing them around. Alerio greeted them both and started a conversation with Cali. Leo leaned closer to Tilly. "How were your first few days, Til?"

"Alerio scared the hell out of me with his eagle and Faris is still mad at me," she said. She took a long sip from her drink.

Leo laughed. "That sounds about right." He dropped his voice so only she could hear. "Have you been okay? It's taken every ounce of my self-control not to come and see you."

"I'm okay, it's been hard though. I really miss you," she said quietly. "How about you? You seemed pretty angry at Piper the other day."

His eyes darkened. "In one breath, she insulted you and tried inviting herself to my room. I won't let anyone speak badly of you and I would never touch that woman."

Tilly gave him a small smile, she was glad he was honest with her, she knew Piper was bad news. Leo's eyes lingered on her short skirt. "I almost didn't recognise you when you walked in, you look stunning."

She laughed, pointing to her outfit. "You can thank Cali for this."

He leaned closer to her ear. "I'll write Cali a song, thanking her for that."

Tilly felt even hotter suddenly. She finished her drink, trying to hide her flushed face. Leo downed the rest of his, not taking his eyes off her. "Dance with me?"

Tilly couldn't hide her surprise. "Aren't we meant to be staying away from each other?"

He smirked, holding his hand out for hers. "We are showing that we can co-exist together like adults, there's nothing wrong with that."

Tilly glanced over at Cali, she nodded enthusiastically. Tilly took Leo's hand, feeling buzzed from the drinks. "I'm not sure about this, I don't want you to get into more trouble."

Leo walked backwards, pulling her towards the stage. "Conrad said I couldn't be with you, he didn't say I couldn't be the best friend you ever had." He spun her onto the dance floor.

Tilly laughed. "You know he's not going to like that."

"Maybe he should have chosen his words more carefully," Leo said cheerfully.

Tilly shook her head. "You're unbelievable," she said laughing. She looked at him nervously. "I should probably warn you, I'm a really bad dancer."

Leo shimmied his shoulders around. "So am I," he said. Tilly watched him with amazement as he took her hand and spun her again, then brought her back towards him. They both smiled at each other like idiots.

They danced terribly together, seeing who could do the worst moves and laughing at each other. The singer sang about one last dance—it felt fitting. Tilly couldn't get the smile off her face, how could she ever act like she wasn't madly in love with this man? She glanced over and noticed that Alerio and Cali were dancing together, her jaw dropped. Leo followed her gaze and his eyebrows shot up.

They were both incredible dancers.

They danced their way towards Tilly and Leo. Once they were close, Cali leaned towards them. "You two should stick to fighting," she said seriously.

Alerio leaned forward. "Yes, you're embarrassing us," he added.

Tilly and Leo were taken aback, they looked at each other and burst out laughing. Leo motioned towards the bar and Tilly nodded. He took her hand and led her through the crowd. She noticed that wherever they went they drew a lot of attention. Leo didn't seem to take any notice, so she tried not to either. She was surprised by how he was acting tonight. The thought of still being friends with him made her heart feel a little lighter. She wanted him in her life no matter what.

"Do you want another drink?" Leo asked.

"Maybe just water?" She was happy with the buzz she had gotten from the other two.

He asked for two glasses of water and they went and sat in one of the small booths around the edge of the room. "I hope Cali doesn't mind me stealing you," he said.

Tilly smiled, shaking her head. "Cali encouraged it."

Leo smiled. "She seems really nice. I'm glad you're making friends."

"She is nice, I really like this city," she said earnestly. "Thank you for paying for the suite, you didn't have to do that. Can I give you money for it?"

"No, Til," he whispered. "I'll always take care of you."

Leo placed his hand under the table and took hers, he stroked the back of it softly. Tilly smiled sadly at him. She wanted to tell him everything, she wanted to crawl into his arms, she wanted to kiss him, but all she could do was hold his hand and hope he could see how much she loved him.

Cali and Alerio made their way over to the table, they were both smiling and trying to catch their breath. The four of them spent the rest of the night talking and laughing. Tilly had to admit she was enjoying herself. She glanced between Leo, Cali and Alerio and smiled, realising she had found her place in this city—it was with them.

Chapter Thirteen

The Rematch

Tilly woke up with a massive headache. She sat up and grabbed her phone as Cali groaned beside her. She glanced at the time, she was supposed to be at Headquarters in thirty minutes. "Shit!" Tilly sprung from the bed and ran to the bathroom. She quickly showered and put on her uniform. She headed to the kitchen and peeked towards the bedroom—Cali still hadn't moved. She quickly conjured a tray of pastries and went to wake her.

"What time is it?" Cali yawned.

"Almost ten—I have a session with Leo in fifteen minutes," Tilly said.

Cali shot up from the bed, still in the pink mini-dress. "Let's go," she said, looking determined.

Tilly laughed. "Do you want to borrow some clothes?"

Cali looked down. "That's probably a good idea," she agreed.

"Help yourself to whatever, you can keep that dress," Tilly said. She grabbed an apple danish from the tray and took a bite.

"Are you sure?" Cali asked uncertainty.

"Definitely, I'll never wear it."

Cali changed and Tilly offered the tray to her. They both loaded their hands with pastries before rushing out the door. They ate and walked as quickly as they could. "Mm these are so good," Cali groaned.

"So good," Tilly agreed. "I love food."

Cali watched her with amusement. "I'll have to take you to meet my family one day, they have a cake stall."

Tilly froze and looked at Cali. "Why have you only just mentioned this? Let's go right now," she joked.

They both burst out laughing and ran up the steps to Headquarters. "Do you know where you're going?" Cali asked.

"I have no idea."

"When Leo is here, he works in a room attached to the armoury. If you go through the arena, it's behind that."

"Thanks, Cali. I had so much fun with you last night," she said honestly.

Cali beamed at her. "So did I. I'd never really spoken to Alerio before. We're going dancing again one night, uh without...you guys," she said nervously.

Tilly laughed hard. "That's probably a good idea."

They said goodbye and Tilly bolted through Headquarters, earning a lot of puzzled looks from the soldiers. She found the armoury and stopped to catch her breath. She felt a pull towards one of the rooms and knew Leo was in there. She went to knock, but he opened the door just as she raised her hand. Tilly never would have guessed that he was up half the night, his uniform was crisp and he looked well-rested and ready to go. He took in her appearance and a small smile crept up his face. She looked down at her shirt, it was covered in pastry crumbs and she hadn't done up the top few buttons. She quickly brushed the crumbs off and fixed her buttons.

"You can leave it like that, I don't mind," he said cheerfully.

"I'm sorry, we slept in."

Leo stepped back to let her inside before shutting the door. "It's okay, you're right on time."

"Who does lessons on a Saturday morning?" she sulked.

Leo laughed. "Well, you didn't exactly have a typical sign-up, I had to fit you in somewhere."

Tilly looked around his training room, it was simple and modern. There was a table to the side and the walls were covered in various weapons, one wall just held random objects. Tilly walked over and picked up a crowbar and a pair of handcuffs, she turned to Leo and held them up. "What do you teach exactly?"

Leo bit his lip as he tried not to laugh. "When I'm not on assignment I give specialised weapon training. We also go over different scenarios, like how to escape if you're captured or ways to use items around you if you're unarmed," he explained.

Tilly stared blankly while she imagined him using the handcuffs on her, then putting his skilled mouth all over her body. She didn't even notice he was still speaking.

"Tilly?—Tilly?" he said, looking delighted.

She glanced up at him, then back towards the handcuffs. She passed them to him quickly as her cheeks turned bright red. "Sorry, I think I'm still waking up."

Leo laughed loudly. "Would you like to share what you were daydreaming about?"

"Definitely not," she said embarrassed.

He went and stood behind her—a little too close—he wrapped his arms around her and fastened the handcuffs around her wrists. Tilly's heart started racing. Leo leaned down and whispered in her ear. "Why does it look like you're enjoying this?"

"Because it's you doing it," she answered softly.

"There are so many things I'd like to do to you," he whispered. "Tell me what you were thinking about."

Tilly could feel his body pressed up against hers. He slowly trailed his nose along her cheek. She closed her eyes, her voice barely above a whisper. "Your mouth."

He spun her around, lifting her off the ground so fast she didn't have time to react. He sat her on top of the table and spread her legs. She wrapped them around his waist and pulled him closer. Leo stopped, they were both breathing fast, studying each other. Tilly could see the inner battle he was having with himself, it was the same one she was having.

Someone knocked on the door.

Tilly dropped her legs and Leo quickly uncuffed her. She jumped off the table and grabbed the closest thing she could reach, pretending to practice with it and trying to calm her racing heart. Leo went to open the door and Conrad strolled inside. "Good morning Leopold, Tilly, I was just checking in to see how you were both doing in your first session together. I hope it hasn't been too awkward for you both."

"Not at all Conrad, Tilly and I have agreed we can be friends," Leo said calmly.

Conrad looked down at Tilly's hands—she was holding a mop. He glanced back at Leo, looking puzzled. "You're not forcing the poor girl to clean, are you?"

Leo cleared his throat and took the mop from Tilly. "We were just discussing how to use everyday objects if your weapons are taken from you. Tilly was asking how this mop could be used offensively," he stated.

"Hmm, that is a useful lesson." Conrad examined Tilly's face thoughtfully. "Very well, I'm sorry for the interruption. Please continue where you left off." He turned and strolled out of the room.

Leo and Tilly both sighed in relief. "That was too close," Tilly said softly. "We're lucky he even knocked."

Leo hung the mop back up. "I know, I'm sorry, I shouldn't have done that. It's hard acting like I'm not in love with you."

Tilly's heart sank. "It's hard for me too, do you want me to drop these sessions?"

"And miss out on watching you fight with a mop? Never," he teased.

They both started laughing, she loved how he always lightened the mood with his humour, they were so alike in that way and many others. Leo spent the rest of the morning showing her how to use different weapons, he even showed her ways she could use the mop in an emergency. At the end of the lesson, they both left together, heading out through the arena. Tilly looked over at the stage wistfully, remembering the morning they had shared before her trial. She missed being with him.

Leo noticed her mood change. He glanced up towards the stage. "You know, we've never actually had a real fight."

"We did, I elbowed you in that handsome face of yours," she teased.

Leo smirked. "If I remember correctly, I was just standing there waiting for you to finish your tantrum so I could talk to you."

How dare he.

Her face shot to his. "Tantrum? I thought you were a stalker, and you kind of were," she pointed out.

Leo's eyes sparkled mischievously, he was trying to rile her up—it was working. He jumped onto the side of the stage and pulled himself over the ring, then he turned to face her. "There's no one around, loser buys lunch?"

Tilly felt the excitement build in her stomach. She looked around, the arena was completely empty. "And dessert," she added, pulling herself onto the stage.

"Deal, the first one to tap out loses."

Tilly went and stood in front of him, they were both grinning at each other. She pulled her magic from her chest and let it flow through her body, giving her strength. There was no way she was going to let him win, not when there was food at stake—and her reputation.

Wow, Matilda.

They started circling each other. Leo couldn't wipe the smile off his face. Tilly lunged towards him. He blocked every hit and she evaded each of his, they were moving so fast it looked like they were dancing around each other. Tilly noticed a small crowd starting to form around the stage.

Leo tried to grab her, but she slipped under his arm and elbowed him in the back, making him stumble forward. He quickly shot up and spun around, grabbing her arm and pulling her towards him. Tilly grabbed his wrists and pulled down hard, sliding herself through his legs so he had to let go or go down with her—he let go. Before she could get up, he pounced on top of her, knocking her to the ground. She pushed her magic and bucked him off, rolling so she was now on top of him. Leo's eyes turned to fire, she could tell he was enjoying this as much as she was.

"Go, Tilly!" Cali yelled. Tilly glanced up, the crowd was now half the size as it had been the day of her trial.

Leo pushed her off and they both scrambled to their feet. He feigned left and grabbed her around the waist. She kneed him in the stomach and slipped out of his hands. She tried to kick him but he sidestepped—they were too equally matched. She pretended to go for his face and instead, wrapped her leg around the back of his. She grabbed his shoulders and brought her magic to her arms, pulling him over her leg and pushing him to the ground. On his way down, he grabbed her ankle and yanked it out from underneath her. Tilly went flying down with him. They landed in a heap on the stage, both of them in fits of laughter.

"I think it's a tie," Leo said, still laughing.

"I nearly had you," Tilly sulked. This made him laugh harder.

There were cheers and whistles around the arena, they both sat up and Tilly noticed Conrad, Faris and Alerio standing together at the back of the crowd. Conrad's lips were pressed in a tight line, he didn't look happy. Faris had a small smirk on his face and Alerio looked intrigued.

"We love you, Tilly!" Cali whistled, and a few others joined her.

Tilly gave an embarrassed laugh as Leo helped her up. "Guess I'm not the only one," he murmured.

"So, who buys lunch?" Tilly asked confused. Her stomach rumbled loudly and Leo chuckled.

The crowd began to dissolve. Alerio walked up the steps towards them, he looked worried. Leo's face instantly dropped. Once Alerio reached them he glanced around, it was just the three of them now. "I hate being the one to say this, but I think you two might need to keep your distance for a while."

"What's going on?" Leo asked.

"Conrad heard about our night out together—Piper saw us." He hesitated. "There's a big assignment that's come up, he's considering sending you to get you away from Tilly. You'd be gone for months."

"But I just got back," Leo said pained. "We usually take turns."

Alerio placed his hand on Leo's shoulder. "I know, I offered to go. I said I could use the fresh air, but he hasn't made up his mind yet."

"Thanks for letting me know," Leo said miserably.

Alerio nodded at him, he turned to Tilly and his face softened. "I've never seen anyone knock Leo down. It's now a memory I will always cherish, thank you," he said sincerely. Tilly tried not to laugh.

"It was a tie," Leo said in disbelief.

Alerio sighed happily. "Not to me it wasn't."

He turned and walked away before Leo could say anything else. Leo turned to Tilly looking disappointed. "I'm sorry, looks like we might have to do lunch another time."

"I understand," she said quietly. "We haven't been very good at staying away from each other."

His eyes hardened. "I never want to be away from you." He glanced around quickly before he gave her a small kiss on the forehead and hurried away.

"Bye Leo," she whispered.

Tilly felt like she was going to cry, she hurried to the bathroom and stopped at the sink, grabbing some tissues and wiping her eyes. Piper walked out of one of the stalls, her eyes lit up when she saw Tilly. Tilly quickly washed her hands, wanting to get out of there as fast as she could. Piper looked in the mirror and fixed her tousled red hair. "I heard Leo's leaving again soon. Conrad said I might be able to go too, just to keep an eye on him."

Tilly kept washing her hands.

"Can you imagine? Just Leo and I, travelling together, probably sharing hotel rooms."

Tilly dried her hands and threw the towel in the basket.

"I'm sure he gets lonely and desperate when he's away. It's the only reason he would have brought you back here."

Tilly knew none of it was true, she turned and started to walk out when Piper blocked her path, looking mad. "I'm talking to you bitch."

Tilly stared at her calmly. "Move."

Piper sneered at her. "Why don't you make me, or is the tough girl thing just an act."

She knows she can't take you, she's trying to get you into trouble.

Tilly slowly shook her head. "I have no interest in your games."

Piper crossed her arms and eyed her down. "I don't get the big deal about you, you aren't even that good. Everyone knows Faris let you win because you slept with him."

Tilly's eyes widened in surprise, she threw her head back and laughed hysterically. Piper stepped back, looking startled. Tilly wiped a tear from her eye and shook her head, still laughing. "Thanks, Piper, I needed a good laugh today." Tilly pushed past her and walked out, still grinning.

"Crazy bitch," Piper muttered.

You dealt with that better than I would have. I would've had her beheaded.

Tilly went back to her suite and blacked out the windows before she called Annora out. Annora stretched beside her.

153

Tilly went and grabbed an apple out of the fridge. "Do you want anything to eat?"

I'm a spirit, Matilda, I'm technically dead.

Tilly sighed and slumped back on the couch, Annora went and curled up beside her. Tilly reached over and scratched behind her furry ears. "If you're dead, can you feel that?"

Yes, it's the same as any other physical body. I just don't ever feel hunger or thirst, I always remain the same.

"What if you were attacked?" Tilly asked suddenly. "Could you die if you're already a spirit?"

We are very hard to kill, but it can happen. Our link would be severed and I would return to the spirit realm.

Tilly felt a wave of worry roll through her body. She had to protect Annora, she was a part of her.

Calm down, I am quite capable of keeping myself alive. Nobody even knows I exist, so there's no need to worry over nothing.

She was right. Tilly stared up at the crystal chandelier, thinking about Jaini's dinner tonight, she wasn't in the mood for a party. She was too worried about Leo leaving, she couldn't imagine being in this city without him.

You should go, Jaini has been a kind friend to you.

"I'll definitely go, it wouldn't be fair to let her down." She glanced at the time, they still had hours until she had to be there. "Will you teach me more magic?"

Annora stood eagerly and made her way to the other side of the room.

One of the most useful spells in battle is the shield charm. You summon an invisible force around you and nothing solid can enter. Anyone who touches it will feel something similar to an electric shock.

That's very useful, Tilly thought excitedly. Annora explained it to her and Tilly practiced until she could easily cast it over her entire body.

I'm impressed, your magic has come quite naturally to you. Soon we'll be able to start training together. The soldiers of Panthera fought alongside their guardians and they were a force to be reckoned with.

Tilly checked the time—Jaini would be expecting her soon. She showered and sorted through the formal dresses Jaini had brought her, before pulling out the least ridiculous one. It was navy blue, floor length with a high neckline, an open back and lace sleeves. She hid her daggers under the skirt and pulled her hair down, letting it flow down her back. She grabbed the closest pair of earrings—a cluster of diamonds. "God I hope these aren't real," she muttered. Tilly glanced in the mirror and took a deep breath. It was going to be a long night.

Chapter Fourteen

The Councillors

Tilly took the lift up to the penthouse. When she arrived, one of Jaini's guards led her to a golden door at the back of the suite and knocked. "Come in," Jaini called.

Tilly entered an elegant beauty room. Everything was white and gold, matching the rest of Jaini's home. Make-up and jewellery filled an entire wall, all sorted into glass cabinets. A double-sided vanity ran down the middle of the room, with two scoop-back chairs on either side. Jaini was seated in one of them, wearing a sleeveless emerald gown which matched her green-tinted skin. Her purple hair was tied in a neat bun. She twisted a chain of diamonds around the base. "I've missed you, Tilly," she muffled, as she held a hairpin between her teeth.

Tilly smiled. "I've missed you too. Thanks for sending the clothes, you really didn't have to."

Jaini waved a hand dismissively. "Oh, it's nothing—and I really did." She finished with her hair and turned to face Tilly, eyeing her down. "I guessed your size right, you look perfect," she said approvingly. She studied Tilly's face and her silver eyes softened. "You also look as miserable as Leo did earlier."

Tilly's smile dropped, she was hoping Jaini wouldn't notice her mood. "Conrad's threatening to send him away. I'm guessing he told you already."

Jaini's face turned grim. "You haven't heard then," she said softly. "Conrad has given Leo the assignment. He wanted him to leave tonight, but Leo said there was no way he'd miss my ceremony tomorrow. He's leaving straight after, I'm so sorry." Tilly squeezed her eyes shut, she didn't know what to say. Jaini stood up and took Tilly's hands in hers. "It's going to be okay. You are not alone in this city. I will be here for you," she said earnestly. "And at least you'll get to say goodbye to Leo at the ceremony, I know he isn't allowed to see you anymore."

Tilly hated that Leo wasn't allowed to tell her himself. She put the thought aside and tried putting on a brave face for Jaini. "Thank you, I'll be alright. I'm here for you tonight remember, tell me about this dinner party."

Jaini straightened up and a look of determination crossed her face. "It's tradition for the newest Councillor and their family to host dinner for the other Councillors. As I obviously don't have any family, I've told them you're my guest of honour," Jaini explained.

Tilly's stomach fluttered, she had no idea how was she going to make conversation with six Councillors—all she knew how to do was fight and be sarcastic. "That's a huge honour," she said, giving Jaini an encouraging smile. "I didn't realise your ceremony was so soon."

Jaini beamed and rubbed her hands together. "It couldn't come soon enough for me. I've got a lot of work to do around here," she said. "I hope you haven't made plans tomorrow. There's a festival at the marketplace in the morning and then the ceremony starts late afternoon, followed by a ball."

Tilly grinned. "No plans. I wouldn't miss your big day."

"You're welcome to bring a plus one, preferably someone sexy so Leo realises he's an idiot and knocks Conrad out for keeping you apart," Jaini said, not taking a breath.

Tilly laughed in surprise. "I'll think about it." She loved how Jaini didn't sugarcoat things.

She will be an excellent voice for this city, they need her.

Jaini glanced in the mirror and fixed her make-up. "God I'm not looking forward to this dinner, most of them give me violent thoughts the moment they open their mouths."

"Well now I am looking forward to it," Tilly teased.

They both grinned. Jaini linked her arm through Tilly's and led her out. Tilly thought she would take her to the same dining room as last time, but Jaini led her to a sweeping ballroom with a breathtaking view of the city. Two golden swan statues hung above them, with feathers made of diamonds. Their wings spread so wide they nearly took up the entire ceiling. A long dining table stood in the centre of the room, decorated with candles and flowers. Jaini noticed the shock on Tilly's face and laughed. "This is for my formal events—the other dining room is just for friends."

Tilly shook her head. "And I thought the last one was fancy."

An Orbarian woman was setting up on a small stage, surrounded by white crystal bowls and other instruments Tilly had never seen. Jaini nodded to her and she began to play. Tilly felt the music vibrate through her body. Jaini leaned towards her, smirking. "It's meant to help keep everyone calm. I'll try anything at this point."

Smart girl.

A guard entered and announced Jaini's guests had arrived. "Please escort them in," Jaini said.

Tilly's heart quickened, she felt so out of place here. She would rather fight Faris again than sit through a dinner like this.

Don't feel intimidated. You should have been their Queen.

Tilly still found that hard to believe. The guard returned with six Orbarians trailing behind him. One woman and five men. Jaini greeted each of them and introduced them to Tilly. Tilly had met a few of them at her trial, but there was no way she would remember all of their names.

I'll try to help.

Thank you, Annora, Tilly thought gratefully. They all took their seats and Jaini took her place at the head of the table. Tilly sat to her left, opposite a balding Orbarian man with purple-tinted skin and a deep blue suit with a collar made of sapphires. Tufts of hair grew from his ears and his silver eyes drooped.

Councillor Zoth.

Jaini had really outdone herself, there was a server for each guest and every plate of food looked like a piece of art. Tilly glanced down in front of her, there were four different sets of cutlery and three different glasses, she had no idea what she was doing. She picked up a bread roll and a butter knife, which felt like the safest option.

Jaini stood up and raised her champagne flute. "Thank you all for joining me this evening and for your support leading up to my inauguration. I look forward to helping this incredible city flourish even further," she said passionately. She turned to Tilly and smiled. "And thank you to my wonderful new friend

Tilly, for joining our celebrations. Our city has been blessed by your presence."

Everyone clapped politely. Councillor Zoth met Tilly's eyes and muttered under his breath. "Just a friend, is she?"

Jaini luckily hadn't heard him, but Tilly gripped her butter knife tighter than necessary. She didn't care if he thought they were together, she was mad he was disrespecting Jaini. Tilly glared at him and he gave her a patronising look. Her magic flared in her chest. She didn't think this day could get any more annoying.

Put down the butter knife Matilda.

Councillor Ezra stood from his seat. He had sharp silver eyes, green-tinted skin and short, white hair combed to the side. A sparkling tie coated in emeralds was tucked under his green velvet jacket. He held out his glass and smiled, but the smile didn't reach his eyes. "Thank you, Lady Zirk, we are confident you will quickly find your place within our council," he said snidely.

Tilly clenched her fist. Councillor Zoth snickered as Jaini stared Councillor Ezra down. He remained stone-faced, but it was obvious he was already trying to assert his dominance. It had been less than twenty minutes and Tilly already understood what Jaini had meant about violent thoughts.

Jaini beamed down at him pleasantly. "As you can see Councillor Ezra, my place is at the head of the table. I'm sure with all of my support, it will remain so," she challenged back.

Councillor Zoth scoffed loudly, staring at her in disbelief. "You think having love from those commoners will give you more power? They have no say in this council."

"Those people grow restless," Jaini seethed. "Their basic needs are not being met. How long will it be until they become so desperate and resentful that they burn our towers to the ground? I'm surprised it hasn't happened already."

Councillor Ezra sighed loudly. "You are young, Lady Zirk, you don't know what you're talking about. Our people are thankful for what we provide them, as they should be."

Tilly turned to Councillor Ezra. "Have you spoken to them? You must have been so touched when they told you this."

Councillor Ezra was speechless. Jaini smirked and a couple of the Councillors chuckled. Councillor Zoth eyed Tilly down. "What do you know of this city or its people? You're a nobody, you're only here for decoration."

Tilly went to open her mouth, but another Councillor spoke first. "She is a guest. I do believe I saw you at her trial Councillor Zoth, we all know we are lucky to have her in Everorb City. You would do well to remember your manners," he said calmly.

Councillor Ginz, I like him.

The council members looked embarrassed, except for Councillor Zoth, who was fuming. Tilly gave him the sweetest smile she could manage, making him even angrier.

I don't think the crystal bowls are working.

Councillor Della stood from her seat. She wore a simple black gown and ruby earrings, her silver hair curled to her shoulders. She held up her glass, giving Jaini a kind smile. "I for one, am thrilled to have you join us. This council could do with your strong leadership and fresh ideas. I believe some of the Councillors have been here so long they are beginning to go stale."

Jaini nodded to her appreciatively. Tilly watched Councillor

Zoth and Councillor Ezra exchange glances—she didn't like them at all. The remainder of the night was more civil, they all seemed to hold a lot of respect for Councillor Ginz. Tilly wondered how he felt about Jaini joining them. At the end of the night, everyone thanked Jaini for dinner and made their way out. All but Councillor Zoth, who left without saying a word.

Jaini sighed as she picked up her champagne flute and sat back in her chair. "That went well, I think. You've enough sass to be a very entertaining politician."

I agree.

"I'm not sure if that's a compliment," Tilly teased, as she picked at the leftover dessert.

Jaini looked excited all of a sudden. "I almost forgot, I have a surprise for you." Jaini grabbed her hand and dragged her back to the beauty room, stopping in front of two large fabric bags hanging beside each other—dresses. Tilly worried about where this was going. "I received my gown this morning for the ball," Jaini said. She motioned towards the bag, almost bouncing with excitement. "I knew you wouldn't have one, so I had it made with mine."

Tilly eyed the bag nervously. "That was very thoughtful of you."

Jaini laughed. "I promise you'll like it, it's even your favourite colour." She undid the clasp and pulled the bag off the dress. It was a black ball gown with skin-tight, sheer long sleeves and cuffs thinly lined in black gemstones. It had a sweetheart neckline and the entire corset was covered in small black gems, which spiked in different directions and shone in various colours under the light.

"I don't know what to say, it's the most beautiful dress I've ever seen," Tilly said in awe.

Jaini clapped her hands. "I knew you'd love it." She lifted a pair of heels from a box. "These go with it—oh you're so fun to dress." The black heels had a simple thin strap above the toes and another that went around the top of the ankle, the straps were covered in gemstones that matched the dress.

"You've outdone yourself, can I see yours?"

Jaini looked horrified. "Of course not, mine is a surprise. Now go get your beauty sleep and I'll see you at the festival."

Tilly laughed and shook her head. "Thanks for tonight, dinner was—interesting." Jaini laughed with her and walked her to the lift before giving her a tight hug goodbye.

Tilly walked down the corridor towards her suite, as she drew closer her body grew warm and tingles ran down her neck—Leo. She pulled off her heels and hurried inside, finding him sitting on the couch with a bouquet of flowers. "Leo," she cried, as she ran over to him.

He stood up and wrapped her in his arms. Tilly let out a sob as he kissed her head. "I hope I didn't scare you," he said softly. "Gera helped me sneak in."

Tilly pressed her face into his chest. "I'm so happy to see you, but will Conrad notice you're gone?"

"He's busy with Faris, they're organising security for tomorrow." He glanced down and met her eyes. "You look beautiful Til, how was Jaini's dinner?"

"It was interesting, Jaini seemed happy at least."

Leo let out a small laugh. "She was excited you agreed to go. I knew she'd love you." He let go of her and passed her the flowers. "These are for you."

Tilly took the flowers and admired them. They were

burgundy dahlias, surrounded by soft green foliage. "I've never been given flowers before, thank you."

His eyes softened. "Did Jaini tell you about the assignment?"

"Yes," she whispered, wishing it wasn't true. "I wish I could come with you."

"I've been thinking about it all afternoon," he said sadly. "Conrad would never allow it and if you left the city after I did, he'd know exactly where you'd be going."

"It would be my choice," Tilly said confidently.

Leo ran his thumb along her bottom lip. "No Til, you were right to break it off with me. Being exiled is not the life I want for you, it wouldn't be fair."

Tilly rested her face back against his chest. "It's not the life I want for you either, I'd never expect you to give up everything for me."

He lifted her chin and met her eyes. "I would in a heartbeat if I could give you a better life than that."

Tilly squeezed her eyes closed as tears ran down her cheeks. Leo took the flowers and placed them on the bench. He lifted her up and sat down on the couch, burying his face into her neck. Tilly cried softly while he held her tight. "Do you know what upsets me the most?" Leo said. Tilly shook her head. "Alerio still thinks you won our fight," he said seriously. Tilly laughed through her tears. Leo's eyes lit up, he trailed small kisses across her face. "I'm going to miss that laugh—and the rest of you," he said. His lips brushed down her neck.

Tilly's heart started racing. "I'll probably forget all about you after a week," she teased.

He laughed against her neck. "What can I do to make sure you don't forget me?"

Tilly closed her eyes. "Everything."

He brought his lips to hers and stood up, carrying her to the bedroom without breaking the kiss. He gently dropped her feet to the floor and searched her eyes. "Is this what you want Til?"

"Yes, I want you," she said with certainty. She didn't care what anyone else said, they were meant for each other. She knew once he left, she'd always regret not having this moment with him. Tilly leaned up to kiss him. Leo's hand slid behind her neck as the kiss deepened, his other hand gliding down her bare back, sending shivers down her body.

He rested his forehead against hers. "I love you, with all of my heart." He kissed down her neck. "I'm completely yours," he whispered, his voice tickling her skin.

The world stopped around her, her heart swelled and magic burned through her body. "I've been yours since the moment we met in the forest," she whispered.

He chuckled and kissed her again with more intensity. Tilly reached up and started unbuttoning his shirt—he grabbed it and pulled it over his head. She slid her hands up his toned chest, he was too sexy to be real. Leo reached over and undid the clasp around the back of her neck before sliding her dress down. She stepped out of it, now only wearing lace underwear. His eyes wandered over her body, drinking in every part of her.

"Enjoying the view?" she teased.

"I could look at it all day, you're the most beautiful thing I've ever seen." Tilly could see in his eyes that he meant it.

She undid his pants, letting them fall to the floor. He placed his lips back over hers and gently lifted her up. Tilly wrapped her legs around his waist as he carried her over to the bed and laid her down. He trailed kisses from her neck down to her breasts, teasing her nipples with his tongue. He slid her underwear down and she moaned softly as he gently stroked her. He pushed his finger in, rubbing slowly while his mouth kept moving over her breasts. She closed her eyes, it felt like heaven.

Leo laid on top of her, bringing his mouth back to hers and pressing his body against her. She could feel how hard he was, her body was aching for him. Tilly arched her back, rubbing herself against him as she ran her hands up the back of his neck. He groaned and leaned up, staring down at her with fire in his eyes. She knew her expression matched his, she wanted him more than anything. Leo laid on the bed beside her and pulled her on top of him. "We can go as slow as you like," he said gently.

Tilly gave him a small smile, she loved how safe he made her feel. She slid his cotton boxers down and positioned herself over him. Leo gently placed his tip inside her and she moaned as she slowly eased herself down around him. She closed her eyes, it was slightly painful.

Leo laced his fingers through hers and she opened her eyes, looking down at the man she loved more than anything. Nothing in her life had ever felt so right. She started moving slowly, until it no longer hurt. She flowed her magic through her body and pushed herself against him faster. Leo groaned, not taking his eyes off her. His hands caressed her backside before he grabbed her and pulled her down hard. Tilly cried out willingly as he kept going, she could feel the pleasure building. Leo sat up, teasing her breasts with his tongue as she kept moving, she needed him as deep as possible. He held her as she cried out, feeling a release of pure, blissful pleasure. Before she could catch her breath, he laid her back on the pillow and slowly drove himself in and out of her. She wrapped her legs around his waist, moving with him. She squeezed the pillow as she felt the pleasure building again. He moved harder and faster and she shuddered as she felt another release. Leo stopped and groaned as he finished with her.

He laid beside her, wrapping his arms around her as they both tried to catch their breath. Tilly peeked up at him, he was watching her with eyes full of love. Her magic flared softly, he meant everything to her and this moment with him had been perfect.

"How do you feel?" he asked, stroking a lock of hair from her face.

"Like I want to do that with you every minute of every day," she said quickly. Leo laughed, she could see the happiness in his eyes. "Was it okay for you?" she asked nervously. It may have been her first time, but she knew it wasn't his.

He kissed her head and chuckled. "Better than okay, if it were up to me, I'd spend the rest of my life worshipping you and your body."

Tilly's heart fluttered in her chest, how could she ever say goodbye to him. "What do we do now?" she whispered.

He pulled her closer. "We sleep, I'll leave early in the morning. I want to spend my last night holding you while I still can."

Her body ached at the thought of him leaving. She ran her fingers down his stomach, stopping between his legs. She felt him start to harden again. "Maybe we don't have to sleep right away."

Leo laughed and climbed on top of her. "Tilly, I am shocked."
As am I.

Oh my god, Annora.

Chapter Fifteen

The Festival

Tilly opened her eyes and sighed, Leo was already gone. She grabbed the pillow he'd slept on and squeezed it against her chest—it still smelt like him. She rolled onto her back and stared at the ceiling, replaying every part of last night in her mind. It had been the best night of her life.

Mine too.

Tilly laughed and called Annora out. Annora stretched and curled up beside her on the bed. "I'm so sorry, sometimes I get caught up in the moment and forget you see everything I do."

Don't apologise, I was a woman once too, remember. I had many lovers and the bond you share with Leo is purer and more intense than anything I ever felt.

Tilly paused. "Wait a second, you had many lovers? Tell me everything."

Another time, it would take too long to remember them all.

Tilly scoffed. "I am shocked, and impressed." Annora chuckled. Tilly got out of bed and ran herself a bath, she laid back against the smooth crystal. Her heart hurt at the thought of saying goodbye to Leo today. She finished up and slipped into her fluffy robe. Tilly walked around her closet aimlessly, trying to figure out what to wear. There was a loud knock at the door. Tilly quickly pulled Annora back in and went to open it. Cali stood in the doorway, wearing a flowery sundress and tiny flowers through her white hair—she looked like a fairy. "I wasn't expecting you, you look gorgeous," Tilly said.

Cali beamed at her. "I thought we could go to the festival together if you aren't busy?"

Tilly laughed. "Your timing is amazing. I have no idea what to wear—can I wear pants?"

Cali wiggled excitedly and ran to the closet. "You are so fun to dress—no pants."

"That's what Jaini said," Tilly muttered, as she closed the door. She followed Cali to the closet. "That reminds me, do you have plans tonight? Will you be my plus one to the ceremony? There's a ball afterwards."

Cali squealed. "You're going to Lady Zirk's ceremony? She's the champion of our people, we have been waiting forever for this day to come."

Tilly laughed in surprise. "Yeah, she's the friend who gave me all of this," she said, motioning the clothes.

Cali's jaw dropped. "I can't believe she's your friend, we are all obsessed with her." She passed Tilly a mulberry-coloured, midi-dress with spaghetti straps and a tulle skirt. Tilly studied it uncertainly, at least the skirt would hide her daggers she thought. She pulled on the dress and her combat boots before fastening her daggers around her thighs. Cali gave her a strange look. "You're very odd, we're going to a festival."

Tilly grinned. "I don't feel like myself without them."

They walked through the city towards the marketplace, the dome shined a little brighter than usual. Cali leaned towards her enthusiastically. "There are rumours Lady Zirk might make an appearance."

"Jaini is coming, she's really looking forward to it."

The music was growing louder. Tilly could sense Cali's excitement as they drew closer to the festival. Tilly glanced up at the purple lanterns and small white flowers hanging all around them. Cali noticed her admiring them. "They are Lily of the Valley," Cali said, pointing to the flowers. "They symbolise hope—our gift to Lady Zirk." Tilly felt tears build in her eyes, she hardly knew Jaini, yet she was so proud of her. They wandered through the crowded markets and Cali pulled her towards one of the stalls. It had an assortment of exquisitely decorated cakes and biscuits on display. Two white-haired Orbarian men smiled up at them from behind the stall. Cali motioned towards them. "Tilly this is my dad, Jari, and my little brother, Xan."

Tilly beamed at them. "It's lovely to meet you both. These cakes look incredible."

Jari smiled and shook her hand politely. "Thanks, Tilly, we've heard so much about you."

Xan stared at Tilly with wide eyes, he hadn't moved since Cali introduced them. Cali waved her hand in front of his face. "Hello? Xan?"

Xan shook his head and ran around to the front of the stall. He knelt in front of Tilly and kissed her hand. "It's an honour to meet you, we've heard stories of your beauty and your skill in combat."

He's as cute as Cali is.

"Uh—"

Tilly turned red and looked to Cali for help. Cali elbowed him. "Get up, you're making her uncomfortable and you're freaking me out."

He quickly scrambled to his feet. Tilly gave him an embarrassed smile. "Thanks, Xan, do you help make the cakes?" she asked awkwardly.

His chest puffed out proudly. "Dad makes the cakes, but the biscuits are all mine. We are looking at expanding our business."

"That's so exciting. I have to buy some from you."

Cali lowered her voice. "Don't feel pressured to buy something just because they're my family."

"I never feel pressured to buy cakes," Tilly whispered back seriously. "They are my one true weakness. You must never tell my enemies." Cali laughed and shook her head at Tilly. Tilly left with a bag of biscuits and cakes, and a massive grin on her face. They headed out of the markets and went to stand by the stage. A band played upbeat music and people danced in front of them. They finished their song and Gera strolled over to the microphone. "What's Gera doing up there?" Tilly asked curiously.

Cali smiled towards him. "He helped organise the festival. He does quite a lot for our people when he's off duty."

Gera beamed at the crowd. "What a fantastic day this has turned out to be, thank you all for coming," he said joyfully. "I've just been told Lady Zirk has arrived. Can we all give her a warm Orbarian welcome." He motioned towards the back of the crowd. Jaini stood there in a simple black suit, accompanied by four guards and Leo.

The crowd parted for her, they threw flowers and cheered her name. Jaini waved and shook hands with some of them as she made her way through the crowd. Leo followed behind her and locked eyes with Tilly, they both gave each other a sad smile. Jaini stepped up onto the stage, her hair was now covered in flowers. She laughed and pulled one off, she was glowing with happiness. Tilly glanced over at Cali, she was watching Jaini adoringly.

"Thank you all for your support and for this beautiful festival, I am truly humbled," Jaini said, placing her hands over her heart. "You have all inspired me beyond words. I want you to know that I see you and I hear you. I have big plans for this city and they are all for you."

Tilly looked around, the people were hanging on to her every word, some of them were crying hysterically.

Matilda, look.

Tilly noticed eight tall, hunched figures, slowly stalking towards the back of the crowd. They wore black leather armour with deep red hoods. Their faces were hidden behind some kind of skull, and they were all armed. A shiver ran down her body. They looked like reapers of death.

Calvarian Assassins.

"Cali, get to Leo, tell him to get Jaini out of here!" Tilly yelled. She pulled her daggers out and passed one to Cali. Tilly turned and ran towards the assassins as they began to separate into the crowd. Everyone started to panic. They fled in all directions, making it harder for Tilly to reach them. The assassin closest to her raised his axe before a woman who had stumbled in front of him. Tilly wasn't close enough to stop him. Without thinking, she flowed her magic and pushed her shield around the woman. He brought his axe down and was jolted back. Tilly ran over and helped the woman up.

"Thank you," she sobbed.

Tilly sped towards the Calvarian and froze. Up close she could see that his mask was a leopard skull.

That is the skull of a guardian, these assassins came from Panthera.

Annora snarled and Tilly's vision blurred in red fury.

Kill them all.

She felt Annora's magic mix with her own, turning to a feral rage. She lunged towards him as he stood up. His limbs all moved unexpectedly, as if they had a mind of their own. He swung his axe towards her and she ducked, his other hand shot to her throat. She slipped under his arm and sank her dagger into his neck. He dropped to his knees in front of her and she kicked him in the chest, watching him fall to the ground.

"One," she seethed.

She heard a loud roar and looked back. Leo had shifted and was mauling an assassin on the stage.

"Two."

She noticed another dead at his feet.

"Three."

Two guards were protecting Jaini from the largest one and Cali had just joined them. Tilly ran back towards the stage as fast as she could. She saw an assassin trying to climb up the side and pounced on top of him. She sank her dagger into the back of his head and they both fell to the ground. She pulled it out and tossed his body aside.

"Four."

Leo ran over to help Cali. "Where are the others?" Tilly called desperately. Three of them jumped up from behind the stage, springing towards Jaini with their weapons raised. "No!" Tilly shrieked, racing towards them.

Jaini turned just as the closest assassin brought his sword

down. Tilly sent a shield around Jaini at the last second, and the Calvarian went flying off the stage, knocking the other two back with him.

Jaini turned to Tilly, her face in shock. Tilly reached her on the stage just as the largest assassin fell before Leo.

Five.

She glared at the last three on the ground. They sat up as she dropped from the stage, stalking towards them. She was burning with magic and rage, the blood of their brothers running down her arms. The closest Calvarian scrambled backwards, trying to get away from her. "It's not possible," he rasped.

She charged towards him, hitting him in the face with the hilt of her dagger. His leopard skull cracked in half, revealing his face. His narrow eyes were black and soulless, with a symbol tattooed under each of them. He had greying skin and sunken cheeks. His scream was cut off as she swiped her dagger across his throat.

"Six," she snarled.

The two remaining assassins stood and circled her. She heard a furious roar as Leo flew over and pounced on top of one of them. The last Calvarian aimed his spear at Tilly's chest. Annora growled, pushing her magic through with Tilly's. Tilly pulled the spear from his hand and threw it aside. She lunged towards him and pushed him to the ground. He let out a raspy scream as she held his wrists down and dug her knee into his throat. "Who sent you here?" she yelled. She could see the fear in his black eyes. "Who sent you?" He tried to shove her off, but his strength was no match for hers.

She ripped the panther skull from his face and he flinched. "You're all going to die," he croaked.

Her magic burned through her body, all she could feel was blinding rage. She released his arms and punched him over and over.

Tilly felt a weight on her shoulder, she stopped and glanced back—breathing heavily. It was Leo's paw. He was watching her calmly, his mane matted with blood. Jaini stood behind him with Cali and a dozen soldiers—all staring at her in shock. She looked down at the Calvarian, he was unconscious. She clambered off him as a winged horse and eagle flew down and landed in front of them. Tilly backed away from the assassin and tried to calm herself down, as a group of soldiers ran over to handcuff him.

You would have made your people proud today.

She felt a warmth spread through her chest, easing the rage. Tilly didn't mean to use so much magic, she couldn't help it.

You did what you had to do. Jaini wouldn't be here if you hadn't.

The Calvarians were as terrifying as Alerio had said, but Tilly wondered how they were able to take down a whole city of Spirids, it didn't make sense.

I was just wondering the same thing.

Conrad hurried towards them, his hair was untidy and his badge crooked. He examined the Calvarian and checked for a pulse. "He's still alive. Faris, take him back to Headquarters for questioning."

Faris nodded. The soldiers lifted the assassin over his back and strapped him down. Faris turned and flew off into the city. Two soldiers handed Leo and Alerio clothes as they shifted back to their human forms. Leo rushed straight over to Tilly. "Are you alright?" he asked quietly. "What happened? He looked afraid of you."

Tilly wrapped her arms around herself. "I'm not sure, I just wanted to protect Jaini."

Leo's eyes softened. "She's safe Til, you were amazing."

Conrad stood beside Leo and glanced between them. "What happened here?"

Leo looked down at the dead assassins and frowned. "They showed up while Jaini was making her speech—eight of them. Tilly took half of them down on her own and we got the rest."

Alerio gently squeezed Tilly's shoulder. "You did well little one, you would have saved a lot of lives today."

"Eight," Conrad said in shock. "That's unheard of. We need to get Lady Zirk out of the city immediately. Who would want to harm her enough to hire assassins?"

"Councillor Zoth and Councillor Ezra were openly rude to her at dinner last night," Tilly recalled.

Conrad's face shot to hers. "We will question them. When Faris returns I'll have him escort Lady Zirk to a safe house. Alerio and Leopold, you take Tilly and the soldiers. Sweep the city, we need to make sure it was just the eight of them. Find out how they got in."

Leo's face looked livid. "No."

"I beg your pardon Leopold?" Conrad said in astonishment.

"I'm not leaving Jaini's side," he said firmly. "She is family to me. No one will protect her better than I will. Where was Faris when she was attacked today?"

"I'm not leaving her either," Tilly said.

Conrad raised his eyebrows at Leo. "Absolutely not, you're leaving on assignment tonight. We will stick to the plan."

Leo stepped towards him. "Fuck your plan," he seethed. "I'm not the only person in this team, I know Alerio offered to go. I'm staying with Jaini, we'll be leaving after her ceremony, not before, and Tilly will be coming with us. She's more than proven her loyalty."

"This is exactly why you're not supposed to attach yourself to anyone," Conrad spat. "You're putting your personal relationships before your duty."

Leo stood over him. "I'm not your puppet, Conrad. I'm a human being with loved ones just like everyone else. Right now, my duty is to Jaini. Your plan can be carried out by any of the Five."

Alerio cleared his throat. "Leo's right, Faris and I are more than capable of searching the city. We'll increase security for the ceremony and I can take Leo's place on assignment after that."

"It's too risky," Conrad sputtered.

Tilly glanced towards Jaini, Cali was comforting her. "There's no way Jaini will leave before her inauguration," Tilly added.

Conrad sighed in frustration, running his hands through his hair. "We will let Lady Zirk decide."

They all turned to Jaini, she was still shaking. Conrad approached her slowly. "We need to get you out of the city as soon as possible. Leopold is insisting you stay until after your inauguration, I believe it's too risky. The choice is yours."

"I will not miss my ceremony." Jaini looked horrified that he even suggested it.

Conrad threw his hands in the air and stormed off, shouting orders to the soldiers. Leo and Alerio looked relieved. Tilly ran towards Jaini and Cali, they both threw their arms around her. "I'll never make fun of your daggers, ever again," Cali sobbed.

"I was so worried about you both," Tilly said.

Jaini gave an anxious laugh. "I'm okay, my friends happen

to be badarses."

Tilly laughed and let them go. "Thank you for protecting her," she said to Cali.

Cali peeked over at Jaini. "Anytime," she said quietly.

Leo put his arms around Tilly and Jaini's shoulders. "We need to get off the street."

They all headed back towards the stage. "I can't believe you just said that to Conrad," Tilly said quietly.

"It was well overdue. Alerio has been getting frustrated with him as well," Leo replied.

Tilly bit her lip, trying to hide her smile. "So, you're not leaving?"

He grinned at her. "I'm not leaving."

They walked through the ruined festival. Soldiers were patrolling and cleaning up the assassin's bodies. Some of the guards had been badly injured, but no one had been killed. They had been very lucky. Tilly glanced towards the stalls and stopped. "Shit," she cried.

"What's wrong?" Leo asked, looking around.

"I dropped my cakes," Tilly said sadly.

Matilda!

Leo and Jaini laughed. Cali gave her a small pat on the shoulder. "I'll get you some more cakes. I think you've earned them."

Chapter Sixteen

Jaini's Inauguration

Tilly, Leo and Cali escorted Jaini home, along with a dozen soldiers. The soldiers patrolled the penthouse while Jaini led the others to her beauty room. As they walked in, Leo pulled Tilly aside. "I need to organise a few things before we leave. Do not let her out of your sight."

Tilly nodded. "I wasn't planning to. Don't worry, this place is crawling with soldiers. No one will touch her."

He smiled and gave her a quick kiss before rushing out the door. She heard him giving orders to the soldiers staying behind. Tilly turned to Cali and Jaini—they were both grinning at her. "What?" she asked cautiously.

Cali wiggled her eyebrows. "My friends never kiss me like that."

Tilly laughed as a flush warmed her cheeks. Jaini stepped closer to her. "I was just thinking the same thing, is there something you'd like to share with us, Tilly?"

Tilly was sure she was as red as her dress now. "Jaini, you were almost killed, how can you be thinking about this right now?"

Jaini smirked. "I'm always thinking about this. One of my life goals is to see you two together—it's on my vision board," she added casually.

Jaini and Cali watched her expectantly. Tilly glanced between them. "You two are as bad as each other," she sulked.

"Stop avoiding the question," Cali pushed.

"Oh my god." Tilly hid her face behind her hands. "Yes, we did it, but it doesn't change anything, we still can't be together."

Cali squealed and Jaini threw her arms out wide. "I knew it!" Jaini cried.

"What was it like?" Cali asked, trying to pry Tilly's hands off her face.

Tilly dropped her hands and closed her eyes, she couldn't make eye contact with either of them right now. "It was—perfect."

They both sighed.

"Is he big?" Cali whispered. "Does he have a tail?"

Tilly's eyes shot open. "Okay, this conversation is over." She walked away from them, fanning her face while they cried with laughter behind her.

Once they calmed down, Jaini turned to Cali. "I can't thank you enough for today, will you join us for the rest of the celebrations?"

Cali smiled shyly. "Thank you for the offer, Tilly actually already asked if I'd be her plus one."

"Good, good." Jaini opened the door and called for a guard. "Take Cali to my wardrobe, allow her to use my bathroom and assist her with choosing a gown and whatever else she needs." Cali looked at Jaini with wide eyes and thanked her. Jaini closed the door behind them and strolled over to

Tilly—placing her hands on her hips. "Where have you been hiding that woman?" she asked accusingly. "I did say to bring someone sexy, but I was expecting a man. I am pleasantly surprised."

Tilly laughed. "Cali's just a very good friend."

Jaini looked thoughtful. "I need to ask you something," she said. Tilly took a deep breath, she had a feeling this was coming. "What happened today?" Jaini asked. "How did you save me like that?" Tilly studied Jaini's face. She didn't know whether to tell her the truth. Jaini's expression softened. "You saved my life. Whatever it is, I won't tell a soul."

You can trust her. Tell her who you really are.

"I'm a Spirid," Tilly said quietly.

Jaini's eyebrows shot up. "That's impossible," she whispered.

Tilly placed her hand out towards Jaini, she flowed her magic and conjured a Lily of the Valley. Jaini gasped and took the flower as her other hand covered her mouth. "My real name is Matilda Hazelwood. I was born the day Panthera was attacked. My mother had her friend hide me with a human couple," Tilly said. "I only just found out before I came to Everorb City."

Tears glistened down Jaini's translucent cheeks. "I'm so sorry. I was only a child when it happened, but I remember our people in mourning." Realisation dawned on her face. "Hazelwood? Don't tell me your mother and father were—"

Tilly nodded. "King Namir and Queen Alwyn."

"You should have been our Queen," Jaini said with shock.

"That's the part I find hardest to believe," Tilly joked.

"Does Leo know?"

"No," Tilly said. "You're the only person I've told."

"This is huge." Jaini wrapped her arms around Tilly and held her. "Your secret is safe with me." She stepped back and held

Tilly by the shoulders. "Gross, I forgot you were covered in blood," she complained. Tilly laughed as Jaini glanced down, checking there was none on her.

Jaini showered in the ensuite attached to the beauty room, while Tilly stood guard at the door. Cali returned not long after in a shimmering silver gown—it looked striking against her purple skin and white hair. Tilly hurried into the bathroom to wash the blood off as quickly as she could, she pulled on the purple silk robe Jaini had left out for her. When she came out of the bathroom, Jaini and Cali were having their hair and make-up done. Two Orbarians were waiting for Tilly expectantly. Jaini patted the chair beside her and Tilly hesitated. "It's okay, I can get myself ready."

Jaini frowned at her. "You sit in that chair right now—everything has to be perfect."

Tilly laughed and shook her head as she sat down. "You're so bossy," she complained. Jaini grinned back at her.

The hair and make-up team finished up and Jaini passed Tilly her gown, shuffling her into the bathroom. "You first."

Tilly pulled on the black, jewelled ballgown and looked in the mirror. Her hair was in an elegant updo, with a few curls left out. Her eye make-up was dark and her lips were painted burgundy. Jaini had given her dainty, black diamond earrings to match her dress. Tilly slipped her now clean daggers around her thighs. "That's better."

You are breathtaking. I would cry if I could.

"Hurry up Tilly, we want to see," Cali shouted. Tilly walked out of the bathroom and they both gasped. "Who even are you? You look like a princess," Cali said, wiping her eyes. Tilly's eyes shot to Jaini's and they both laughed awkwardly.

Jaini took Tilly's hands and eyed her down. "I've done so well. You'll be my first gift to this great city." She sighed happily as Tilly scoffed. "Leo is going to lose his mind when he sees you—Cali is he back yet?" Cali ran to the door to check.

"No, that's okay," Tilly said embarrassed, she was starting to regret introducing Cali and Jaini.

Hush Matilda, I want to see Leo's reaction too.

Unbelievable, Tilly thought. She could hear Cali talking to the soldiers. "We need Leo right away," she said seriously. Tilly's heart started racing, she didn't even understand why she was nervous. She sensed Leo close by. "He's coming!" Cali said, running back to stand with Jaini.

Leo hurried into the room wearing a formal black suit. "What's going—"

He stopped when he saw Tilly and a grin spread across his face.

"Say something," Jaini said annoyed.

Leo made a face at Jaini before he stepped towards Tilly, bringing her hand to his lips. "You're too beautiful for words, Til."

Tilly's stomach fluttered. "So are you." Leo chuckled as Jaini and Cali watched on happily.

"My turn," Jaini said, running into the bathroom.

Leo couldn't take his eyes off Tilly. "Stop it," Tilly said embarrassed.

He laughed loudly. "I can't help it—I'm struggling to keep my hands off you."

"Alright, I'm coming out," Jaini said. She walked out of the bathroom with a huge smile on her face. Her long purple hair was curled and her gown was glittering lilac and off the shoulders. A halo of flowers rested on her head, made of coloured crystals and diamonds.

"You are dazzling," Cali whispered.

"You look perfect," Tilly agreed.

Leo looked unimpressed. "Are you sure you want to wear that? I don't think it's shiny enough."

Jaini ignored him. "Let's get this party started," she said excitedly.

Twelve guards escorted them through the glass bridge that led to the Emerald Tower. Leo walked ahead, while Tilly and Cali stayed behind Jaini. Tilly felt ridiculous guarding her in a ballgown. They waited outside the ballroom until it was time for Jaini to make her entrance. Jaini paced around nervously, muttering to herself. Leo gripped her shoulder. "You're going to be fine. We'll be with you the whole time."

Jaini waved him off. "Oh, I'm not worried about that—I'm worried about the ballroom. I didn't get to sign it off after what happened today. What if they used the wrong colours? What if they seated Councillor Della next to Councillor Ezra? She despises him."

Annora chuckled. Leo scoffed and looked to Tilly for help. Tilly went and took her hands. "None of those things matter, all that matters is that you made it here," Tilly said. "So, take a deep breath, and go in there as the fearless leader we know you are."

Jaini squeezed her hands and took a deep breath. "Thank you. I needed that." She glanced at Cali, who gave her an encouraging smile.

"And if that doesn't work," Leo added. "You can always annoy them to death, like you do with me."

Jaini laughed as a smartly dressed Orbarian woman entered

the room. "They're ready for you Lady Zirk."

Leo stepped into the ballroom first and glanced around, he turned and nodded. Jaini followed him and Tilly and Cali stayed behind her. The chatter died down as they entered.

The ballroom was twice the size of Jaini's. Shimmering emeralds hung from the ceiling like vines, giving the room a green glow. The six Councillors were seated on a large stage at the front of the room. Conrad stood behind the podium, watching Jaini expectantly. In front of the stage were round tables, decorated with green silk. The ruling family members were seated around them. There was a dance floor at the back of the ballroom, with an orchestra arranged on another stage. Leo led them all to a table up the front. Alerio and Faris were already seated around it. Tilly noticed a golden eagle ring on Alerio's hand and a golden horse on Faris'. She found her place card and took a seat between Alerio and Cali. Leo sat on Alerio's other side, with Faris next to him. Tilly leaned towards Alerio as Jaini made her way onto the stage. "Why is Conrad up there with them?" she asked.

Alerio smiled, he looked incredible in his black suit. "These events must be officiated by a Historian. Conrad's the only one in Everorb City."

Conrad tapped the microphone. He wore a crisp, dark red suit and his black hair had been neatly tied back, his shield badge glimmered on his chest. "Welcome Councillors, Lords, Ladies and Friends. We are gathered here today to witness Lady Jaini Zirk accept her new role as Councillor. She will, in fact, be the youngest member of council in the history of Everorb City." he said grandly. "Would you please stand and give her a round of applause."

They all stood and clapped as Jaini took her place behind

the podium. Tilly noticed Councillor Zoth remained in his seat with a bored look on his face.

Jaini beamed at the crowd. "Thank you, you may be seated," she said. "I can't tell you all how blessed I feel to be standing here before you. There was a moment today where I feared I may not make it." She glanced back at the Councillors, some of them moved uncomfortably in their chairs. Tilly's eyes narrowed, at least one of them had to be responsible for the attack.

Jaini's smile dropped and her eyes hardened. "Today may not have gone how I had hoped, but it has only shown me how strong my voice really is, and I will not be silenced. I will make sure that every family in this city has a home, every child will have a school and every Orbarian will have a voice. I take my place today, knowing that the next chapter of Everorb City will be greater than any of those come to pass and that chapter begins today."

"Thank god there's so many napkins," Cali whispered, dabbing her eyes.

Tilly laughed quietly, she had tears in her eyes too, she felt so proud of Jaini. When Jaini finished her speech, she bowed to each of the Councillors and they bowed in return. Alerio told Tilly it was to show they would respect her voice equally, as one of them.

Conrad presented Jaini with a golden pin in the shape of an eight-point star, she wore it proudly on her dress. He gestured towards her as she stood at the front of the stage. "I present to you, Councillor Jaini Zirk." Jaini held her head high as the crowd cheered for her. Tilly and Cali whistled loudly—it was official.

The Councillors each joined their families at the tables. Conrad took his place next to Faris and Jaini sat between Conrad and Cali. Cali leaned over to Tilly and lowered her voice. "Why'd they have to seat us right in front of Faris? I'd rather look at a donkey," she sulked. Tilly couldn't help it, she burst out laughing and had to cover her mouth with a napkin. Luckily Faris had been talking to Conrad and hadn't heard, but Leo was grinning at them.

"That was an excellent speech, Jaini," Alerio said kindly.

"You'll have the Councillors wrapped around your fingers in no time," Leo added.

Jaini laughed and glanced around. "Were you able to find out who ordered the attack?" she asked quietly.

Faris looked at Conrad. Conrad's eyes flicked to Tilly before he glanced back at Jaini. "The Calvarian we arrested hasn't told us anything yet. We think he's in shock, he hasn't said a word since he woke up," Conrad said.

Alerio beamed at Tilly. "Who knew you could be so scary." Tilly forced a smile, she hadn't wanted to draw attention to herself.

"Do you know how they got in?" Leo asked.

Faris frowned. "We found guards tied up at the entrance of the city. The Assassins got in quickly and headed straight for the festival before anyone could be alerted, it was well timed."

Alerio nodded with frustration in his eyes. "We have soldiers searching the entire city, so far they haven't found any others."

"They could be hiding," Conrad responded quietly. "Leopold will still take Jaini out of the city tonight. We can't be too careful until we know for sure."

Six courses were served for dinner. Each time another course came out Tilly's face lit up excitedly. Leo glanced over at her, holding back a smile. Drinks were served after dinner and everyone gathered around the dance floor, while the band played slow, elegant music. The Orbarian women were a glittering display in dresses covered in coloured jewels. The men were almost as flashy, with small details of gems on their collars, ties or shoes. Alerio joined Jaini for her introductory dance and more couples joined in after that. Tilly thought back to the night at the club when Leo had danced with her. She looked over at him and he grinned. She could tell he was thinking about it too.

"Oh, what good fun," Conrad commented. "Faris, you must take Tilly for a dance."

Faris looked at Conrad in shock. Tilly nearly spat out her drink. Conrad raised his eyebrows back at Faris expectantly. Faris' lips tightened, he stepped in front of Tilly and held out his hand. "May I have this dance?" he asked through clenched teeth.

Tilly looked to Cali and Leo for help. "It's okay Faris, you don't have to. I'm a really bad dancer," Tilly said.

"She honestly is," Cali agreed.

Conrad took Tilly's drink. "Nonsense, it's about time you two started getting along."

Tilly hesitated and placed her hand in Faris', he squeezed it a little too tight. She felt annoyed already. She burned her magic and squeezed back, watching his jaw tighten. He led her onto the dance floor and Tilly started to panic. Everyone was doing the same slow dance, she was going to make a fool of herself in front of Faris, and everyone else.

Just follow his lead.

Faris did not look happy, he placed an arm around her waist

and stared past her like she wasn't there. Tilly peeked back at Leo, he was watching her with a small smile as Conrad spoke close to his ear. Faris started dancing and she tried to follow. He stepped back, to the side, then forward—it seemed easy enough. "So, are you enjoying your classes?" he asked, sounding irritated.

"All of them except yours," she said without thinking.

His face tightened. Tilly cleared her throat and avoided eye contact with him.

Give him a compliment, Matilda, you have to make an effort.

She met his eyes, he was glaring at her. Tilly started to panic. She quickly noticed how tight his suit looked over his bulging arms. "You have—excellent arms, Faris. They look huge in that suit."

That was the stupidest thing I've ever heard.

Faris stopped dancing and stared at her in disbelief.

What have you done?

He threw his head back and laughed loudly. Tilly laughed nervously and looked around—everyone was watching them curiously. She glanced at Leo, he covered his mouth with his hand as his shoulders shook with laughter. Faris looked back at her with amusement. "No one has ever said that to me before."

Tilly felt so confused. "Well, whatever you're doing, it's definitely paying off," she added uncertainly.

Faris spun her around. "I have to admit, it was satisfying watching you knock Leo down yesterday."

"Uh, thank you Faris," she replied. That was the strangest thing that had ever happened, she thought.

Definitely not what I expected.

They finished the dance and bowed to each other. Faris

walked off without saying another word. Tilly was relieved it was over. She headed back towards Leo when someone grabbed her arm. She looked back and Councillor Zoth stood there swaying, with his top button undone. "My turn for a dance," he said arrogantly.

Tilly eyed his hand wrapped around her arm. "No thank you, I've had enough dancing for tonight."

He rolled his droopy eyes. "Oh, come on. I didn't mean what I said at dinner, you're more than a decoration." His eyes wandered down her body. "I bet you're a feisty one."

"Get your hand off me or you'll see how feisty I can be," Tilly seethed.

He leaned closer, smiling. "I'll pay you. I've got a lot more money than Leo does, maybe we can come to an arrangement."

How dare he.

Her magic flared. "I don't give a shit about your money, or anyone else's."

Other guests were starting to stare at them. He looked around angrily. "Just one dance, you're embarrassing me." He gripped her arm tighter and tried pulling her towards the middle of the dance floor. Tilly yanked his hand off and twisted it behind his back—he yelped in pain. Guards began running over, but Leo reached them first, his eyes burning furiously.

"I think Councillor Zoth has had a bit too much to drink," Tilly said sweetly.

He looked up at Leo in fear. "Forgive me," he whispered. "I heard you were finished with her."

Leo's face began to shift, his teeth lengthening into fangs. Councillor Zoth gasped and cowered away from him. The guards approached nervously. Leo closed his eyes, breathing slowly as his face returned to normal. "Councillor Zoth is drunk," he growled. "He needs an escort home." Tilly let go of him and he scrambled away as quickly as he could.

Leo eyed Tilly with concern. "I know you can take care of yourself, but are you okay?"

"I'm furious that he didn't take no for an answer," she said annoyed.

They both watched him being escorted out. "Councillor Zoth is an entitled arsehole." Leo looked down at her and his eyes turned playful. "He's definitely no Faris."

Tilly squeezed her eyes closed. "I was trying to make peace with him and I panicked alright."

"So, you like his arms. Should I be worried?" he teased.

"I don't like his arms," Tilly said annoyed. "You can just tell he works really hard on them."

Leo laughed at her with adoring eyes. "I'm so glad I found you," he said quietly. "I don't think I could ever live without you now."

"I never want to live without you either," she whispered. "Even if I have to spend my life being your casual nighttime companion."

Leo shook his head. "You're so much more than that, you always have been." They smiled at each other. Tilly glanced over at Jaini, she was having the time of her life dancing with Alerio and Cali. "I have to ask you something," Leo said seriously.

"Oh god, please don't ask me to dance."

He chuckled. "Not that, our dancing probably isn't suitable for a place like this. It's about what happened to Jaini today." Tilly's face shot to his. "I saw you Til, I saw you save her. I was trying to get back but I wasn't quick enough. How did you do that?"

He was going to find out eventually.

Tilly looked around nervously. "I promise I'll tell you soon," she said, "but not here."

"That's okay, it can wait, but whatever you did, thank you."

She looked back at Jaini, feeling her magic spark in her chest. "I'd never let anyone harm her."

Leo reached up and pushed a lock of hair from her face. "I know you wouldn't," he said. "It's one of the things I love about you."

Chapter Seventeen

Escaping Everorb City

Tilly and Leo slipped out of the ball with Jaini, unnoticed. Leo took them to an empty suite in the Emerald Tower and passed them each a backpack. "Alerio and Faris are doing a final sweep of the city," he said. "We need to be ready to leave when they give the signal."

Jaini unzipped the backpack and pulled out a T-shirt—her nose scrunched in disgust. "You packed clothes for us?"

Leo raked his hand through his hair. "Conrad had Piper pack them. We won't be gone long Jaini, just until we know the city is completely safe." Jaini still didn't look happy about it. She took the backpack and headed to the bathroom to change.

"Do we have to leave?" Tilly asked. "She has a lot of protection here."

Leo lowered his voice. "The assassin in custody finally started talking, he told Conrad today was only the beginning and more would come."

She glanced at Leo in shock. "Do you believe him?"

He nodded. "Remember the night we flew to the safe house?

I heard them, camping in the forest. I didn't realise it was them until we saw them today." His eyes darkened. "I heard a lot more than eight voices."

They both watched Jaini walk out of the bathroom. If not for the situation, Tilly would have found it amusing seeing her in jeans and a T-shirt. "Poor Jaini," Tilly said. "Will she be alright out of the dome?"

"She'll be fine for a few days, just uncomfortable—like we are in here," Leo said.

Tilly and Leo took turns changing as Jaini scoured the fridge for food. It had been almost an hour and they still hadn't heard from Faris or Alerio. They all paced around the suite, waiting anxiously. Leo's phone finally buzzed, he glanced at the screen before meeting Tilly's eyes. "It's time."

Tilly's heart pounded as they made their way down the lift, she couldn't even imagine how Jaini was feeling. Leo kept glancing towards them both, his jaw tense. They stepped into the foyer and found it crammed with soldiers. They looked out of place in the posh room with glittering chandeliers hanging above them.

Gera made his way towards Jaini with a grave look on his face. "I am deeply sorry, Councillor Zirk. Today should have been a day of celebration. I shouldn't have invited you out in the open like that." He bowed his head in shame.

Leo placed his hand on Gera's shoulder. "It wasn't your fault this happened. You were just doing something kind because you care about Jaini and your people."

"He's right Gera, that was not your fault. It was a lovely occasion otherwise," Jaini agreed.

Gera nodded appreciatively and motioned towards the door. "At least I can make it up to you now, by getting you out of here safely."

"You're taking us out?" Tilly asked surprised.

"I asked him to," Leo said. "He knows this city better than anyone."

Everyone was quiet as they awaited Leo's orders. The soldiers left first, exiting in small groups and heading out in different directions to patrol the city. Leo gave the signal and they followed Gera out into the darkness, staying close to the towers. Leo and Gera walked ahead, while Tilly stayed beside Jaini and kept an eye on their surroundings. Inside the dome was eerily quiet, all she could hear was water splashing from the fountain nearby.

Gera took them to the mine and stopped at the entrance. "It's a safety precaution for the mine to have multiple exit points," he whispered. "Some of them are hidden outside of the city. I'll lead you out that way in case the main entrance is being watched."

From the corner of her eye, Tilly saw a dark figure dart behind a tree. She pulled out her daggers and blocked Jaini. "We're being followed," she whispered, just low enough for Leo to hear.

"Gera, have the tunnels been checked?" Leo asked quickly.

"Yes, just before we left the foyer," Gera answered.

Tilly could feel Jaini shaking behind her. Leo steered her down into the mine. "Let's go, we don't know how many there are. We can block them off inside."

They followed Gera into the shadows. He led them to a small office and flicked a switch. Lamps flickered on throughout the mine, lighting up the cave walls.

"How did they know we'd be here?" Jaini whispered. "I

thought the city had been cleared?"

How indeed.

Tilly saw something fly towards them, she pushed her magic and shielded them all. A dagger dropped at her feet. Gera gasped. "What just happened?"

Leo stood beside Tilly, blocking Jaini and Gera from view. Another dagger flew towards them and she blocked it again. Leo shifted and growled, baring his teeth.

Two hunched figures approached them slowly. Two was okay, Tilly thought, they could handle two.

As long as they stay in sight.

Leo snarled and shot towards them. The assassins fled in different directions. "Shit," Tilly muttered, she couldn't see any of them now, but she could hear Leo fighting.

Shield.

Tilly threw her shield up just in time. Another dagger fell in front of her. Leo was running back to them when a Calvarian sprang from the darkness towards Jaini, his mask the skull of a cheetah. Annora growled as he raised his sword. Tilly crossed her daggers and blocked it, she flared her magic and kicked him in the stomach. As the assassin fell back, Leo lunged towards him and ripped out his neck.

Tilly counted five more assassins stalk into the mines. She glanced back at Jaini. Gera was holding her behind him, she could see the fear in both of their eyes.

You have to hide them. Make them invisible.

Tilly turned to them quickly. "Hold hands and don't freak out," she whispered.

Jaini nodded shakily and grabbed Gera's hand. Tilly ran her finger down their foreheads, focusing her magic over them. They disappeared before her eyes.

"Ah!" Gera cried.

"Shh, it's okay Gera," Jaini whispered.

Tilly couldn't see them, but she could sense her magic surrounding them. "Go, we'll catch up."

"Lead the way, Gera, do it quickly," Jaini said.

Leo flew towards the assassins. Tilly held her daggers out and followed behind him. Two of the assassins bypassed Leo and advanced towards her. Annora snarled furiously as they drew closer.

More guardian skulls.

Tilly felt the magic build in her chest, she sent it burning through her body, making her stronger. The Calvarians brought their axes up. Tilly shot between them, slicing their thighs on her way through. They both shrieked wrathfully and kept swinging their weapons towards her. Tilly could see the frustration in their black eyes as she darted around them both. An axe swung towards her chest. She quickly crouched down and dug her dagger into the assassin's foot, making him scream and drop to the ground. She pulled it out and sank it into the side of his neck. Tilly pulled her dagger free and was grabbed from behind. She felt the sting of an axe at her throat. She flowed her magic and pushed her shield around herself. The assassin jolted back and she lunged on top of him. His eyes widened beneath his mask as she plunged her dagger into his chest.

Tilly heard Leo snarling behind her and the sound of ripping flesh. She turned to see the last assassin fall to the ground. Leo ran to her side as another group of assassins entered the mine.

"Shit." Tilly eyed them in shock. She didn't understand how so many of them had slipped into the city.

And stayed hidden for so long.

The Calvarians suddenly tensed. They all spun around as Alerio and Faris appeared in the entryway behind them. Alerio was armed with a curved sword and Faris held an axe in each hand—an army of soldiers marched in behind them. Alerio nodded to Leo before he sprang towards the assassins. Leo didn't waste any time, he crouched next to Tilly and she climbed onto his back.

Tilly directed Leo as he sprinted through the caves, chasing after Jaini and Gera. Tilly could still sense her magic around them. "Stop," she whispered.

She climbed off his back and called out to them, a hand wrapped around her arm. "We're here," Jaini whispered.

"Don't move," Tilly said. She found Jaini's forehead and drew the magic from her. Gera took her arm next and she did the same with him. He eyed Tilly anxiously as he reappeared.

Jaini threw her arms around Tilly. "Thank god you're both alright."

Leo shifted back and quickly pulled on his pants before joining them. "You're a Spirid," he said in disbelief. Tilly nodded at him nervously.

"That's impossible," Gera said.

Tilly met Leo's eyes. "I only found out recently." She glanced at Gera. "Please, you can't tell anyone."

Gera placed a hand over his heart. "I swear on my life."

Leo smiled and cupped her cheeks in his hands. "Why didn't you tell me?"

She gave him a shy smile. "I was going to tell you eventually."

His brow furrowed. "I didn't know it was possible—it does explain a lot though." He looked at Jaini, studying her face. "You knew?" he asked with surprise.

Jaini gave him a smug look. "I asked her after she saved me

today. Don't be jealous though, I was always going to be her favourite." They all laughed. Tilly peeked up at Leo, he was still smiling at her. Relief washed over her, she was glad he knew the truth.

"We better keep going," Gera said.

They walked for over an hour before Gera stopped them. He ran his hands along the side of the cave until he found a hidden lever. When he pulled it down, the cave wall opened into the night. The cool breeze rushed past their faces. "Oh my god," Tilly cried happily. "Fresh air!"

Leo laughed loudly. "I thought you loved the dome?" he teased.

Tilly grinned at him. "If it wasn't so hot, I could probably live there forever."

They stepped out onto the rocky cliffside as the waves crashed around below them. "This is where I leave you," Gera said. He turned to Jaini and bowed. "We look forward to your return when the city is safe once more."

Jaini pulled him into a hug, surprising him. "Thank you, Gera, we couldn't have done it without you," she said. "Please come and see me when I return. I've been looking for an adviser, someone to be the voice of our people. I believe it would be an excellent role for you."

Gera's eyes filled with tears. "Thank you," he sobbed. "It would be my greatest honour."

Jaini stood back and patted his shoulder. "Be safe, I'll see you soon." Gera gave them one last bow and disappeared into the cave.

"Alright you two, hold on tight," Leo said. He crouched down to shift and they both climbed onto his back. His dark wings stretched out and he shot off the cliff, flying away from

Everorb City. Jaini let out a sigh of relief as she held Tilly tight around her waist.

Poor Jaini, this must have been awful for her.

At least she was safe now, Tilly thought.

Leo flew up the cliffside, he landed on a bed of leaves in the overgrown forest. Jaini peered around curiously, while Leo hid behind a tree and shifted back. He stepped out just in military pants. Jaini frowned at him as he pulled on a shirt. "I can see why you don't like shifting all the time," she said. "You must rip a lot of pants." Leo looked at Tilly and smirked. Tilly shook her head with amusement as Jaini glanced between them. "Gross. You two won't be all over each other the whole time we're here, will you?" she sulked.

Leo laughed. "If that makes you uncomfortable, then yes, definitely."

Tilly scoffed. "No, we're here to protect you."

Leo looked disappointed. He strolled towards the towering tree and placed his ring against the trunk. Jaini gasped as the door appeared. They entered the safe house and Leo made sure the door had completely disappeared before he followed them down the winding staircase. Tilly glanced around fondly, it looked exactly how they had left it. She placed her hand over one of the jagged crystals and watched as they lit up the house. Jaini ran straight to the back window. "It's incredible! Look how beautiful our city is," she said excitedly. "I've never seen it from the outside."

Tilly laughed. "That's exactly how I felt seeing it for the first time."

Jaini's face dropped. "I can't believe someone wanted me dead so badly that they put all of those Orbarians in danger."

"Conrad will find out who it was," Leo said confidently. "It's what he does, nothing slips past him."

Jaini wrapped her arms around herself. "I hope so, it's freezing in here," she complained.

"There's heaps of blankets in the bedroom, you should go get some rest," Leo said.

Jaini turned to meet their eyes. "I honestly can't thank you both enough, you saved my life more than once today."

"You don't need to thank us, Jaini, you're our family," Tilly replied.

Jaini's silver eyes shone with tears. She gave them both a tight hug, before disappearing into the bedroom at the end of the hall.

Leo took Tilly's hand and kissed it as he pulled her onto the couch. They laid down together and looked out the window towards the night sky. "Who would have thought we'd end up back here," he whispered. Tilly's stomach growled and they both laughed quietly. "Well, I'm glad some things haven't changed," he joked.

Tilly bit her lip, she held out her hand and conjured a honey cake, waiting for Leo's reaction. He stared in wonder before realisation dawned on him. A loud laugh escaped his lips. "So that's where the birthday cake came from. I thought you were so strange carrying it all this way."

Tilly burst out laughing. "That was the first time I used my magic—it scared the hell out of me."

They both shook with laughter. Leo took the cake and placed it on the coffee table before he eyed Tilly seriously. "I can't believe you're a Spirid, we thought they were all gone," he said softly. "I'm so sorry Til, that's a huge secret to carry on your own. You're even more special than anyone realises."

"I'm not really on my own," she said quietly. "I have a guardian, Annora."

"Annora? What's she like? Have you ever brought her out?"

"Only when I'm alone." Tilly grinned. "Mostly she's quite dignified, but she does have a twisted sense of humour."

Tell him I was a great beauty when I was alive, there were many songs about me.

Tilly tried not to laugh, there was no way she was telling him that.

"Can I meet her?" Leo asked.

Yes.

She could feel Annora excitedly trying to come out. Tilly panicked. "No, I think she's asleep right now."

Liar.

She could meet Leo tomorrow when she calmed down, Tilly thought.

Leo's face dropped. "Maybe another time."

I can't believe you lied to him.

Annora was sulking, but Tilly was too tired to bring her out tonight, she yawned sleepily. Leo leaned down and kissed her neck. "Feel like a bath?"

"What about Jaini?" Tilly whispered.

"She's safe here, only the Five can get in," he said.

They went into the first bedroom—the same room Tilly had stayed in last time. Leo closed the door as Tilly sat on the edge of the bath and ran the water. She watched him stalk towards her—suddenly she wasn't tired anymore. She grabbed his face and kissed him hard. After the day they'd both had, she needed him more than ever. Leo responded just as eagerly. He pulled her shirt off and leaned down to kiss her breasts. Tilly unbuttoned his shirt and pushed it off him before reaching for his pants. Leo stepped out of them and knelt in front of her to slide her pants and underwear down. He trailed kisses over her thighs and stopped to kiss her between the legs. Tilly bent her head back and moaned softly. She ran her hand through his black hair as he deepened the kiss with his tongue.

Leo stood abruptly and lifted her up. He climbed into the bath and sat down in the hot water. Tilly wrapped her hand around him and positioned herself over him. She pushed herself down, hard. Leo watched her with dark eyes as his hands gently caressed her backside. She placed her arms around his neck, slowly gliding herself back up and pushing herself down again. She closed her eyes and kept going, she wanted to feel him again and again.

"You're too sexy for your own good," Leo whispered. He pulled her hips down harder and she moaned quietly. "Do you like that?" he said against her ear.

"Yes," she breathed. "I want more."

He kissed her before turning her around. She leaned up on her knees and held onto the edge of the bath. Leo knelt up behind her, rubbing his tip between her legs. He kept rubbing and teasing her before sliding inside. Tilly bit her lip to stop herself from crying out. Leo grabbed her hips, thrusting deeper. She felt the pleasure building and gasped as it spread through her body. Leo held her tight as he finished with her. Tilly leaned back against him, her heart was pounding. Leo kissed her forehead as she smiled contentedly against his chest.

They dried off and Leo pulled on a T-shirt and cotton boxer shorts. Tilly conjured a pyjama top and shorts as Leo watched in amazement. They went and laid back on the couch, both too on edge to sleep in the bedroom while Jaini was under their watch. Tilly could hardly keep her eyes open now. Leo stroked her hair slowly. "I can't get enough of you," he whispered.

"I feel the same about you," she said sleepily.

He sighed and rested his forehead against hers. "I want to be with you more than anything. It kills me that every moment we have together feels stolen. You're the love of my life, Til, you deserve so much more than this."

Tilly felt a tear glide down her cheek. "We'll work it out," she whispered. "We have to. For now, we just have to make the most of the time we get together."

Leo kissed her and held her close as they both drifted off to sleep.

Tilly started to stir. She opened her eyes and Jaini was sitting on the couch opposite them—with a massive grin on her face. "Ah!" Tilly cried, waking Leo. "You scared me."

Tilly noticed her star badge proudly pinned to the collar of her flannel pyjamas. Jaini laughed. "You're pretty jumpy for a badarse Spirid."

Leo yawned. "What are you doing, Jaini?"

"Admiring you two, wrapped in each other's arms," Jaini said cheerfully. "Now, since we have plenty of free time, let's plan how we're going to get you two together."

"We just woke up," Leo groaned.

"I've made a list." Jaini pulled out a sheet of paper and cleared her throat. "What if I buy you a house in the mountains? You could just disappear. Then I can visit in the warmer months?"

Leo pulled a cushion over his face while Tilly laughed. "I do like mountains," she joked.

"Do you have to visit?" Leo asked.

"I'll put that as a maybe." Jaini scribbled on the paper. "What if we fake your death? We'd make it heroic of course."

Matilda, listen.

Leo's face shot towards the staircase as a silver object was thrown down towards them. Tilly jumped over to Jaini and Leo sprang on top of them both.

A thick smoke released from the object.

Tilly pushed her shield around them, but it was no use, the smoke passed through and everything faded to black.

Chapter Eighteen

The Confession

Tilly opened her eyes, the room slowly came into focus. She was still in the safe house. Her wrists and ankles were tied to a chair in the living room, with her back facing the window. She tried to build her magic, but she couldn't feel it, she could barely feel Annora with her. Using what little strength she had, she tilted her head to the side. Leo and Jaini were tied to chairs beside her, they were both unconscious. Her head drooped back down.

"Ah, I thought you might be the first to wake up."

Tilly's heart sank as she clenched her eyes shut. "Conrad," she whispered. She should have known.

"You sound surprised. I thought you may have been smart enough to work it out."

She peered up at him as he strolled towards her, dressed in the same dark grey military uniform she was given. His black, peppered hair was tied back. Faris stalked into the room and stood beside him with a strained look on his face. He crossed his burly arms over his chest. Realisation dawned on Tilly. "It was you who arranged the attacks on Jaini."

Conrad's blue eyes glinted dangerously. He waved her off. "Yes, yes of course, but that was just as a favour for Councillor Ezra." He gave her a chilling smile. "This is about you."

"You bastards," Leo snarled. "What do you want with Tilly?"

Their faces all shot to Leo. He pulled at his ropes as his eyes burned with rage. Conrad tutted. "Ah, Leopold," he said sadly. "You should have left when I told you to, then we could have avoided this mess."

Leo bared his teeth and growled. Conrad chuckled at him. "Don't even bother trying to shift. I've injected each of you to keep your bodies weak." He rubbed his hands together and glanced between Leo and Tilly. "Now, we have much to discuss. It was most fortunate that you brought Tilly back to Everorb City with you Leopold." Conrad's eyes locked onto hers. "I knew who you were the moment we first met, you're almost a spitting image of dear Queen Alwyn."

Leo frowned. "Queen Alwyn?"

Tilly kept her eyes on Conrad. "She was my real mother."

Conrad looked down his nose at her. "I put you against Alerio and Faris to see what you could do—it was stupid of you to use your magic in that trial. And then you came to my office, fixated on the painting of Panthera. I told you about Torben just to see your reaction."

Tilly clenched her fists. "What do you want?"

His eyes flashed angrily. "What I've always wanted," he seethed. "Torben was meant to bring the Queen to me before you were born."

Leo's face fell. "Torben? Tell me it wasn't you who brought down Panthera."

Faris turned to Conrad in shock. "You did what?"

Conrad rolled his eyes, looking bored. "Of course it was me. Torben was a fool, he wasn't smart enough to pull off something like that."

"Why would Torben do that for you?" Faris asked.

Conrad scoffed. "I blackmailed him. He found his soulmate and wanted to leave the Five to be with her—so I had her held hostage and made him a deal he couldn't refuse." He glanced at Leo pathetically. "Sound familiar?"

"What was the deal?" Faris pressed.

Conrad frowned at him. "He was to rid the realm of Spirids and bring me the Queen, or I'd kill the woman he loved. It was the price he chose to pay to be with her." He strolled over to Leo, looking at him in disgust. "Love is the most powerful and dangerous thing of all, it makes it too easy to bend someone to your will. Is that how far you would go, Leopold? For Tilly?"

"Never," Leo snarled. "I would have killed you without a second thought."

Tilly gritted her teeth. "How did you do it? How did you bring down Panthera?"

Conrad looked at her smugly. "I'd read of a great army that sailed the seas. I sent Torben off to find them with crates of gold and the promise of living in a city of riches." Conrad paused, gazing out the window. "I gave them everything they needed. I created a compound that weakened Spirid magic and I weaponised it. The Calvarians gassed the city, once the Spirids lost their magic it was almost too easy."

"And the attacks around Valuna?" Faris asked.

Conrad sighed happily. "All brilliantly planned by me. How else do you think the assassins were able to track down every last Spirid the Guard was hiding?" He walked over to Tilly and lifted her chin. She jerked her head away. "Everything went to plan until Torben reached the palace. Alwyn met him at the door and blew it up in front of his eyes, we all thought you'd died in there with her."

"No," Tilly whimpered. She dropped her head as anger and despair burned through her body.

"You're a murderer," Leo shouted. "I can't believe I ever trusted you. You betrayed Panthera and you betrayed us."

Faris' eyes narrowed. "Why did you kill them?"

Conrad's face shot to his. "Why all the questions?" he spat. "They were dangerous. One bad Spirid could bring down a city if they wished to. I did Valuna a great service, we are safer without them."

Tilly lowered her voice threateningly. "You will pay for what you did to my mother and my people."

Leo raised his head shakily, his eyes fixed on Conrad. "You were jealous of their power, weren't you? You've never liked anything you couldn't control."

Conrad looked livid. "I never met a single Spirid who deserved that power. Why should they be capable of things we could only dream of?"

"And you think you deserve that power?" Jaini asked furiously. Tilly used all her strength to turn her face to Jaini. She looked groggy but she was unhurt.

Conrad bared his teeth. "It's my birthright!" he yelled.

"You're a Spirling," Tilly realised. "How?"

Conrad's jaw clenched. He paced in front of them. "My father was a Spirid and my Mother a pathetic human. She was so disappointed I didn't have magic, that she never even noticed my ability. She left me at a church when I was eight and never came back." He watched Tilly as he paced. "I spent the remainder of my adolescence living in that church, learning everything I could about Valuna. My knowledge and my photographic memory had me appointed as the youngest Historian there's ever been."

Leo shook his head in disgust. "Your mother's disappointment and abandonment are not a good enough reason for genocide. You killed an entire race."

Conrad stopped at the kitchen bench and lifted a needle from a small case. "Not all of them," he said casually. "I've one thing left to do before that happens." He walked over to Tilly and stood beside her.

"What are you doing? Don't touch her!" Leo growled.

"I'm taking what is rightfully mine," Conrad said. "The magic runs in my blood, it just needs a boost for me to access it."

Tilly's heart raced, she tried to move, but her body was too weak. She still couldn't feel her magic or Annora, the drugs were keeping them blocked. She felt the sting of the needle as Conrad jabbed it into her arm and drew her blood. "There's no way this is going to work Conrad," Tilly said.

Conrad's eyes shone wickedly. "I have a feeling it might. It didn't work with the other Spirids, but you have a powerful royal bloodline." He smiled gleefully. "And, you share my blood."

They all looked at Conrad in shock. "You're lying," Tilly hissed.

Conrad's grin widened. "As I said, almost a spitting image of Alwyn." He reached out and twirled a lock of Tilly's hair through his fingers. "Except for your black hair—you get that from me."

Faris shook his head. "That can't be true."

Conrad looked insulted. "Why would I lie? It wasn't a secret that Namir couldn't have children. Alwyn was so desperate for a baby she came to the Historians for help. They arranged a team to attempt artificial insemination and I switched the DNA. She never even knew."

Tilly squeezed her eyes shut, she felt like she was going to be sick.

"That's why you wanted the Queen's baby," Leo said. "All of this was for the magic."

"Of course it was, I saw an opportunity and I took it," Conrad said. "Tilly means nothing to me, she's just a tool to get what I need." He dug the needle deep into his skin and released the blood into his arm. They all watched in horror as Conrad's eyes turned white. He shuddered and fell to the ground.

"No," Tilly cried, she tried to build her magic again. She could feel it stir, but it wasn't enough.

Slowly he sat up and looked at his hands in awe. "I can feel it, it's weak from the drugs but it's finally mine." Conrad stood and met her eyes. "This magic was wasted on you. I will do greater things than anyone could possibly imagine. I will be worshipped." He paused dramatically, glancing between the three of them. "It's a shame none of you will be around to see it."

Leo pulled at his restraints. "There's no way you'll get away with this," he said. "Faris stop him, it's not too late."

Faris stepped towards them uncertainly. Conrad shot him a look. "You will stick to the plan or die with them. I've worked too hard for this."

"What's your plan?" Jaini asked. "You better not touch my city."

Conrad gave a hearty laugh. "No, I'll return to Everorb as a hero. Everyone will hear the tale of how I couldn't save you from the assassins, but with Tilly's dying breath she blessed me with her magic to save the city. Then I'll clear out Panthera and rule it along with the rest of the realm."

"You're delusional," Jaini whispered.

"A complete psychopath," Tilly agreed.

Conrad rested his hands on Tilly's chair, he was so close his nose almost touched hers. "I'm a little disappointed to be honest. Being my daughter and the last of your royal bloodline, I expected you to be capable of so much more."

Tilly felt magic and rage burn through her body, she glared at him with pure hatred in her eyes, not even recognising her own voice. "You have no idea what I'm capable of."

Release me.

A low growl erupted from Tilly's throat. Everyone cried out in shock as Annora shot from her chest and knocked Conrad to the ground. Her claws dug into his torso, she sank her teeth into the side of his face and ripped away the skin. Conrad's scream was cut off as he passed out cold. Annora tossed him aside and stalked towards Faris with blood dripping down her chin. Faris held up his hands and slowly backed away from her.

They heard the door fly open. Alerio came running down the stairs with his curved sword. He took one look around the room and lunged towards Faris, at the same time Annora pounced. Faris shifted and shot himself out the window. They all ducked as glass shattered around them.

Alerio landed at Annora's feet. He stared up at her in surprise and quickly bowed before her. Leo cleared his throat. "I think the bowing can wait Alerio, a little help would be great," he said casually.

Alerio hurried over to untie them. "I'm sorry I wasn't here sooner. Conrad sent me off on assignment but something didn't feel right, so I came straight back. Are you hurt?"

"We're fine," Leo said. "Just weak from the drugs."

Tilly rubbed her wrists as she watched Conrad bleed out on the stone floor. Tears burned her eyes, how could that disgusting man be her father? She thought back to when she had asked Celia who her father was—she had hesitated—now Tilly wondered if Celia had known the truth. Annora rubbed up against her gently.

Blood isn't everything. You are nothing like that man, Jack will always be your father.

"Thank you, Annora," Tilly whispered, hugging her against her chest. When she looked up everyone was watching them silently.

"What?" She looked down at herself, feeling a little ridiculous in her pyjamas.

Leo wrapped his arms around her and held her tight. "We've never seen a guardian like Annora," he said softly. "Snow leopards were incredibly rare, only the greatest rulers had them."

That is true. I had a snow leopard and I was a fierce ruler.

Alerio approached Annora slowly and ran his fingers down her back. "Annora as in Queen Annora? She was legendary." Annora bowed her head to him.

Leo rested his nose in Tilly's hair. "I'm so glad you're alright. I can't believe Conrad was behind all of this."

They looked down at Conrad's body. Alerio knelt beside him and clutched his wrist. "There's a pulse, it's weak but it's there." He glanced up at Tilly. "What would you like to do?"

Her magic flared, he deserved to die, but he also deserved to suffer for what he had done.

I agree, death would be a gift.

"Bandage him up. We'll publicly announce his crimes so he can suffer the consequences of his actions. If he does die on the way it's no real loss," she added coldly.

Leo kissed her forehead. "You even sound like a Queen."

Jaini smirked. "I knew she was out of your league."

Tilly slowly shook her head. "I'm no Queen."

"No," Alerio said quietly. "But you should have been, and you are still our Princess."

"Princess Tilly," Leo said. A flicker of playfulness returned to his eyes. "It has a nice ring to it."

Jaini patted him on the shoulder, looking smug. "It's actually Princess Matilda—you have a lot of catching up to do."

Leo glanced at Tilly in surprise. "Matilda?"

"Yes, Leopold, my name is Matilda," she said seriously.

Leo chuckled. "You'll always be my Tilly."

Leo caught Alerio up on everything that had happened after they left Everorb. Alerio frowned while he spoke, shaking his head. "The assassins all cleared out after you left and Conrad sent me on my way, it didn't make any sense."

Once the drugs had worn off, Alerio and Leo shifted. Alerio carefully lifted Conrad with his talons and flew out the broken window. Tilly and Jaini climbed onto Leo and he followed.

The sun shone down on them as they flew by the seaside. Tilly could feel Jaini behind her hiding from it. They landed on the cliff just before the bridge and Alerio and Leo wandered off to shift. Jaini looked at Tilly thoughtfully. "You should bring Annora back out," she said. "With Conrad out of the way, you don't need to hide who you are anymore."

Tilly looked at her uncertainly as Alerio emerged from behind a tree, carrying Conrad over his shoulder. "She's right," he said, as he headed towards them. "Not only that, the two of you would bring hope back to the Orbarians—and the rest of Valuna."

Leo's eyes met Tilly's as he joined them. "It's your choice, Til. Only do it if you're ready."

Tilly glanced up at the dome city, she didn't know if she was ready. Once the truth was out, everything would change. "What do you think Annora?" she whispered.

I think Conrad has been controlling the realm for too long. It's time for Valuna to know we are still here.

Tilly called Annora out. Alerio smiled and bowed his head. "You are brave to do this. You have no idea how much the royal family meant to this realm."

She gave him a small nod. Leo took her hand and they followed Alerio into the foyer. Two dozen soldiers lined the room. Tilly's eyebrows rose, the atmosphere was completely different from when Leo had first brought her to Everorb. The soldiers froze as they saw Annora, they quickly dropped to one knee and bowed their heads.

"What are they doing?" Tilly asked.

"They know you're royalty," Leo said amused.

Tilly felt her heart quicken. "Please stand up," she said.

They stood and stared at her in wonder. Alerio placed Conrad down on the desk. "Take Conrad to the hospital and keep him heavily guarded. Once he has recovered, he is to be arrested for the attempted murder of Princess Matilda, Councillor Zirk and Leopold of the Valunan Five. As well as the mass murder and destruction of Panthera."

There were gasps around the room. A group of soldiers took Conrad and rushed off to one of the black carriages. An Orbarian guard escorted Tilly and the others to a different carriage. The guard trembled as Annora stalked past him to climb in first.

I could get used to this.

Leo took the seat beside Tilly as Jaini and Alerio sat opposite them. Annora sat in the aisle. She kept a close watch on the nervous guard as the carriage shot towards the city. They all sat in silence, still shaken up by what had happened. Tilly was relieved they hadn't put Conrad in the same carriage, she never wanted to see him again. Leo stroked her hand as he gazed out the window, lost in thought. Jaini looked over at him with a confused look on her face. "Who will lead the Five now?" she asked.

"Alerio will," Leo said confidently. "He's the oldest and wisest of us. I think it's obvious that we should not be controlled by men."

Alerio considered. "I would be honoured, but I'll contact our brothers first and tell them what's happened. We will have a discussion between us." He glanced at Tilly. "Although, I think they will agree there are changes needing to be made."

They came to a stop and Alerio stepped out of the carriage first. He took Jaini's hand and helped her down before he reached for Tilly's hand. "I think we need to have a chat, will you come and see me later?"

Tilly nodded. "Of course, Alerio, whatever you need."

Leo looked between them and Alerio smiled at him. "Yes Leo, you too."

Annora stalked ahead, she nipped at one of the guards playfully, making him yelp. Tilly laughed. "Annora!"

He didn't bow before me.

Tilly shook her head. "I'll send you back in," she threatened. Annora went and stood beside her sulkily, but Tilly could sense her amusement.

Alerio and Leo stopped to speak to the guards. Jaini pulled Tilly aside and lowered her voice. "While we were tied up and almost murdered, I was wondering something," she said nervously. "Do you think Cali would go on a date with me?"

Tilly looked at her in surprise. "I think Cali would squeal her head off if you asked her."

Jaini smiled fondly. "She is very cute like that."

"Cali is fun and kind and so are you, you should definitely ask her."

Jaini nodded to herself uncertainly.

They followed Leo and Alerio into the dome and froze. A crowd had already gathered around the entrance, some of them holding up cameras and phones. The Orbarians gasped and whispered as they saw Annora. Jaini gave an amused laugh. "News travels fast in the dome—the guards who took Conrad must have told everyone."

Orbarians and humans spilled out of their towers. Tilly watched the ruling families approach with wide eyes. She spotted Cali standing with other soldiers. Cali smiled in disbelief and gave her a small wave. Tilly smiled back and tried not to laugh at her expression. Piper stood near Cali and looked as if she were about to faint.

Annora stood forward and raised her head proudly. Tilly tried to shrink back but Jaini nudged her forward. Alerio came and stood beside her and the crowd fell silent. "You are in the presence of Her Royal Highness, Princess Matilda Hazelwood, daughter of the late Queen Alwyn Hazelwood," he said loudly. "Our Military Historian, Conrad Golding, has been taken into custody after he confessed to orchestrating the attack on Panthera. As well as the assassination attempt of Councillor Jaini Zirk on Councillor Ezra's behalf." Jaini lifted her chin as guards pushed through the crowd and took Councillor Ezra away. Alerio glanced down at Tilly. "Let it be known that from this day forward, the Valunan Five officially remove ourselves from the Historian's rule. We pledge our allegiance to Princess Matilda and vow to protect her, along with the rest of Valuna, on our own terms. This is the start of a new era."

The crowd cheered as Tilly glanced at Alerio in shock. He placed his hand over his heart and knelt on one knee. Leo and Jaini followed, along with the people of Everorb City. Tilly didn't know what to say, she had the city at her feet. She had never expected this and she never asked for it, but looking around at the people bowing before her, she knew she would do anything to protect them.

This is who you were born to be. You don't have to say anything, but maybe you could show them.

Tilly smiled, she wasn't sure if it would work, but she held out her left hand and closed her eyes. She imagined lily of the valley flowers floating down over the city. She flowed her magic and slowly waved her right hand down. When she opened her eyes it looked like snow was falling inside the dome. Orbarians cried her name and children jumped and giggled as they tried to catch the tiny flowers. Leo stood beside her and took her hand. "And to think I found you barefoot in the forest—bullying the trees."

Tilly laughed as he brought her hand to his mouth and kissed it softly.

That was perfect, Matilda.

Chapter Nineteen

The Future

Tilly, Leo and Alerio arrived at Headquarters. Jaini had insisted she was fine and just needed to rest, so they'd sent her home with a small army of soldiers—Cali had joined them. Alerio turned to them both as they walked through the foyer. "Give me an hour, then meet me in Conrad's office." He gave them a small smile before he hurried off.

Leo took Tilly's hand and led her down the corridor towards the Five's suites. She glanced up at him anxiously, he'd hardly said a word since they'd returned to Everorb. He stopped at a black door at the end of the hall and entered a code in the keypad. A warmth filled Tilly's chest as she stepped inside. Leo's apartment had a calm, industrial feel, with an exposed brick wall, raw timber furniture and a lot of black. Black and white framed photos decorated the rooms and a black, caged pendant light hung over the timber dining table. She spotted his bedroom and headed towards it curiously. His king-sized bed rested against the bricks, with a large black and white photo of a mountain range hung above it. Timber bookshelves took up the whole side wall, they were crammed full of books. Tilly looked at them with amazement and stopped to read some of the titles. "I could spend weeks in here," she muttered.

Leo stopped behind her and wrapped his arms around her waist. "I'd like that," he said softly.

She glanced down at his bed and laughed. "I meant reading your books."

He shook his head seriously. "No, you've already said it. You want to spend weeks in my bedroom."

Tilly turned to face him, holding back a smile. "Is that all you think about?"

"Hmm, not always," he said. He kissed her forehead. "Just when I'm near you, or see you, or think about you."

She grinned and leaned up to kiss him. His arms tightened around her. She suddenly noticed the worry in his eyes, it was the same look he'd had after finding her in Lord Dalton's mansion. "Are you okay?" she asked gently.

He gave a half smile. "You mean, after finding out a man I've looked up to my whole life is a lying, psychopathic murderer? And the woman I love was born to be Queen of us all? It's just another day for me." He sighed and buried his face in the curve of her neck. "I can't tell you how sorry I am. I feel so stupid for bringing you here and showing you off to everyone, I just wanted to help you follow your dreams. If I knew you were a Spirid I would have kept you hidden."

Tilly's heart sank. "Hey, it's not your fault," she said. "You couldn't have known about Conrad, you have nothing to be sorry for."

He eyed her sadly. "What about you? Are you okay?"

She frowned and sat on the edge of the bed, sinking into the soft, black sheets. "Surprisingly I am," she said. "Don't get me wrong, I'm horrified by what Conrad did and what he tried to do to us, but I know he will suffer for it." Leo sat beside her as she shook her head slowly. "It makes me sick to think he's my biological father, but honestly, I'll never think of him that way. Jack and Edith are my parents and he can't ever take that away from me."

Leo watched her affectionately. "You're an incredibly strong woman, do you know that?"

Tilly grinned and flowed her magic, she pushed him down onto the bed and straddled him. Leo laughed in surprise. "You mean this kind of strong?" she teased.

His eyes darkened. "You've been holding out on me, here I was trying to be gentle with you."

She raised her eyebrows. "You were being gentle?"

In one move he flipped them over so he was lying on top of her. "You have no idea," he said against her neck. He kissed her while pushing his body against hers, making her moan softly. Leo sat up and studied her face. "I can't believe you're our Princess, no one even knew you were born," he said sadly. "So much has been taken away from you, you should have had an incredible life."

Tilly leaned up on her elbows. "I'm happy with my life, Leo, everything that's happened has led me to you. I didn't even know I was a Princess until recently." She glanced away and frowned.

"But?" he asked softly.

She thought about Torben and the Calvarian Assassins living in Panthera, her magic sparked with anger. Annora growled as her own rage mixed with Tilly's. Tilly took a deep breath and tried to calm herself down. "I want to see Panthera with my own eyes. I want to find Torben and avenge my people."

Spoken like a true Queen.

"I don't care about wearing a crown," Tilly added, "but if there's a chance to save Panthera, I'll take it."

"You really mean it," he said. A look of determination crossed his face. "If that's what you want, we'll do it together. I'll be by your side, no matter what."

"You would come with me?" she asked in surprise.

Leo looked offended, he placed his hand over his heart and held her gaze. "I Leopold, of the Valunan Five, pledge my life to you, Princess Matilda Hazelwood. I vow to love, protect and worship you every day, for as long as I live."

Tears filled Tilly's eyes. "Can you do that?" she whispered. "Will you be allowed to come with me?"

He smiled. "Alerio already pledged us to you, this is how it should be. Before Panthera fell we worked with Conrad, but we answered to the Crown. Besides, I'd like to see anyone try and stop me."

Where was this man when I was alive?

Tilly laughed through her tears. "I think Annora is as much in love with you as I am." Leo chuckled and jumped off the bed. "Hey, come back," she sulked.

"You just reminded me, I want to show you something." He scanned through his bookshelf and pulled out a worn, leather-bound book with gold letters embossed on the front. He flicked through the pages and passed it to her. Tilly peered down at a drawing of a warrior Queen with her sword raised. She wore impressive plate armour and a matching crown. A pile of dead bodies laid at her feet and her snow leopard guardian was attacking a soldier in front of her. Tilly read the caption, 'Queen Annora and her Guardian Myra. The battle for Moonee Cove.'

That drawing is inaccurate, there were many more dead bodies.

Tilly looked up at Leo, he was smiling. "Queen Annora saved the Orbarians from greedy humans, it was her idea to build Everorb City to protect them. She never took a husband, but she had four children and ruled on her own. She's a legend."

I would have taken him as my husband if he were alive.

Tilly scoffed.

"What?" he said amused.

"She said she would have taken you as a husband."

Leo laughed loudly. "I'm flattered."

Tilly called Annora out and she sat by Leo. She rubbed her head against him as he stroked behind her ear. Tilly shook her head at them both. "You were quite a rebel Annora, you never told me any of this."

I didn't want to intimidate you. I knew you'd find out eventually.

Tilly closed the book and held it to her chest. "You can keep that," Leo said. "It's the history of Panthera."

She hugged it tighter. "I love it, thank you."

They walked through Headquarters hand in hand as Annora stalked ahead. Soldiers pressed up against the wall and bowed their heads as she passed. Tilly leaned towards Leo, lowering her voice. "I don't think I'll ever get used to this."

"No, I've been getting bowed to since I was a child and I'm still not used to it," he admitted.

They reached Conrad's office and knocked. Alerio opened the door and led them over to the bar. "Can I make you both a drink?" he asked.

Annora curled up on a soft rug as Tilly and Leo took a seat around a small table. "Sure, thank you," Tilly said.

Alerio's face lit up. He pulled out different bottles and

poured them into three glasses. Leo watched curiously as Alerio passed the green drinks around and took a seat opposite them. "I've always wanted to do that," Alerio said happily. Tilly took a sip of her drink and tried not to spit it out—it was awful—she placed it on the table.

Leo laughed. "You're full of surprises Alerio."

Alerio smiled at him fondly, he glanced over at Tilly and his smile dropped. "I'm very sorry little one, about everything. I must admit, I'd also guessed who you were when you arrived."

Leo threw his hands up in disbelief. "Did all of you know?"

Tilly's eyes widened. "You knew?"

"Yes," Alerio said. "We lived in Panthera remember, we fought alongside Spirids. I'm sure Faris would have guessed too."

"Why didn't you say anything?" Leo asked.

Alerio ran his hand over his shaved head. "It wasn't my place. I knew how dangerous it would be for Tilly if it were true," he said. "To be honest with you both, I've been watching Conrad for the past few years. It's why I asked to stay here and be more involved in military training."

"You suspected him?" Tilly asked.

He nodded. "The Historians benefited more than anyone from the fall of Panthera—Conrad in particular. Having control of the Five is a lot of power for one man. I was never able to prove anything though, he was very careful." Alerio's eyes darkened. "As I was leaving last night, I realised he was the only one who could have hidden the Calvarians in the city."

"How is he?" Leo asked quietly.

"Alive, but in an induced coma while he heals. When he's strong enough we'll transfer him to a high-security prison."

"Any word from Faris?" Leo asked.

Alerio leaned forward, resting his elbows on his thighs. "Nothing, I'd be surprised if that traitor ever shows his face again."

"I always thought he was a bastard," Leo said bitterly, "but I never thought he'd turn his back on his brothers."

Tilly glanced between them. "I'm not sure Faris was involved in everything. He didn't know about Torben and he seemed to genuinely consider coming to free us."

"I noticed that too," Leo admitted.

"Until we can find him, we won't know for certain what part he played." Alerio sat up straight. "Now, the reason I've asked you here. I've spoken to our brothers. Hojin and Denz have both asked if I will lead the Five."

He will make an excellent leader.

"That's perfect, you deserve this," Leo said enthusiastically.

Alerio nodded to him gratefully. "Thank you, we all agree that the Historians will have no part in our future. We also agreed that Faris will be replaced," he said. "By Princess Matilda."

"Me?" Tilly asked in shock.

Annora came and sat by her side as Leo beamed at her. Alerio's eyes softened. "I don't have the authority to give you your rightful crown, but I can offer you a place with us. You've had everything taken from you and have still shown your dedication to protecting our people. There's no one who deserves this more."

He's proving me right already.

"Thank you, I don't know what to say," she whispered.

"Obviously we can't make you a shapeshifter. I doubt it would even work since you're already a Spirid, but you would be one of us in every way that mattered," Alerio said.

"That would be a dream come true."

Alerio's eyes gleamed mischievously. "There's something else. When you join the Valunan Five, you commit yourself to your brothers and to the realm. If you're one of us, I don't see any reason why the two of you couldn't be together—you're technically more than honouring your commitment to each other."

Leo took Tilly's hand and kissed it. Tilly beamed at him. "I'll join you," she said excitedly.

Alerio chuckled. "Good, because the other two are already on their way here for your ceremony."

Leo grinned at Alerio. "This means everything to us, I can't thank you enough."

Alerio looked between them. "It's obvious nothing can keep you two apart and I wouldn't want it to. You're soulmates."

Leo frowned. "Conrad shrugged it off when I told him about it, he said I was sensing a strong mate and it happened all the time." He met Tilly's eyes. "I knew it was more than that."

"He lied to you," Alerio said. "Spirids can sense their soulmates, our blessing means we can too." His eyes turned distant. "I only know because I found mine as well."

Tilly's smile faded. "Where are they?"

"She's gone. She lived in Panthera, I would have married her in a heartbeat, but I knew my duty and the consequences, so I ignored it." He dropped his face into his hands. "I regret it every day of my life."

"I'm so sorry Alerio," Tilly said.

Leo leaned forward and held his arm. "I never knew."

Alerio smiled sadly. "Thank you both. I never got my chance at love, but at least I can give you yours." Tilly stood and hugged him, catching him by surprise. He chuckled and patted her on the back. "Alwyn would have been so proud of you," he whispered.

"We want to go there," Leo said suddenly. "To Panthera. Tilly wants to see it with her own eyes and I want to go with her."

Alerio's expression turned amused. "I was expecting this—and I agree. None of us have seen it since it was taken over. Conrad's so-called scouts never survived the trip. Of course, it makes sense now as to why he refused to send one of us."

"I can hide us," Tilly said. "We can sneak in and find out what we're up against."

"Yes," Alerio said. "I think we all need to see it for ourselves, I know Hojin and Denz will want to come too. We'll make the arrangements after your ceremony, but this stays between us."

Leo glanced at Tilly and squeezed her hand. They discussed the details of her ceremony before Alerio sent them on their way.

Tilly and Leo walked back to Tilly's suite, once inside, Leo pulled her to his chest and kissed the top of her head. "That chat with Alerio was not what I expected at all," he admitted.

"Are you disappointed?" she teased.

"Are you kidding? This is the best day of my life." They beamed at each other and he leaned down to kiss her, she pulled him closer, not wanting the kiss to end. "There's something I want to do," he said with a low voice.

"Yes," she breathed. "Right now."

Leo chuckled, gliding his lips along her neck. "Is that all you think about, Matilda?"

"Only since I met you," she admitted, closing her eyes.

Leo laughed. "It's not that, go get ready and I'll be back soon."

"Ready for what?"

"You'll see." He kissed her forehead and hurried out the door.

Tilly looked at Annora. "Any idea what he's talking about?"

No, but you definitely can't wear pants.

Tilly smiled and shook her head. She went and took a long shower before changing into a black, backless midi-dress. She picked out some green earrings, matching green heels and dark red lipstick. As she got ready she played back the conversation with Alerio in her mind. Despite everything that had happened, she was feeling on top of the world. She never could have imagined she would be joining the Valunan Five and spending her life with Leo. Everything felt like it was falling into place.

It's the life you deserve.

Tilly pulled her hair down and brushed it into light waves around her. She felt tingles down her neck and glanced up. Leo stood in the doorway wearing a black shirt and pants, the top button of his shirt undone. He eyed her body in the mirror and ran his finger down her bare back. "I'm nearly tempted to keep you here all night."

Tilly closed her eyes. "That's fine by me."

He laughed softly and spun her around, his eyes glinting excitedly. "I'll spend the rest of my life devouring you. Tonight we're celebrating."

"What's the occasion?"

He grabbed her backside and pulled her against him. "That I can now tell the whole of Valuna you're mine, and you're so badarse that you'll be the first woman in history to join the Five."

I'm so proud.

Leo took her to the Ruby Tower—the same tower Cali had taken her clubbing. This time they went inside and took the lift up to the top floor. They entered a rooftop restaurant where the glass walls and ceiling were shaped like a dome, showing off the night sky and the rest of the city. Soft, shining orbs hung at different heights above the tables, giving the room a warm glow. An Orbarian waiter appeared and bowed before them nervously. "Good evening your Highness, Sir, please follow me."

Tilly looked at Leo with excitement. "We're eating."

He threw his head back and laughed. "I knew you'd be excited. You might recall, I actually owe you a meal."

Tilly grinned at him. "Does this mean you admit defeat?"

He bit his lip. "Pulling your ankle out from under you was pretty desperate."

Tilly laughed as the waiter took them to a private booth beside the window. Dark candles and dahlias decorated the table. They sat opposite each other and Leo reached across the table for her hand. "Do you mind if I order for us?" he asked.

"Go ahead," she said curiously. He asked for the five-course set menu and Tilly's eyes lit up.

"I thought you'd enjoy trying a bit of everything."

"I am definitely in love with you," she whispered.

"And all I had to do was feed you," he teased.

She smirked. "You've done a lot more than that."

The waiter cleared his throat, his eyes lingered on the ceiling—he looked like he would rather be anywhere else but there. "Can I get you something to drink?"

Leo smiled politely. "Champagne please." The waiter nodded and rushed away.

Tilly cringed. "I forgot he was standing there."

"So did I. You're very distracting."

She laughed and glanced out the window, she was starting to feel nervous about the ceremony tomorrow. "What are Denz and Hojin like?"

"They're a lot of fun, you're going to love them. Denz is too charming for his own good. He calls himself the sexiest of the Five and will probably try to steal you from me. Hojin is quiet and friendly, but he's also sneaky."

Tilly smiled. "You sound fond of them."

"They're like real brothers to me, they taught me everything I know."

"Denz is a lynx, right? And Hojin a tiger?"

Leo nodded. "They're our best hunters, which is why they're almost always on assignment."

"I'm excited to meet them," Tilly said.

The waiter returned with their champagne and Leo lifted his glass. "To you, Til. You've accomplished so much. You should be proud of yourself, I certainly am."

Tilly's heart swelled in her chest. "I couldn't have done it without you."

He took her hand and brought it to his lips. "I think you could have, but I'm glad you let me come along for the ride."

"I'm the one who's glad, you could have left me in Silverleaf City," she teased.

Leo shook his head. "I'd still be there if you hadn't left. Your parents would definitely be sick of me visiting by now," he added.

Tilly laughed and then her face dropped. "I never asked, how did you keep Lord Dalton distracted for so long?" Leo lifted his glass and took a long sip. Tilly raised her eyebrows.

"Was it bad?" she asked with surprise.

He stared up at the orb lights above them. "I shifted and chased him around his ridiculously large mansion."

Tilly burst out laughing. "You didn't! Can't you get in trouble for that?"

His eyes darkened. "He was the one in trouble. I ordered a search after seeing those disturbing photos and he was arrested a few days later. He had women locked up in the basement."

"He didn't," Tilly whispered.

Leo's jaw clenched. "It's no wonder you were afraid of him. He was an evil bastard."

"Those poor women," Tilly said, wrapping her arms around herself. "I'm glad he's locked away."

Leo met her eyes. "I would have killed him if he'd hurt you."

She reached over and squeezed his hand. "He didn't though, you saved me." Her eyes turned playful. "And now that I'm joining the Five, you can teach me how to make an entrance like you did."

Leo laughed loudly. "Of course, right after you learn the power poses."

They both laughed as the waiter returned with their entrees, he was trying hard not to look either of them in the eye. Tilly looked out towards the city. She wondered how much longer they would stay here, she'd grown to love Everorb. "We'll come back," Leo said. "I want to show you the whole realm, just like you've always wanted."

She tucked her hair behind her ear. "How did you know what I was thinking?"

"I could tell by the look on your face."

Leo stood up and shuffled into the booth beside her. They ate and drank together, talking about their friends and everything that had happened while they were apart. It was the best food she'd ever had. The final course was a tray of small, assorted cakes, decorated with colourful sugar crystals and gold foil.

Leo took her hand and led her out to a balcony, it was even more humid that high up in the dome. Tilly rested her head on his shoulder as they watched the glowing city together. "So how did I do?" he asked. "On our first date?"

She gave him a playful smile. "It was almost perfect."

His eyebrows shot up. "Almost?"

Tilly leaned up and kissed him. "Now it's perfect."

Chapter Twenty

The Happy Ending

Tilly paced Jaini's beauty room restlessly. She'd heard that Hojin and Denz had arrived earlier that morning—as well as countless citizens of Valuna. Alerio had told her that the news of a surviving Spirid royal had spread far and wide. Flocks of people had shown up in Everorb City, all wanting to see for themselves. Tilly stopped in front of the mirror and examined her reflection. Her eye makeup was dark and her black hair ran down her back in soft curls. Jaini had dressed her in a black, floor-length embroidered dress with a high neckline and short sleeves. The dress almost looked like armour. Tilly hung her mother's moonstone amulet around her neck and clasped her dainty charm bracelet around her wrist. She wasn't sure how she felt about wearing a dress to the ceremony—considering the Valunan Five were elite soldiers. Jaini draped an arm around Tilly's shoulders. "Stop worrying, it's perfect. You're an icon for badarse women around the realm."

She's right.

Cali appeared on her other side. "Are you sure you won't wear the matching crown?" she asked hopefully.

Tilly felt her chest tighten. "Definitely not."

Cali looked disappointed, but Jaini smirked and shook her head. "You'll have to wear it one day, Princess."

Tilly pulled an unimpressed face and they both laughed. Jaini and Cali left her alone in front of the mirror while they kept getting ready.

Will you just try it on? I'd like to see it.

Tilly glanced down at the crown, it was made of delicate gold and embellished with black gemstones. She slowly lifted it from the cushion and placed it on her head. Her heart quickened as she stared back at her reflection, she still hadn't come to terms with this side of herself.

Princess Matilda of the Valunan Five. I've never been prouder.

"It feels like a bit much," Tilly whispered.

She hadn't noticed Cali behind her, watching. "You may not feel like a Princess," Cali said quietly, "but you definitely look like one."

Jaini pulled her phone out excitedly and took a photo of Tilly. "For my vision board," she stated. "Tilly as Queen."

Tilly scoffed—the thought made her feel nauseous. An Orbarian guard appeared in the doorway and cleared his throat. "They are ready for you, your Highness."

Tilly closed her eyes, she pictured the snowy mountains of Panthera and tried to centre herself for a moment, she felt a calmness settle over her body. Tilly took a deep breath before she followed the guard out of the room.

They all took the lift down to the ground floor. The ceremony was being held near the marketplace, allowing anyone to attend. Jaini and Cali gave her a quick hug and left to take their seats under the dome. Leo was waiting by the door, his playful expression turned to astonishment when he saw Tilly. He approached her slowly and knelt at her feet, taking her hand. "What are you doing?" she asked nervously.

"Worshipping you," he whispered.

"You're freaking me out."

You're still wearing the crown.

"Oh my god, I totally forgot."

She went to pull the crown off, but Leo jumped up and grabbed her hand. "Don't you dare," he said seriously.

Tilly laughed. "I am not leaving this thing on Leo. Annora just wanted to see it."

He steered her towards the door. "Yes you are, you look perfect. This is part of who you are."

Her smile dimmed and she stopped in the doorway. "I feel like I don't deserve it," she said quietly. "The crown, that is."

Leo's eyes softened in understanding. "I know what you mean," he said. "I felt the same when I first joined the Five."

She raised her eyebrows, she hadn't expected him to say that. "How did you deal with it?"

"By proving to myself every day, that I did deserve it and you can do the same. It's not about wearing the crown, it's about what you can do with it—how many people you can help."

Tilly smiled at him, wondering if it was possible to love him any more than she already did. "And you call Alerio the wise one," she teased.

Leo grinned and took her hand. "I have my moments."

Tilly had never seen so many people in Everorb City. Soldiers had to part the crowd and form a path to the marketplace. Tilly held her head high, smiling and waving as they made their way through the lively crowd. The streets had been decorated with garlands of purple dahlias and twinkling lights. The stage slowly came into view, with the same garlands wrapped around the base. Alerio was waiting for them at the top of the stairs. When they reached him, he gave her a tight hug. "Our Princess, this will be a memorable day for Valuna."

"Thanks, Alerio, for everything," Tilly said earnestly.

He gripped her forearm and leaned closer. "Leo's been quite busy too." Alerio motioned towards the front row and Tilly almost jumped off the stage. Her mother and father were seated next to Jaini and Cali. They smiled up at her with tears running down their cheeks.

Tilly smiled back tearfully and turned to Leo. "Thank you," she whispered.

He kissed her forehead and went and took his place beside Hojin and Denz. The brothers were dressed in black with their hands crossed in front of them, showing off their gold rings. Hojin and Denz were both well-built and almost as tall as Leo. Hojin had warm skin, cunning, dark brown eyes and long black hair tied up behind his head. Tilly could see why Denz called himself the sexy one. He was tanned with dark blonde, neatly styled hair and a chiselled face. He had bright green eyes that any woman could lose herself in—the cocky expression on his face told her that he knew it too. Tilly joined Alerio behind the podium and Denz's face dropped, he leaned over to Leo looking stunned. "How the hell did you manage that?" he asked. Leo beamed at him, his eyes shining with pride. Tilly glanced away, feeling her face flush.

Alerio held up his hand to silence the crowd. "Welcome friends," he said loudly. "Thank you all for joining us on this monumental day. It is my great pleasure to introduce you all to our chosen sister, Princess Matilda Norris-Hazelwood and her guardian, Annora. Matilda has proven herself in heart and in battle. We accept her today as one of us, pledging our lives to her, until our last breath. While our past may be shadowed in darkness, our future will be blinding with her by our side."

Tilly took her place at the front of the stage and called Annora out. Annora pounced from her chest, materialising before the crowd. They cheered as she stalked up and down the stage before standing at Tilly's side. Tilly placed her hand over her heart and glanced down at her parents, she could see the pride in their eyes. As she looked over at Jaini, Cali and the rest of the crowd, she saw the same, a mix of pride and hope. Her magic burned steadily in her chest. "I, Princess Matilda Astara Norris-Hazelwood, stand before you today to pledge my life to the Valunan Five. I promise to protect Valuna with everything I have and vow to uphold the values of the Five. I will stand beside them in war, and in celebration, and give my life freely for theirs. I pledge my life today, knowing the honour and sacrifice that comes with this duty."

Leo stepped forward and pulled a velvet box from his pocket. His lion ring gleamed on his hand as he pulled out a dainty ring from the box. Tilly watched his eyes turn to fire as he slowly slid it over her finger. Her heart quickened, and for a moment she forgot about everyone around them, it was just her and Leo. When he stood back with his brothers, she glanced down at the golden ring—two crossed daggers beneath a snow leopard's face, its eyes made of opals.

Perfect.

Alerio joined his brothers and Tilly approached each of them. They placed a hand on each other's shoulder and repeated the same sentence. "I pledge myself to you, Brother, I will protect

Valuna by your side, until my last breath," she said.

When it was Leo's turn, she noticed his eyes sparkle as she said Brother—it took all of her strength not to laugh. After the pledge, they each shifted into their animal forms. Alerio the wise, harpy eagle. Leo the powerful, regal lion. Hojin the majestic tiger and Denz the free-spirited lynx. Tilly stood beside them while Annora stalked to each brother and pressed her forehead against theirs. Tilly raised her eyebrows when she lingered around Leo longer than the others.

I'm so happy he's ours.

Tilly cleared her throat to cover her laugh. When Annora finished, the four brothers spread their wings and took off over the crowd. People cheered and threw flowers in the air while they soared around the dome. Tilly beamed up at them, she wanted to remember this moment forever.

Get on my back.

Annora stopped in front of her and crouched down. Tilly climbed onto her back and held on as she pounced off the stage, startling the crowd. Annora stalked down the aisle, moving from side to side so people could run their hands through her fur. Leo landed beside her and she rubbed her head up against him. The crowd parted and Leo took off through the city. Annora sprinted after him, quickly catching up while Tilly held on for her life. "This is terrifying," Tilly said.

Yes, we probably should have practiced this.

She laughed and watched Leo take off into the air. "What a showoff!"

He looked back and bared his teeth in a grin. Annora took Tilly back to the stage and stopped in front of her parents. Tilly jumped off and threw her arms around them.

"Just look at you," Edith sobbed. "We had no idea you were

our Princess—Celia told us after you left."

Jack chuckled beside her ear. "You should have seen your mother when she found out, she was fretting about her parenting and all the chores she used to make you do."

Tilly laughed. "Your parenting was great—I didn't care about the chores."

Jaini joined in on the hug, wrapping her arms around the three of them. "This is excellent. I've always wanted a big family."

Cali squealed and joined in too. "This is the best day of my life," she bellowed. Tilly laughed tearfully, she couldn't remember ever feeling so happy.

Leo appeared back in human form, now wearing his dark military uniform. Edith noticed him and stepped back to fix her hair.

See, it's not just me. That man is perfection.

Leo held his hand out towards them. "Mr and Mrs Norris, I'm Leo, it's great to finally meet you both."

Jack smiled and pulled him into a hug, surprising them all. "Thank you for looking after our girl, and for bringing us here." Leo took Edith's hand and kissed it, she fanned her face and Jack chuckled at her.

"I can't believe you're here," Tilly said to her parents. "Where are you staying?"

"With me of course," Jaini said. "We have a lot to discuss. Did you bring baby photos, Edith?"

Edith looked at her in surprise. "Actually, I did. I thought Leo would like to see them."

"Shit," Tilly muttered.

Leo laughed and wrapped his arm around Tilly's waist. "You were right, we would love to see them." Tilly's eyes narrowed.

Leo bit his lip, barely holding back a smile. "Has anyone told you you're adorable when you're mad?"

She shook her head at him. "Unbelievable." Annora nudged Edith's arm, Edith nervously reached out to stroke her ears. "I tried to call you yesterday. When did you get here?" Tilly asked.

"This morning," Edith said, she looked at Leo gratefully. "Leo arranged everything for us."

"We got to fly in one of the military planes," Jack said excitedly.

Tilly glanced at Leo. "How did you pull that off?"

He shrugged. "I said they were precious cargo."

Tilly laughed at him. "What are you both doing now?" she asked. "Can I show you around?"

Jaini cut in. "Excuse me? We have an after-party to attend."

"What after-party?" Tilly asked.

Jaini looked horrified. "Obviously yours. Leo tried to plan it but don't worry, I jumped in and saved the day."

Leo sighed, shaking his head. "I do know how to throw a party, Jaini."

Tilly elbowed him playfully. "Well, thanks for trying."

Jaini shooed them away. "Off you go, I'm taking Mum and Dad back to mine so we can freshen up. You two go get ready—I've had a dress delivered to your suite."

Tilly groaned. "Another dress? What's wrong with this one?"

Jaini looked her up and down. "That's much too formal, we're going clubbing."

Tilly scoffed and gave her parents a tight hug. "I'll see you soon," she whispered. "Sorry about Jaini."

Edith chuckled. "We really like her, see you soon dear."

Tilly pulled her heels off as they arrived back at her suite. "Finally," she said, feeling instantly relieved. Leo made his way to the bar to grab a bottle of champagne. Annora went and sat by the window, watching the city below. Tilly sat on the couch and pulled her daggers out from under her dress, placing them on the coffee table. Leo chuckled at her. "You are the strangest girl I've ever met."

She smirked. "Thanks, you're not too bad yourself."

He took a seat beside her and passed her a glass. She took a slow sip as he trailed kisses up her shoulder. "We have a bit of time before we have to leave," he said. "What would you like to do, your Highness?"

She placed the glass down on the opal coffee table. "I can think of a few things," she whispered. She leaned forward to meet his lips, kissing him deeply and slipping her tongue between his teeth. He groaned and pulled her on top of him.

I'll be having a nap in the other room if you need me.

Tilly laughed and they watched Annora stalk off to the bedroom. "I'm surprised she didn't try to stay and watch," she joked.

I can come back if you like.

Tilly's eyes widened. "No, that's fine! Thank you, Annora."

Leo laughed as he pulled her dress up over her head and threw it to the floor. Tilly reached for his pants, undoing them and springing him free. His fingers tightened around her underwear, he ripped them off and tossed the pieces of lace aside. Tilly raised her eyebrows. "Did they offend you?"

Leo smirked. "Yes. They were in my way." Tilly laughed, she went to pull the crown off and he stopped her. "Leave it," he whispered. He unhooked her bra, kissing her breasts as she positioned herself on top of him. She burned her magic and pressed down hard against him. Leo's arm snaked up her back, he held the back of her neck as he ran his mouth along her throat. Tilly arched her back, gliding herself over him again and again.

Leo laid her back on the couch. He wrapped her legs up around his neck and pushed himself deep inside her. She cried out loudly, making him pause. "Don't stop," she said.

He kept going, staring down at her as he went. He definitely wasn't being gentle anymore and she loved it. Tilly felt the pleasure begin to build. Leo stroked her with his fingertip while thrusting in and out. She couldn't hold on any longer, her body tightened and she shuddered as she came around him.

Tilly pulled her legs down and tried to catch her breath, her body was still tingling. Leo lifted her up and brought his lips to hers, he carried her to the bathroom without breaking the kiss. He set her down in the shower and turned the tap on. Tilly squealed as the cold water hit her shoulder. Leo laughed loudly as he pulled his clothes off and hopped in with her, holding her against him as the water warmed up. Tilly's heart was racing, she loved the feeling of Leo's body against hers. She looked up into his eyes, she could see the love in them, as well as the joy. She knew she would never get enough of this man.

She leaned up to kiss him. He lifted her against the wall, holding her up by her thighs and sliding inside her. She moaned and wrapped her fingers through his hair. Leo held her tight, pushing himself in and out of her as the water ran down his back. Tilly closed her eyes, crying out as she felt herself release again. Leo finished with her. He sighed with contentment and rested his forehead against hers. Tilly smiled to herself, if the rest of her life was spent fighting for her realm and loving him, it would be a fulfilling life.

"What are you thinking?" he asked quietly.

She opened her eyes. He was watching her with his shy smile that she loved. "That I couldn't have asked for a better life than this," she said.

His smile widened, he placed her down and stroked her back under the water. "I was just thinking the same thing."

Tilly and Leo took the bridge to the Opal Tower—deciding to avoid the crowded city. Tilly was wearing the slate blue, silk mini-dress Jaini had left for her, it had thin straps with a bodice coated in diamonds. Leo wore chinos with a tight-fitting white shirt and boots. They caught the lift down to the basement, entering a room with neon lights running under a transparent floor. Muffled music could be heard behind a large, silver door. A security guard opened it and ushered them inside.

Tilly felt like she had entered a cave rave, the nightclub was packed and the music pulsed through her body. Neon lights ran underneath the entire floor. The walls were made of rock and the largest crystal formations she had ever seen. Orbarians glittered in every direction, dancing to the hypnotic beat, their silver eyes glowing in the dim light. Leo took her hand and led her to a staircase. Orbarians bowed their heads as they passed. They went upstairs to a private room with glass walls overlooking the rest of the club. Tilly's family and friends were all standing around small bar tables, holding drinks.

"Surprise!" Cali yelled, holding up her drink. From the look on her face, Tilly guessed it wasn't her first. Tilly burst out laughing as everyone looked at Cali strangely. "Wasn't it a surprise?" Cali asked confused. Jaini glanced at her lovingly before smiling at Tilly. Tilly noticed they were holding hands.

Edith and Jack pulled Tilly into a hug. They were both very nicely dressed—she was sure Jaini had something to do with it. "You two look amazing, I can't believe you're in a nightclub," Tilly teased.

Jack started dancing awkwardly and Edith bobbed her head. "You should have seen us back in our day," she said. "We did this all the time."

Leo's eyes sparkled. "I can see where Tilly gets her dance moves from." Tilly held back her laugh, but Jack and Edith both looked pleased. Leo kissed her cheek and went to join Alerio.

"I'm so happy to see you both, thank you for coming all this way," Tilly said softly.

Edith smiled. "We've missed you every single day. We were so thrilled when Leo called us to arrange it. We do love the photos you've been sending, but it's not quite the same."

Jack wrapped his arm around her. "You look happy Tillio. We love seeing how much you're thriving here, you're a different woman."

Tilly beamed at them. "I am happy, I've just missed you both so much. I'm surprised Celia didn't want to come along."

Jack's brow furrowed. "We haven't heard from her. She left the day after you did, she wouldn't say where she was going."

Tilly's smile dropped, she hoped Celia was okay. "I guess she did always love an adventure."

Edith patted her hand. "Go say hello to your friends dear, we're staying with Jaini for a week, so we'll have plenty of time together."

Tilly hugged them again. "That's perfect, there's so much I

want to show you."

She walked over to Jaini and Cali, they were both in glittering dresses similar to hers. Jaini gave her a tight hug and Cali passed her a drink. Tilly's stomach growled as she noticed the canapes arriving. Jaini grabbed her hand and inspected her ring. Cali leaned forward to have a look too. "It's no engagement ring, but it's not bad," Jaini said.

Tilly laughed. "Is that next on your vision board? Because I think that might be pushing it a bit—we're lucky to even be together."

Cali leaned closer, swaying slightly. "The vision board always comes true," she said seriously. Tilly and Jaini both laughed. Jaini noticed a confused waiter enter the room and excused herself.

Tilly raised her eyebrows at Cali. "Did I see you and Jaini holding hands?" she teased.

Cali beamed at her. "We went on a date, can you believe it? I've admired this woman for years and she asked me on a date. I could barely give her an answer I was so shocked."

Tilly dropped her voice. "You should know Cali, when Conrad had us tied up, Jaini was thinking about you. You're an amazing person and she sees that."

Cali's eyes shone happily. "I'm amazing? You're the amazing one, just look at that photo. Princess Matilda," she said with a sigh.

Tilly glanced behind her, noticing the large photo of herself hung on the wall—the photo Jaini had taken of her in the crown. "Oh my god," Tilly sputtered, she lunged towards it.

Leo grabbed her around the waist, laughing. "I was wondering when you'd notice that."

"It needs to come down immediately," she sulked.

Leo chuckled, bringing his mouth to her ear. "No way, after tonight I'm hanging it above my bed."

"That's really creepy," Tilly said, still sulking.

Leo grinned and pulled her towards Alerio and the others. "Time to get to know your brothers," he teased.

Alerio gave her a kiss on the cheek. He was nicely dressed in a button-up shirt and chinos. "We were just talking about how well the ceremony went."

"It was perfect Alerio, you did an amazing job," she said.

Hojin stepped forward in a dark shirt and jeans, his long, black hair tied back. He gave her an awkward hug. "Welcome little sister, we have heard many stories of your bravery."

Denz threw an arm around her shoulder, he wore ripped jeans and a white fitted T-shirt. She glanced up at him, his green eyes studied hers. "We weren't expecting you to be so beautiful. Are you sure you're up for this life? It's not a glamorous one."

Leo shook his head at Denz while Alerio and Hojin watched quietly. Tilly gave him a tight smile. "I wouldn't have agreed to it if I wasn't ready."

Denz scrunched his face. "But you're so little and cute."

Tilly felt her magic flare in her chest.

Deep breath Matilda, he's your brother now.

"You've never seen her fight before," Leo pointed out.

Denz shrugged. "I fought with Spirids in the past, they were impressive, but I've yet to be beaten by one."

Tilly gave him a sweet smile. "Would you like to be?"

The men all laughed and Denz smiled wide. "I'd let you do anything you wanted to me, sweetheart."

Alerio tilted his head. "You know, Faris underestimated Tilly and got knocked out cold. Maybe you two should get in the

246

ring."

Yes, please.

Denz sighed dramatically. "Faris was always too busy trying to show off. I don't really want to fight her—I might mess up her hair." Tilly's magic burned through her body. In one swift move, she knocked him down onto his backside. Denz threw his head back and laughed loudly. "Finally, I was wondering how long it would take you to crack." Tilly squeezed her eyes closed and laughed, she couldn't believe she had fallen for that. They were going to have a lot of fun together. Hojin shook his head at Denz disapprovingly. "Is she quicker than you, Leo?" Denz asked curiously.

Tilly and Leo glanced at each other, a smile crept up their faces. "We did have a match once," Leo said, "but it was a tie."

Tilly scoffed as Alerio cleared his throat. "I believe Tilly won, Leo pulled her ankle out as he went down." Denz and Hojin both laughed.

Tilly patted Leo on the back. "Don't worry, you'll get another chance someday," she teased.

"I won't go easy on you next time," he joked. Tilly laughed as he leaned down to kiss her. When he pulled away, she noticed the others watching wistfully. Her heart sank, she wondered if they all would have found love if they'd been allowed to, it didn't seem fair.

They spent the rest of the night drinking and laughing. Cali pulled Jaini down to the dance floor and they all followed. Leo took Tilly into his arms and spun her around. "Are you having fun?" he asked.

She looked over at her mum and dad, dancing happily together, her mother smiled as she met her eye. Alerio and the others had joined Cali and Jaini, they'd formed a dance circle and were laughing and cheering each other on. She looked back up into Leo's eyes. "It's the best day of my life," she said softly. He smiled and leaned down to kiss her. She wrapped her arms around his neck and pulled him closer.

"You two are the cutest!" Cali screamed, throwing her arms around them both. Tilly and Leo burst out laughing.

Tilly patted Cali on the arm while shaking her head. "No one is cuter than you, Cali."

Tilly woke up in Leo's room, she glanced beside her, he was still fast asleep. She sat up and stretched, feeling surprisingly good after the big night they'd had. She had a sudden craving for her favourite coffee from Veer's bakery in Silverleaf. She tried to remember exactly how it had tasted and held out her hand, conjuring a tray with two cups. Her face lit up as she inhaled the smell of fresh coffee, and she reached out to take one.

"Don't you feel like that's cheating sometimes?" Leo said amused.

"Ah!" She wobbled the tray, almost dropping it.

Leo laughed loudly. "See, you even act like you've been caught out."

"I thought you were asleep," Tilly said laughing. "One of these was actually for you, but now I think I'll keep it."

He shot out from under the blanket, sitting on top of her so she couldn't move. "Don't you dare." He took one of the cups and sipped it slowly, watching her carefully.

"Why are you acting weird?" she asked suspiciously.

"Have you noticed anything different?"

"You slept in your party clothes?" Tilly asked.

Leo looked down in surprise. "That is different. But no,

something else."

Tilly looked around, her eyes widened as she noticed the large photo of herself from the party, badly hung on the wall. "How?" she asked in disbelief.

Leo grinned. "I had it hidden under my shirt when we left the club."

Tilly burst out laughing. "You went to a lot of effort to keep that."

He glanced at it happily and sighed. "It was worth it. Besides, Edith may have let it slip that you had a picture of me in your bedroom. Seems like it's only fair."

She felt her face flush. "That traitor, I'll be having words with her." Leo laughed as Annora stalked into the room, she jumped up on the bed next to them. "When did you come out?" Tilly asked surprised.

Last night, you tried to ride me home from the nightclub, it was very amusing.

"Oh my god." Tilly dropped her face into her hand, she was so embarrassed. She did kind of remember trying to do that. Leo laughed and tried to pull her hand away from her face. "I'm not coming back out, I can't believe I did that in front of everyone."

"We were all drunk, Til, I'd be surprised if anyone remembers."

She peeked through her fingers. "Do you remember?"

He bit his lip. "Yes, it was hilarious. You tried to get me on too."

Tilly groaned. "I'm so sorry, Annora." Annora rested her head on the pillow.

We all need to have a bit of fun sometimes Matilda, don't worry about it.

Tilly pulled her hand away from her face.

"So, I've been thinking," Leo said casually. "I know we'll be leaving for Panthera eventually, but, do you want to move in with me?" Tilly's eyebrows shot up. Leo gave her a small smile. "I love waking up with you, I always have," he said softly.

"Yes!" she cried happily, she placed her coffee on the bedside table and wrapped her arms around his neck, pulling him down on top of her. He laughed and kissed her face as she tried pulling his shirt off.

I think I'll go back to the other room.

Tilly laughed, she glanced happily between Leo and Annora—her heart felt full. She didn't know what the future held, but she knew they would always be there with her, and that itself was more than she could have ever asked for.

About the Author

Kirsten Ryan lives in Queensland, Australia, with her husband and two little boys. Her love for books began at the age of nine when she was gifted the first Harry Potter novel from a family friend. When Kirsten isn't writing she enjoys travelling, cooking, daydreaming, inappropriate jokes and spending as much time as possible in the forest.

You can connect with me on:
- http://kirstenryan.com
- https://www.instagram.com/kirsten_ryan_author